INTRODUCTION

Clifford D. Simak, no more than a vaguely recognised name to many SF readers today, was among the giants of the Golden Age, in the glory days of John W. Campbell's *Astounding Science Fiction* magazine. Still collecting honours in the 1980s, he was inaugurated as the third Grand Master of Science Fiction in 1977. Robert Heinlein said of him, famously: 'The reader who does not like Simak stories, does not like science fiction at all'.

The accolades will seem strange to a new reader of Simak's quiet, 'pastoral' science fiction: where we find no thrusting rocketships, no worship of gleaming, futuristic technology, and very few fishbowl-helmeted spacemen. Yet arguably, Simak's apotheosis of rural Wisconsin, between the two 'World Wars' of the twentieth century, stands, and always did, at the true heart of the Galactic Empire. Rocketships are the means. The dream is of escape – away from the restrictions and the crowded complexity of planet Earth, to some New World that often recalls the much-idealised pioneer West. Not the Wild West of the gunfights, but a hidden place where *a man* (female characters are rare in Simak's fiction) may live at peace, in a homestead built by his own hands; where he may know every tree and meadow as a friend; government is a distant rumour, and his nearest neighbour's smoke can barely be discerned on the horizon.

Simak was a prolific writer, especially in the short form. Some of his novels, notably *Way Station* (1963) and *Time Is The Simplest Thing* (1961) have been more highly regarded, but *City* (1952, 1980), remains his best read work. The novel is a fix-up –

a term coined by A. E Van Vogt for a collection of published stories using the same scenario, retrofitted into a single narrative. Eight of the tales in *City* were published in the short form in 1944-51. A ninth, written in 1973, was added to the revised 1980 edition, along with a retrospective foreword by the author. The overarching story charts the slow demise of Man, and the fortunes of a successor race of augmented, sentient Dogs. The scene is Simak's beloved rural Wisconsin, with forays to a far-future Geneva, and to the surface (sic) of Jupiter. Links between the stories are provided by whimsical passages of 'Doggish' scholarship, discussing the authenticity of these folktales about the mythical, extinct creature called 'Man'.

The first tale, 'City' describes a future (the date is 1990) in which cities are emptying, and farming has become obsolete (replaced, somewhat improbably, by hydroponics). Modern conveniences mean Americans no longer need to 'huddle together' in the cities Simak personally detested: John Webster, unassuming hero, devises a solution for the human costs of this great change. In the second story, which, significantly, opens with a funeral, the mechanical robots who will serve both Dogs and Men have emerged. Space travel is commonplace, the Martians are well known, but since they deserted the cities Men have become reclusive. A surgeon descendent of the original John Webster fails, partly due to circumstance and partly paralysed by agoraphobia, to perform a crucial operation: and realises he may never leave his home again. In the third episode the first pet dogs are given speech, by another Webster surgeon, and by some means the surgical changes become heritable. The dogs, retaining the amiable character and trusting loyalty of family pets, are contrasted unfavourably with 'Joe' – one of the wayward 'super-thinkers', a naturally occurring human mutant strain, who might seem to be more promising successors. In the fourth episode a Man and his dog discover that humans, if they abandon their human bodies, can live in eternal bliss on Jupiter; in the fifth we return to the Webster dynasty, and another climactic 'failure' (this time, refusal to take a life). The remaining stories tell how the last of the Websters consigns himself to eternal sleep, in a vault under Geneva, with the rest of the last humans, while the Dogs – aided by robot servitors, and guided by Jenkins, the near-immortal robot butler who has served generations of Websters – establish a peaceable kingdom, where no animal (at least, nothing furred or feathered) will kill another, even for food. The Dogs, indifferent to outer space, discover an inner-space means of visiting and colonising other worlds. They battle with the sentient ants, arbitrarily created and then goaded into development by the mutant 'Joe' in episode three; are haunted by evil aliens from the inner space worlds, and tackle a resurgence of the killer instinct. Finally, when the Dogs have long deserted Earth, and even the Ants have vanished, Jenkins returns alone to pronounce Man's epitaph.

There's more plot and incident to these stories than appears in a brief synopsis, but their lasting appeal is a tribute to Simak's understated, laconic style, rather than his content. Like his close contemporary, Ray Bradbury, he is a master of mood and suggestion. In his foreword for the 1980 edition he explains that the *City* stories were written in deep disillusion, when the Second World War and the Atomic Bomb had destroyed his last hope in human nature: 'I was trying to create a world in which I, and other disillusioned people, could, for a moment, take refuge . . .'. Never remotely interested in 'technology', or in factual 'science', he translates the fears and longings of his present day into timeless fable, with only the most perfunctory futuristic trappings. *For a moment*, in these tales, a Man sits in his armchair, his loving Dog at his knee, a glass of whiskey at his elbow; pondering the lives of small creatures in the quiet woods around his homestead. Asking nothing, demanding no reward or second chance for the failed experiment of human civilisation; inventing nothing that isn't already held in this moment, he spins a dream of blameless wonderland.

Clifford Simak, though his stories appear so harmless, is possibly one of those fellows (wasn't it a little dog?) who draws back the mystic curtain, and shows the world what the Wizard really looks like. Perhaps all of science fiction secretly lives in Simak's moment, and is made of the same stuff as *City* – a paradoxical hybrid of nihilism and wish-fulfilment; tempered by a stoic acceptance of the cold equations.

Among the many honours of his long career, he won three Hugos and a Nebula award (for 'The Grotto of the Dancing Deer' in 1980); he was awarded the International Fantasy Award for Science Fiction, for *City*, in 1953. He died in 1988.

Gwyneth Jones

These are the stories that the Dogs tell when the fires burn high and the wind is from the north. Then each family circle gathers at the hearthstone and the pups sit silently and listen and when the story's done they ask many questions:

'What is Man?' they'll ask.

Or perhaps: 'What is a city?'

Or: 'What is a war?'

There is no positive answer to any of these questions. There are suppositions and there are theories and there are many educated guesses, but there are no answers.

In the family circle, many a storyteller has been forced to fall back on the ancient explanation that it is nothing but a story, there is no such thing as a Man or city, that one does not search for truth in a simple tale, but takes it for its pleasure and lets it go at that.

Explanations such as these, while they may do to answer pups, are no explanations. One does search for truth in such simple tales as these.

The legend, consisting of eight tales, has been told for countless centuries. So far as can be determined, it has no historic starting point; the most minute study of it fails entirely to illustrate the stages of its development. There is no doubt that through many years of telling it has become stylized, but there is no way to trace the direction of its stylization.

That it is ancient and, as some writers claim, that it may be of non-Doggish origin in part, is borne out by the abundance of jabberwocky which studs the tales – words and phrases (and worst of all, ideas) which have no meaning now and may have never had a meaning. Through telling and retelling, these words and phrases have become accepted, have been assigned, through context, a certain arbitrary value. But there is no way of knowing whether or not these arbitrary values even approximate the original meaning of the words.

This edition of the tales will not attempt to enter into the many technical arguments concerning the existence or nonexistence of Man, of the puzzle of the city, of the several theories relating to war, or of the many other questions which arise to plague the student who would seek in the legend some evidence of its having roots in some basic or historic truth.

The purpose of this edition is only to give the full, unexpurgated text of the tales as they finally stand. Chapter notes are utilized to point out the major points of speculation, but with no attempt at all to achieve conclusions. For those who wish some further understanding of the tales or of the many points of consideration which have arisen over them there are ample texts, written by Dogs of far greater competence than the present editor.

Recent discovery of fragments of what originally must have been an extensive body of literature has been advanced as the latest argument which would attribute at least part of the legend to mythological (and controversial) Man rather than to the Dogs. But until it can be proved that Man did, in fact, exist, argument that the discovered fragments originated with Man can have but little point.

Particularly significant or disturbing, depending upon the viewpoint that one takes, is the fact that the apparent title of the literary fragment is the same as the title of one of the tales in the legend here presented. The word itself, of course, is entirely meaningless.

The first question, of course, is whether there ever was such a creature as Man. At the moment, in the absence of positive evidence, the sober consensus must be that there was not, that Man, as presented in the legend, is a figment of folklore invention. Man may have risen in the early days of Doggish culture as an imaginary being, a sort of racial god, on which the Dogs might call for help, to which they might retire for comfort.

Despite these sober conclusions, however, there are those who see in Man an actual elder god, a visitor from some mystic land or dimensions, who came and stayed awhile and helped and then passed on to the place from which he came.

There still are others who believe that Man and Dog may have risen together as two co-operating animals, may have been complementary in the development of a culture, but that at some distant point in time they reached the parting of the ways.

Of all the disturbing factors in the tales (and they are many) the most disturbing is the suggestion of reverence which is accorded Man. It is hard for the average reader to accept this reverence as mere story-telling. It goes far beyond the perfunctory worship of a tribal god; one almost instinctively feels that it must be deep-rooted in some now forgotten belief or rite involving the pre-history of our race.

There is little hope now, of course, that any of the many areas of controversy which revolve about the legend ever will be settled.

Here, then, are the tales, to be read as you see fit – for pleasure only, for some sign of historical significance, for some hint of hidden meaning. Our best advice to the average reader: Don't take them too much to heart, for complete confusion, if not madness, lurks along the road.

NOTES ON THE FIRST TALE

There is no doubt that, of all the tales, the first is the most difficult for the casual reader. Not only is its nomenclature trying, but its logic and its ideas seem, at first reading, to be entirely alien. This may be because in this story and the next a Dog plays no part, is not even mentioned. From the opening paragraph in this first tale the reader is pitchforked into an utterly strange situation, with equally strange characters to act out its solution. This much may be said for the tale, however – by the time one has laboured his way through it the rest of the tales, by comparison, seem almost homey.

Overriding the entire tale is the concept of the city. While there is no complete understanding of what a city might be, or why it should be, it is generally agreed that it must have been a small area accommodating and supporting a large number of residents. Some of the reasons for its existence are superficially explained in text, but Bounce, who has devoted a lifetime to the study of the tales, is convinced that the explanation is no more than the clever improvisations of an ancient storyteller to support an impossible concept. Most students of the tales agree with Bounce that the reasons as given in the tale do not square with logic and some, Rover among them, have suspected that here we may have an ancient satire, of which the significance has been lost.

Most authorities in economics and sociology regard such an organization as a city an impossible structure, not only from the economic standpoint, but from the sociological and psychological as well. No creature of the highly nervous structure necessary to develop a culture, they point out, would be able to survive within such restricted limits. The result, if it were tried, these authorities say, would lead to mass neuroticism which in a short period of time would destroy the very culture which had built the city.

Rover believes that in the first tale we are dealing with almost pure myth and that as a result no situation or statement can be accepted at face value, that the entire tale must be filled with a symbolism to which the key has long been lost. Puzzling, however, is the fact that if it is a myth-concept, and nothing more, that the form by now should not have rounded itself into the symbolic concepts which are the hallmark of the myth. In the tale there is for the average reader little that can be tagged as myth-content. The tale itself is perhaps the most angular of the lot – raw-boned and slung together, with none of the touches of finer sentiment and lofty ideals which are found in the rest of the legend.

The language of the tale is particularly baffling. Phrases such as the classic 'dadburn the kid' have puzzled semanticists for many centuries and there is to-day no closer approach to what many of the words and phrases mean than there was when students first came to pay some serious attention to the legend.

The terminology for Man has been fairly well worked out, however. The plural for this mythical race is men, the racial designation is human, the females are women or wives (two terms which may at one time have had a finer shade of meaning, but which now must be regarded as synonymous), the pups are children. A male pup is a boy. A female pup a girl.

Aside from the concept of the city, another concept which the reader will find entirely at odds with his way of life and which may violate his very thinking, is the idea of war and of killing. Killing is a process, usually involving violence, by which one living thing ends the life of another living thing. War, it would appear, was mass killing carried out on a scale which is inconceivable.

Rover, in his study of the legend, is convinced that the tales are much more primitive than is generally supposed, since it is his contention that such concepts as war and killing could never come out of our present culture, that they must stem from some era of savagery of which there exists no record.

Tige, who is almost alone in his belief that the tales are based on actual history and that the race of Man did exist in the primordial days of the Dogs' beginning, contends that this first tale is the story of the actual breakdown of Man's culture. He believes that the tale as we know it to-day may be a mere shadow of some greater tale, a gigantic epic which at one time may have measured fully as large or larger than to-day's entire body of the legend. It does not seem possible, he writes, that so great an event as the collapse of a mighty mechanical civilization could have been condensed by the tale's contemporaries into so small a compass as the present tale. What we have here, says Tige, is only one of many tales which told the entire story and that the one which does remain to us may be no more than a minor one.

I
City

Gramp Stevens sat in a lawn chair, watching the mower at work, feeling the warm, soft sunshine seep into his bones. The mower reached the edge of the lawn, clucked to itself like a contented hen, made a neat turn and trundled down another swath. The bag holding the clippings bulged.

Suddenly the mower stopped and clicked excitedly. A panel in its side snapped open and a cranelike arm reached out. Grasping steel fingers fished around in the grass, came up triumphantly with a stone clutched tightly, dropped the stone into a small container, disappeared back into the panel again. The lawn mower gurgled, purred on again, following its swath.

Gramp grumbled at it with suspicion.

'Some day,' he told himself, 'that dadburned thing is going to miss a lick and have a nervous breakdown.'

He lay back in the chair and stared up at the sun-washed sky. A helicopter skimmed far overhead. From somewhere inside the house a radio came to life and a torturing crash of music poured out. Gramp, hearing it, shivered and hunkered lower in the chair.

Young Charlie was settling down for a twitch session. Dadburn the kid.

The lawn mower chuckled past and Gramp squinted at it maliciously.

'Automatic,' he told the sky. 'Ever' blasted thing is automatic now. Getting so you just take a machine off in a corner and whisper in its ear and it scurries off to do the job.'

His daughter's voice came to him out of the window, pitched to carry above the music.

'Father!'

Gramp stirred uneasily. 'Yes, Betty.'

'Now, Father, you see you move when that lawn mower gets to you. Don't try to out-stubborn it. After all, it's only a machine. Last time you just sat there and made it cut around you. I never saw the beat of you.'

He didn't answer, letting his head nod a bit, hoping she would think he was asleep and let him be.

'Father,' she shrilled, 'did you hear me?'

He saw it was no good. 'Sure, I heard you,' he told her. 'I was just fixing to move.'

He rose slowly to his feet, leaning heavily on his cane. Might make her feel sorry for the way she treated him when she saw how old and feeble he was getting. He'd have to be careful, though. If she knew he didn't need the cane at all, she'd be finding jobs for him to do and, on the other hand, if he laid it on too thick, she'd be having that fool doctor in to pester him again.

Grumbling, he moved the chair out into that portion of the lawn that had been cut. The mower, rolling past, chortled at him fiendishly.

'Some day,' Gramp told it, 'I'm going to take a swipe at you and bust a gear or two.'

The mower hooted at him and went serenely down the lawn.

From somewhere down the grassy street came a jangling of metal, a stuttered coughing.

Gramp, ready to sit down, straightened up and listened.

The sound came more clearly, the rumbling backfire of a balky engine, the clatter of loose metallic parts.

'An automobile!' yelped Gramp. 'An automobile, by cracky!'

He started to gallop for the gate, suddenly remembered that he was feeble and subsided into a rapid hobble.

'Must be that crazy Ole Johnson,' he told himself. 'He's the only one left that's got a car. Just too dadburned stubborn to give it up.'

It was Ole.

Gramp reached the gate in time to see the rusty, dilapidated old machine come bumping around the corner, rocking and chugging along the unused street. Steam hissed from the over-heated radiator and a cloud of blue smoke issued from the exhaust, which had lost its muffler five years or more ago.

Ole sat stolidly behind the wheel, squinting his eyes, trying to duck the roughest places, although that was hard to do, for weeds and grass had overrun the streets and it was hard to see what might be underneath them.

Gramp waved his cane.

'Hi, Ole,' he shouted.

Ole pulled up, setting the emergency brake. The car gasped, shuddered, coughed, died with a horrible sigh.

'What you burning?' asked Gramp.

'Little bit of everything,' said Ole. 'Kerosene, some old tractor oil I found out in a barrel, some rubbing alcohol.'

Gramp regarded the fugitive machine with forthright admiration. 'Them was the days,' he said. 'Had one myself used to be able to do a hundred miles an hour.'

'Still OK,' said Ole, 'if you only could find the stuff to run them or get the parts to fix them. Up to three, four years ago I used to be able to get enough gasoline, but ain't seen none for a long time now. Quit making it, I guess. No use having gasoline, they tell me, when you have atomic power.'

'Sure,' said Gramp. 'Guess maybe that's right, but you can't smell atomic power. Sweetest thing I know, the smell of burn-ing gasoline. These here helicopters and other gadgets they got took all the romance out of travelling, somehow.'

He squinted at the barrels and baskets piled in the back seat.

'Got some vegetables?' he asked.

'Yup,' said Ole. 'Some sweet corn and early potatoes and a few baskets of tomatoes. Thought maybe I could sell them.'

Gramp shook his head. 'You won't, Ole. They won't buy them. Folks has got the notion that this new hydroponics stuff is the only garden sass that's fit to eat. Sanitary, they say, and better flavoured.'

'Wouldn't give a hoot in a tin cup for all they grow in them tanks they got,' Ole declared, belligerently. 'Don't taste right to me, somehow. Like I tell Martha, food's got to be raised in the soil to have any character.'

He reached down to turn over the ignition switch.

'Don't know as it's worth trying to get the stuff to town,' he said, 'the way they keep the roads. Or the way they don't keep them, rather. Twenty years ago the state highway out there was a strip of good concrete and they kept it patched and ploughed it every winter. Did anything, spent any amount of money to keep it open. And now they just forgot about it. The concrete's all broken up and some of it has washed out. Brambles are growing in it. Had to get out and cut away a tree that fell across it one place this morning.'

'Ain't it the truth,' agreed Gramp.

The car exploded into life, coughing and choking. A cloud of dense blue smoke rolled out from under it. With a jerk it stirred to life and lumbered down the street.

Gramp clumped back to his chair and found it dripping wet. The automatic mower, having finished its cutting job, had rolled out the hose, was sprinkling the lawn.

Muttering venom, Gramp stalked around the corner of the house and sat down on the bench beside the back porch. He didn't like to sit there, but it was the only place he was safe from the hunk of machinery out in front.

For one thing, the view from the bench was slightly depressing, fronting as it did on street after street of vacant, deserted houses and weed-grown, unkempt yards.

It had one advantage, however. From the bench he could pretend he was slightly deaf and not hear the twitch music the radio was blaring out.

A voice called from the front yard.

'Bill! Bill, where be you?'

Gramp twisted around.

'Here I am, Mark. Back of the house. Hiding from that dad-burned mower.'

Mark Bailey limped around the corner of the house, cigarette threatening to set fire to his bushy whiskers.

'Bit early for the game, ain't you?' asked Gramp.

'Can't play no game to-day,' said Mark.

He hobbled over and sat down beside Gramp on the bench. 'We're leaving,' he said.

Gramp whirled on him. 'You're leaving!'

'Yeah. Moving out into the country. Lucinda finally talked Herb into it. Never gave him a minute's peace, I guess. Said everyone was moving away to one of them nice country estates and she didn't see no reason why we couldn't.'

Gramp gulped. 'Where to?'

'Don't rightly know,' said Mark. 'Ain't been there myself. Up north some place. Up on one of the lakes. Got ten acres of land. Lucinda wanted a hundred, but Herb put down his foot and said ten was enough. After all, one city lot was enough for all these years.'

'Betty was pestering Johnny, too,' said Gramp, 'but he's holding out against her. Says he simply can't do it. Says it wouldn't look right, him the secretary of the Chamber of Commerce and all, if he went moving away from the city.'

'Folks are crazy,' Mark declared. 'Plumb crazy.'

'That's a fact,' Gramp agreed. 'Country crazy, that's what they are. Look across there.'

He waved his hand at the streets of vacant houses. 'Can remember the time when those places were as pretty a bunch of homes as you ever laid your eyes on. Good neighbours, they were. Women ran across from one back door to another to trade recipes. And the men folks would go out to cut the grass and pretty soon the mowers would all be sitting idle and the men would be ganged up, chewing the fat. Friendly people, Mark. But look at it now.'

Mark stirred uneasily. 'Got to be getting back, Bill. Just sneaked over to let you know we were lighting out. Luanda's got me packing. She'd be sore if she knew I'd run out.'

Gramp rose stiffly and held out his hand. 'I'll be seeing you again? You be over for one last game?'

Mark shook his head. 'Afraid not, Bill.'

They shook hands awkwardly, abashed. 'Sure will miss them games,' said Mark.

'Me, too,' said Gramp. 'I won't have nobody once you're gone.'

'So long, Bill,' said Mark.

'So long,' said Gramp.

He stood and watched his friend hobble around the house, felt the cold claw of loneliness reach out and touch him with icy fingers. A terrible loneliness. The loneliness of age – of age and the outdated. Fiercely, Gramp admitted it. He was outdated. He belonged to another age. He had outstripped his time, lived beyond his years.

Eyes misty, he fumbled for the cane that lay against the bench, slowly made his way towards the sagging gate that opened on to the deserted street back of the house.

The years had moved too fast. Years that had brought the family plane and helicopter, leaving the auto to rust in some forgotten place, the unused roads to fall into disrepair. Years that had virtually wiped out the tilling of the soil with the rise of hydroponics. Years that had brought cheap land with the disappearance of the farm as an economic unit, had sent city people scurrying out into the country where each man, for less than the price of a city lot, might own broad acres. Years that had revolutionized the construction of homes to a point where families simply walked away from their old homes to the new ones that could be bought, custom-made, for less than half the price of a prewar structure and could be changed at small cost, to accommodate need of additional space or just a passing whim.

Gramp sniffed. Houses that could be changed each year, just like one would shift around the furniture. What kind of living was that?

He plodded slowly down the dusty path that was all that

remained of what a few years before had been a busy residential street. A street of ghosts, Gramp told himself – of furtive, little ghosts that whispered in the night. Ghosts of playing children, ghosts of upset tricycles and canted coaster wagons. Ghosts of gossiping housewives. Ghosts of shouted greetings. Ghosts of flaming fireplaces and chimneys smoking of a winter night.

Little puffs of dust rose around his feet and whitened the cuffs of his trousers.

There was the old Adams place across the way. Adams had been mighty proud of it, he remembered. Grey field stone front and picture windows. Now the stone was green with creeping moss and the broken windows gaped with ghastly leer. Weeds choked the lawn and blotted out the stoop. An elm tree was pushing its branches against the gable. Gramp could remember the day Adams had planted that elm tree.

For a moment he stood there in the grass-grown street, feet in the dust, both hands clutching the curve of his cane, eyes closed.

Through the fog of years he heard the cry of playing children, the barking of Conrad's yapping pooch from down the street. And there was Adams, stripped to the waist, plying the shovel, scooping out the hole, with the elm tree, roots wrapped in burlap, lying on the lawn.

May, 1946. Forty-four years ago. Just after he and Adams had come home from the war together.

Footsteps padded in the dust and Gramp, startled, opened his eyes.

Before him stood a young man. A man of thirty, perhaps. Maybe a bit less.

'Good morning,' said Gramp.

'I hope,' said the young man, 'that I didn't startle you.'

'You saw me standing here,' asked Gramp, 'like a danged fool, with my eyes shut?'

The young man nodded.

'I was remembering,' said Gramp.

'You live around here?'

'Just down the street. The last one in this part of the city.'

'Perhaps you can help me then.'

'Try me,' said Gramp.

The young man stammered. 'Well, you see, it's like this. I'm on a sort of . . . well, you might call it a sentimental pilgrimage—'

'I understand,' said Gramp. 'So am I.'

'My name is Adams,' said the young man. 'My grandfather used to live around here somewhere. I wonder—'

'Right over there,' said Gramp.

Together they stood and stared at the house.

'It was a nice place once,' Gramp told him. 'Your grand-daddy planted that tree right after he came home from the war. I was with him all through the war and we came home together. That was a day for you . . .'

'It's a pity,' said young Adams. 'A pity . . .'

But Gramp didn't seem to hear him. 'Your granddaddy?' he asked. 'I seem to have lost track of him.'

'He's dead,' said young Adams. 'Quite a number of years ago.'

'He was messed up with atomic power,' said Gramp.

'That's right,' said Adams proudly. 'Got into it just as soon as it was released to industry. Right after the Moscow agreement.'

'Right after they decided,' said Gramp, 'they couldn't fight a war.'

'That's right,' said Adams.

'It's pretty hard to fight a war,' said Gramp, 'when there's nothing you can aim at.'

'You mean the cities,' said Adams.

'Sure,' said Gramp, 'and there's a funny thing about it. Wave all the atom bombs you wanted to and you couldn't scare them out. But give them cheap land and family planes and they scattered just like so many dadburned rabbits.'

John J. Webster was striding up the broad stone steps of the city hall when the walking scarecrow carrying a rifle under his arm caught up with him and stopped him.

'Howdy, Mr. Webster,' said the scarecrow.

Webster stared, then recognition crinkled his face.

'It's Levi,' he said. 'How are things going, Levi?'

Levi Lewis grinned with snagged teeth. 'Fair to middling. Gardens are coming along and the young rabbits are getting to be good eating.'

'You aren't getting mixed up in any of the hell raising that's being laid to the *houses*?' asked Webster.

'No, sir,' declared Levi. 'Ain't none of us Squatters mixed up in any wrong-doing. We're law-abiding, God-fearing people, we are. Only reason we're there is we can't make a living no place else. And us living in them places other people up and left ain't harming no one. Police are just blaming us for the thievery and other things that's going on, knowing we can't protect ourselves. They're making us the goats.'

'I'm glad to hear that,' said Webster. 'The chief wants to burn the *houses*.'

'If he tries that,' said Levi, 'he'll run against something he ain't counting on. They run us off our farms with this tank farming of theirs but they ain't going to run us any farther.'

He spat across the steps.

'Wouldn't happen you might have some jingling money on you?' he asked. 'I'm fresh out of cartridges and with them rabbits coming up—'

Webster thrust his fingers into a vest pocket, pulled out a half dollar.

Levi grinned. 'That's obliging of you, Mr. Webster. I'll bring a mess of squirrels, come fall.'

The Squatter touched his hat with two fingers and retreated down the steps, sun glinting on the rifle barrel. Webster turned up the steps again.

The city council session already was in full swing when he walked into the chamber.

Police Chief Jim Maxwell was standing by the table and Mayor Paul Carter was talking.

'Don't you think you may be acting a bit hastily, Jim, in urging such a course of action with the *houses*?'

'No, I don't,' declared the chief. 'Except for a couple of dozen or so, none of those houses are occupied by their rightful owners, or rather, their original owners. Every one of them belongs to the city now through tax forfeiture. And they are nothing but an eyesore and a menace. They have no value. Not even salvage value. Wood? We don't use wood any more. Plastics are better. Stone? We use steel instead of stone. Not a single one of those houses have any material of marketable value.

'And in the meantime they are becoming the haunts of petty criminals and undesirable elements. Grown up with vegetation as the residential sections are, they make a perfect hideout for all types of criminals. A man commits a crime and heads straight for the *houses* – once there he's safe, for I could send a thousand men in there and he could elude them all.

'They aren't worth the expense of tearing down. And yet they are, if not a menace, at least a nuisance. We should get rid of them and fire is the cheapest, quickest way. We'd use all precautions.'

'What about the legal angle?' asked the mayor.

'I checked into that. A man has a right to destroy his own property in any way he may see fit so long as it endangers no one else's. The same law, I suppose, would apply to a municipality.'

Alderman Thomas Griffin sprang to his feet.

'You'd alienate a lot of people,' he declared. 'You'd be burning down a lot of old homesteads. People still have some sentimental attachments—'

'If they cared for them,' snapped the chief, 'why didn't they pay the taxes and take care of them? Why did they go running off to the country, just leaving the houses standing. Ask Webster here. He can tell you what success he had trying to interest the people in their ancestral homes.'

'You're talking about that Old Home Week farce,' said Griffin. 'It failed. Of course, it failed. Webster spread it on so thick that they gagged on it. That's what a Chamber of Commerce mentality always does.'

Alderman Forrest King spoke up angrily. 'There's nothing wrong with a Chamber of Commerce, Griffin. Simply because you failed in business is no reason . . .'

Griffin ignored him. 'The day of high pressure is over, gentlemen. The day of high pressure is gone for ever. Ballyhoo is something that is dead and buried.

'The day when you could have tall-corn days or dollar days or dream up some fake celebration and deck the place up with bunting and pull in big crowds that were ready to spend money is past these many years. Only you fellows don't seem to know it.

'The success of such stunts as that was its appeal to mob psychology and civic loyalty. You can't have civic loyalty with a city dying on its feet. You can't appeal to mob psychology when there is no mob – when every man, or nearly every man has the solitude of forty acres.'

'Gentlemen,' pleaded the mayor. 'Gentlemen, this is distinctly out of order.'

King sputtered into life, walloped the table.

'No, let's have it out. Webster is over there. Perhaps he can tell us what he thinks.'

Webster stirred uncomfortably. 'I scarcely believe,' he said, 'I have anything to say.'

'Forget it,' snapped Griffin and sat down.

But King still stood, his face crimson, his month trembling with anger.

'Webster!' he shouted.

Webster shook his head. 'You came here with one of your big ideas,' shouted King. 'You were going to lay it before the council. Step up, man, and speak your piece.'

Webster rose slowly, grim-lipped.

'Perhaps you're too thick-skulled,' he told King, 'to know why I resent the way you have behaved.'

King gasped, then exploded. 'Thick-skulled! You would say that to me. We've worked together and I've helped you. You've never called me that before . . . you've—'

'I've never called you that before,' said Webster levelly.
'Naturally not. I wanted to keep my job.'

'Well, you haven't got a job,' roared King. 'From this minute on, you haven't got a job.'

'Shut up,' said Webster.

King stared at him, bewildered, as if someone had slapped him across the face.

'And sit down,' said Webster, and his voice bit through the room like a sharp-edged knife.

King's knees caved beneath him and he sat down abruptly. The silence was brittle.

'I have something to say,' said Webster. 'Something that should have been said long ago. Something all of you should hear. That I should be the one who would tell it to you is the one thing that astounds me. And yet, perhaps, as one who has worked in the interests of this city for almost fifteen years, I am the logical one to speak the truth.

'Alderman Griffin said the city is dying on its feet and his statement is correct. There is but one fault I would find with it and that is its understatement. The city . . . this city, any city . . . already is dead.

'The city is an anachronism. It has outlived its usefulness. Hydroponics and the helicopter spelled its downfall. In the first instance the city was a tribal place, an area where the tribe banded together for mutual protection. In later years a wall was thrown around it for additional protection. Then the wall finally disappeared but the city lived on because of the conveniences which it offered trade and commerce. It continued into modern times because people were compelled to live close to their jobs and the jobs were in the city.

'But to-day that is no longer true. With the family plane, one hundred miles to-day is a shorter distance than five miles back in 1930. Men can fly several hundred miles to work and fly home when the day is done. There is no longer any need for them to live cooped up in a city.

'The automobile started the trend and the family plane finished it. Even in the first part of the century the trend was noticeable – a movement away from the city with its taxes and its stuffiness, a move towards the suburb and close-in acreages. Lack of adequate transportation, lack of finances held many to the city. But now, with tank farming destroying the value of land, a man can buy a huge acreage in the country for less than he could a city lot forty years ago. With planes powered by atomic there is no longer any transportation problem.'

He paused and the silence held. The mayor wore a shocked look. King's lips moved, but no words came. Griffin was smiling.

'So what have we?' asked Webster. 'I'll tell you what we have. Street after street, block after block, of deserted houses, houses that the people just up and walked away from. Why should they have stayed? What could the city offer them? None of the things that it offered the generations before them, for progress has wiped out the need of the city's benefits. They lost something, some monetary consideration, of course, when they left the houses. But the fact that they could buy a house twice as good for half as much, the fact that they could live as they wished to live, that they could develop what amounts to family estates after the best tradition set them by the wealthy of a gen-eration ago – all these things outweighed the leaving of their homes.

'And what have we left? A few blocks of business houses. A few acres of industrial plants. A city government geared to take care of a million people without the million people. A budget that has run the taxes so high that eventually even business houses will move to escape those taxes. Tax forfeitures that have left us loaded with worthless property. That's what we have left.

'If you think any Chamber of Commerce, any ballyhoo, any hare-brained scheme will give you the answers, you're crazy. There is only one answer and that is simple. The city as a human institution is dead. It may struggle on a few more years, but that is all.'

'Mr. Webster—' said the mayor.

But Webster paid him no attention.

'But for what happened to-day,' he said, 'I would have stayed on and played doll house with you. I would have gone on pretending that the city was a going concern. Would have gone on kidding myself and you. But there is, gentlemen, such a thing as human dignity.'

The icy silence broke down in the rustling of papers, the muffled cough of some embarrassed listener.

But Webster was not through.

'The city failed,' he said, 'and it is well it failed. Instead of sitting here in mourning above its broken body you should rise to your feet and shout your thanks it failed.

'For if this city had not outlived its usefulness, as did every other city – if the cities of the world had not been deserted, they would have been destroyed. There would have been a war, gentleman, an atomic war. Have you forgotten the 1950s and the 60s? Have you forgotten waking up at night and listening for the bomb to come, knowing that you would not hear it when it came, knowing that you would never hear again, if it did come?

'But the cities were deserted and industry was dispersed and there were no targets and there was no war.

'Some of you gentlemen,' he said, 'many of you gentlemen are alive to-day because the people left your city.

'Now, for God's sake, let it stay dead. Be happy that it's dead. It's the best thing that ever happened in all human history.'

John J. Webster turned on his heel and left the room.

Outside on the broad stone steps, he stopped and stared up at the cloudless sky, saw the pigeons wheeling above the turrets and spires of the city hall.

He shook himself mentally, like a dog coming out of a pool.

He had been a fool, of course. Now he'd have to hunt for a job and it might take time to find one. He was getting a bit old to be hunting for a job.

But despite his thoughts, a little tune rose unbidden to his lips. He walked away briskly, lips pursed, whistling soundlessly.

No more hypocrisy. No more lying awake nights wondering

what to do – Knowing that the city was dead, knowing that what he did was a useless task, feeling like a heel for taking a salary that he knew he wasn't earning. Sensing the strange, nagging frustration of a worker, who knows his work is non-productive.

He strode towards the parking lot, heading for his helicopter.

Now, maybe he told himself, they could move out into the country the way Betty wanted to. Maybe he could spend his evenings tramping land that belonged to him. A place with a stream. Definitely it had to have a stream he could stock with trout.

He made a mental note to go up into the attic and check his fly equipment.

Martha Johnson was waiting at the barnyard gate when the old car chugged down the lane.

Ole got out stiffly, face rimmed with weariness.

'Sell anything?' asked Martha.

Ole shook his head. 'It ain't no use. They won't buy farm-raised stuff. Just laughed at me. Showed me ears of corn twice as big as the ones I had, just as sweet and with more even rows. Showed me melons that had almost no rind at all. Better tasting, too, they said.'

He kicked at a clod and it exploded into dust.

'There ain't no getting around it,' he declared. 'Tank farming sure has ruined us.'

'Maybe we better fix to sell the farm,' suggested Martha.

Ole said nothing.

'You could get a job on a tank farm,' she said. 'Harry did. Likes it real well.'

Ole shook his head.

'Or maybe a gardener,' said Martha. 'You would make a right smart gardener. Ritzy folks that's moved out to big estates like to have gardeners to take care of flowers and things. More classy than doing it with machines.'

Ole shook his head again. 'Couldn't stand to mess around

with flowers,' he declared. 'Not after raising corn for more than twenty years.'

'Maybe,' said Martha, 'we could have one of them little planes. And running water in the house. And a bathtub instead of taking a bath in the old washtub by the kitchen fire.'

'Couldn't run a plane,' objected Ole.

'Sure you could,' said Martha. 'Simple to run, they are. Why, them Anderson kids ain't no more than knee-high to a cricket and they fly one all over. One of them got fooling around and fell out once, but—'

'I got to think about it,' said Ole desperately. 'I got to think.'

He swung away, vaulted a fence, headed for the fields. Martha stood beside the car and watched him go. One lone tear rolled down her dusty cheek.

'Mr. Taylor is waiting for you,' said the girl.

John J. Webster stammered. 'But I haven't been here before. He didn't know I was coming.'

'Mr. Taylor,' insisted the girl, 'is waiting for you.'

She nodded her head towards the door. It read:

BUREAU OF HUMAN ADJUSTMENT

'But I came here to get a job,' protested Webster. 'I didn't come to be adjusted or anything. This is the World Committee's placement service, isn't it?'

'That is right,' the girl declared. 'Won't you see Mr. Taylor?'

'Since you insist,' said Webster.

The girl clicked over a switch, spoke into the inter-communicator. 'Mr. Webster is here, sir.'

'Send him in,' said a voice.

Hat in hand, Webster walked through the door.

The man behind the desk had white hair but a young man's face. He motioned towards a chair.

'You've been trying to find a job,' he said.

'Yes,' said Webster, 'but—'

'Please sit down,' said Taylor. 'If you're thinking about that sign on the door, forget it. We'll not try to adjust you.'

'I couldn't find a job,' said Webster. 'I've hunted for weeks and no one would have me. So, finally, I came here.'

'You didn't want to come here?'

'No, frankly, I didn't. A placement service. It has, well . . . it has an implication I do not like.'

Taylor smiled. 'The terminology may be unfortunate. You're thinking of the employment services of the old days. The places where men went when they were desperate for work. The government operated places that tried to find work for men so they wouldn't become public charges.'

'I'm desperate enough,' confessed Webster. 'But I still have a pride that made it hard to come. But, finally, there was nothing else to do. You see, I turned traitor—'

'You mean,' said Taylor, 'that you told the truth. Even when it cost you your job. The business world, not only here, but all over the world is not ready for that truth. The businessman still clings to the city myth, to the myth of salesmanship. In time to come he will realize he doesn't need the city, that service and honest values will bring him more substantial business than salesmanship ever did.

'I've wondered, Webster, just what made you do what you did?'

'I was sick of it,' said Webster. 'Sick of watching men blundering along with their eyes tight shut. Sick of seeing an old tradition being kept alive when it should have been laid away. Sick of King's simpering civic enthusiasm when all cause for enthusiasm had vanished.'

Taylor nodded. 'Webster, do you think you could adjust human beings?'

Webster merely stared.

'I mean it,' said Taylor. 'The World Committee has been doing it for years, quietly, unobtrusively. Even many of the people who had been adjusted don't know they have been adjusted.

'Changes such as have come since the creation of the World

Committee out of the old United Nations have meant much human maladjustment. The advent of workable atomic power took jobs away from hundreds of thousands. They had to be trained and guided into new jobs, some with the new atomics, some into other lines of work. The advent of tank farming swept the farmers off their land. They, perhaps, have supplied us with our greatest problem, for other than the special knowledge needed to grow crops and handle animals, they had no skills. Most of them had no wish for acquiring skills. Most of them were bitterly resentful at having been forced from the livelihood which they inherited from their forebears. And being natural individualists, they offered the toughest psychological problems of any other class.'

'Many of them,' declared Webster, 'still are at loose ends. There's a hundred or more of them squatting out in the *houses*, living from hand to mouth. Shooting a few rabbits and a few squirrels, doing some fishing, raising vegetables and picking wild fruit. Engaging in a little petty thievery now and then and doing occasional begging on the uptown streets.'

'You know these people?' asked Taylor.

'I know some of them,' said Webster. 'One of them brings me squirrels and rabbits on occasions. To make up for it, he bums ammunition money.'

'They'd resent being adjusted, wouldn't they?'

'Violently,' said Webster.

'You know a farmer by the name of Ole Johnson? Still sticking to his farm, still unreconstructed?'

Webster nodded.

'What if you tried to adjust him?'

'He'd run me off the farm,' said Webster.

'Men like Ole and the Squatters,' said Taylor, 'are our special problems now. Most of the rest of the world is fairly well-adjusted, fairly well settled into the groove of the present. Some of them are doing a lot of moaning about the past, but that's just for effect. You couldn't drive them back to their old ways of life.

'Years ago, with the advent of industrial atomics in fact, the

World Committee faced a hard decision. Should changes that spelled progress in the world be brought about gradually to allow the people to adjust themselves naturally, or should they be developed as quickly as possible, with the committee aiding in the necessary human adjustment? It was decided, rightly or wrongly, that progress should come first, regardless of its effect upon the people. The decision in the main has proved a wise one.

'We knew, of course, that in many instances, this readjustment could not be made too openly. In some cases, as in large groups of workers who had been displaced, it was possible, but in most individual cases, such as our friend Ole, it was not. These people must be helped to find themselves in this new world, but they must not know that they're being helped. To let them know would destroy confidence and dignity, and human dignity is the keystone of any civilization.'

'I knew, of course, about the readjustments made within industry itself,' said Webster, 'but I had not heard of the individual cases.'

'We could not advertise it,' Taylor said. 'It's practically undercover.'

'But why are you telling me all this now?'

'Because we'd like you to come in with us. Have a hand at adjusting Ole to start with. Maybe see what could be done about the Squatters next.'

'I don't know—' said Webster.

'We'd been waiting for you to come in,' said Taylor. 'We knew you'd finally have to come here. Any chance you might have had at any kind of job would have been queered by King. He passed the word along. You're blackballed by every Chamber of Commerce and every civic group in the world today.'

'Probably I have no choice,' said Webster.

'We don't want you to feel that way about it,' Taylor said. 'Take a while to think it over, then come back. Even if you don't want the job we'll find you another one – in spite of King.'

*

27

Outside the office, Webster found a scarecrow figure waiting for him. It was Levi Lewis, snaggle-toothed grin wiped off, rifle under his arm.

'Some of the boys said they seen you go in here,' he explained. 'So I waited for you.'

'What's the trouble?' Webster asked, for Levi's face spoke eloquently of trouble.

'It's them police,' said Levi. He spat disgustedly.

'The police,' said Webster, and his heart sank as he said the words. For he knew what the trouble was.

'Yeah,' said Levi. 'They're fixing to burn us out.'

'So the council finally gave in,' said Webster.

'I just came from police headquarters,' declared Levi. 'I told them they better go easy. I told them there'd be guts strewed all over the place if they tried it. I got the boys posted all around the place with orders not to shoot till they're sure of hitting.'

'You can't do that, Levi,' said Webster sharply.

'I can't!' retorted Levi. 'I done it already. They drove us off the farms, forced us to sell because we couldn't make a living. And they aren't driving us no farther. We either stay here or we die here. And the only way they'll burn us out is when there's no one left to stop them.'

He shucked up his pants and spat again.

'And we ain't the only ones that feel that way,' he declared. 'Gramp is out there with us.'

'Gramp!'

'Sure, Gramp. The old guy that lives with you. He's sort of taken over as our commanding general. Says he remembers tricks from the war them police have never heard of. He sent some of the boys over to one of them Legion halls to swipe a cannon. Says he knows where we can get some shells for it from the museum. Says we'll get it all set up and then send word that if the police make a move we'll shell the loop.'

'Look, Levi, will you do something for me?'

'Sure will, Mr. Webster.'

'Will you go in and ask for a Mr. Taylor? Insist on seeing him. Tell him I'm already on the job.'

'Sure will, but where are you going?'

'I'm going up to the city hall.'

'Sure you don't want me along?'

'No,' declared Webster. 'I'll do better alone. And, Levi—'

'Yes.'

'Tell Gramp to hold up his artillery. Don't shoot unless he has to – but if he has, to lay it on the line.'

'The mayor is busy,' said Raymond Brown, his secretary.

'That's what you think,' said Webster, starting for the door.

'You can't go in there, Webster,' yelled Brown.

He leaped from his chair, came charging around the desk, reaching for Webster. Webster swung broadside with his arm, caught Brown across the chest, swept him back against the desk. The desk skidded and Brown waved his arms, lost his balance, thudded to the floor.

Webster jerked open the mayor's door.

The mayor's feet thumped off his desk. 'I told Brown—' he said.

Webster nodded. 'And Brown told me. What's the matter, Carter. Afraid King might find out I was here? Afraid of being corrupted by some good ideas?'

'What do you want?' snapped Carter.

'I understand the police are going to burn the *houses*.'

'That's right,' declared the mayor, righteously. 'They're a menace to the community.'

'What community?'

'Look here, Webster—'

'You know, there's no community. Just a few of you lousy politicians who stick around so you can claim residence, so you can be sure of being elected every year and drag down your salaries. It's getting to the point where all you have to do is vote for one another. The people who work in the stores and shops, even those who do the meanest jobs in the factories, don't live inside the city limits. The businessmen quit the city long ago. They do business here, but they aren't residents.'

'But this is still a city,' declared the mayor.

29

'I didn't come to argue that with you,' said Webster. 'I came to try to make you see that you're doing wrong by burning those houses. Even if you don't realize it, the *houses* are homes to people who have no other homes. People who have come to this city to seek sanctuary, who have found refuge with us. In a measure, they are our responsibility.'

'They're not our responsibility,' gritted the mayor. 'Whatever happens to them is their own hard luck. We didn't ask them here. We don't want them here. They contribute nothing to the community. You're going to tell me they're misfits. Well, can I help that? You're going to say they can't find jobs. And I'll tell you they could find jobs if they tried to find them. There's work to be done, there's always work to be done. They've been filled up with this new world talk and they figure it's up to someone to find the place that suits them and the job that suits them.'

'You sound like a rugged individualist,' said Webster.

'You say that like you think it's funny,' yapped the mayor.

'I do think it's funny,' said Webster. 'Funny, and tragic, that anyone should think that way to-day.'

'The world would be a lot better off with some rugged individualism,' snapped the mayor. 'Look at the men who have gone places—'

'Meaning yourself?' asked Webster.

'You might take me, for example,' Carter agreed. 'I worked hard. I took advantage of opportunity. I had some foresight. I did—'

'You mean you licked the correct boots and stepped in the proper faces,' said Webster. 'You're the shining example of the kind of people the world doesn't want to-day. You positively smell musty, your ideas are so old. You're the last of the politicians, Carter, just as I was the last of the Chamber of Commerce secretaries. Only you don't know it yet. I did. I got out. Even when it cost me something, I got out, because I had to save my self-respect. Your kind of politics is dead. They are dead because any tinhorn with a loud mouth and a brassy front could gain power by appeal to mob psychology. And you

30

haven't got mob psychology any more. You can't have mob psychology when people don't give a damn what happens to a thing that's dead already – a political system that broke down under its own weight.'

'Get out of here,' screamed Carter. 'Get out before I have the cops come and throw you out.'

'You forget,' said Webster, 'that I came in to talk about the *houses*.'

'It won't do you any good,' snarled Carter. 'You can stand and talk till doomsday for all the good it does. Those *houses* burn. That's final.'

'How would you like to see the loop a mass of rubble?' asked Webster.

'Your comparison,' said Carter, 'is grotesque.'

'I wasn't talking about comparisons,' said Webster.

'You weren't—' The mayor stared at him. 'What were you talking about then?'

'Only this,' said Webster. 'The second the first torch touches the *houses*, the first shell will land on the city hall. And the second one will hit the First National. They'll go on down the line, the biggest targets first.'

Carter gaped. Then a flush of anger crawled from his throat up into his face.

'It won't work, Webster,' he snapped. 'You can't bluff me. Any cock-and-bull story like that—'

'It's no cock-and-bull story,' declared Webster. 'Those men have cannon out there. Pieces from in front of Legion halls, from the museums. And they have men who know how to work them. They wouldn't need them, really. It's practically point-blank range. Like shooting the broadside of a barn.'

Carter reached for the radio, but Webster stopped him with an upraised hand.

'Better think a minute, Carter, before you go flying off the handle. You're on a spot. Go ahead with your plan and you have a battle on your hands. The *houses* may burn but the loop is wrecked. The business men will have your scalp for that.'

Carter's hand retreated from the radio.

From far away came the sharp crack of a rifle.

'Better call them off,' warned Webster.

Carter's face twisted with indecision.

Another rifle shot, another and another.

'Pretty soon,' said Webster, 'it will have gone too far. So far that you can't stop it.'

A thudding blast rattled the windows of the room. Carter leaped from his chair.

Webster felt suddenly cold and weak. But he fought to keep his face straight and his voice calm.

Carter was staring out of the window, like a man of stone.

'I'm afraid,' said Webster, 'that it's gone too far already.'

The radio on the desk chirped insistently, red light flashing.

Carter reached out a trembling hand and snapped it on.

'Carter,' a voice was saying. 'Carter. Carter.'

Webster recognized that voice – the bull-throated tone of Police Chief Jim Maxwell.

'What is it?' asked Carter.

'They had a big gun,' said Maxwell. 'It exploded when they tried to fire it. Ammunition no good, I guess.'

'One gun?' asked Carter. 'Only one gun?'

'I don't see any others.'

'I heard rifle fire,' said Carter.

'Yeah, they did some shooting at us. Wounded a couple of the boys. But they've pulled back now. Deeper into the brush. No shooting now.'

'OK,' said Carter, 'go ahead and start the fires.'

Webster started forward. 'Ask him, ask him—'

But Carter clicked the switch and the radio went dead.

'What was it you wanted to ask?'

'Nothing,' said Webster. 'Nothing that amounted to anything.'

He couldn't tell Carter that Gramp had been the one who knew about firing big guns. Couldn't tell him that when the gun exploded Gramp had been there.

He'd have to get out of here, get over to the gun as quickly as possible.

'It was a good bluff, Webster,' Carter was saying. 'A good bluff, but it petered out.'

The mayor turned to the window that faced towards the *houses*.

'No more firing,' he said. 'They gave up quick.'

'You'll be lucky,' snapped Webster, 'if six of your policemen come back alive. Those men with the rifles are out in the brush and they can pick the eye out of a squirrel at a hundred yards.'

Feet pounded in the corridor outside, two pairs of feet racing towards the door.

The mayor whirled from his window and Webster pivoted around.

'Gramp!' he yelled.

'Hi, Johnny,' puffed Gramp, skidding to a stop.

The man behind Gramp was a young man and he was waving something in his hand – a sheaf of papers that rustled as he waved them.

'What do you want?' asked the mayor.

'Plenty,' said Gramp.

He stood for a moment, catching back his breath, and said between puffs:

'Meet my friend, Henry Adams.'

'Adams?' asked the mayor.

'Sure,' said Gramp. 'His granddaddy used to live here. Out on Twenty-seventh Street.'

'Oh,' said the mayor and it was as if someone had smacked him with a brick. 'Oh, you mean F. J. Adams.'

'Bet your boots,' said Gramp. 'Him and me, we were in the war together. Used to keep me awake nights telling me about his boy back home.'

Carter nodded to Henry Adams. 'As mayor of the city,' he said, trying to regain some of his dignity, 'I welcome you to—'

'It's not a particularly fitting welcome,' Adams said. 'I understand you are burning my property.'

'Your property!' The mayor choked and his eyes stared in disbelief at the sheaf of papers Adams waved at him.

'Yeah, his property,' shrilled Gramp. 'He just bought it. We just come from the treasurer's office. Paid all the back taxes and penalties and all the other things you legal thieves thought up to slap against them houses.'

'But, but—' the mayor was grasping for words, gasping for breath. 'Not all of it. Perhaps just the old Adams property.'

'Lock, stock and barrel,' said Gramp triumphantly.

'And now,' said Adams to the mayor, 'if you would kindly tell your men to stop destroying my property.'

Carter bent over the desk and fumbled at the radio, his hands suddenly all thumbs.

'Maxwell,' he shouted. 'Maxwell, Maxwell.'

'What do you want?' Maxwell yelled back.

'Stop setting those fires,' yelled Carter. 'Start putting them out. Call out the fire department. Do anything. But stop those fires.'

'Cripes,' said Maxwell, 'I wish you'd make up your mind.'

'You do what I tell you,' screamed the mayor. 'You put out those fires.'

'All right,' said Maxwell. 'All right. Keep your shirt on. But the boys won't like it. They won't like getting shot at to do something you changed your mind about.'

Carter straightened from the radio.

'Let me assure you, Mr. Adams,' he said, 'that this is all a big mistake.'

'It is,' Adams declared solemnly. 'A very great mistake, mayor. The biggest one you ever made.'

For a moment the two of them stood there, looking across the room at one another.

'To-morrow,' said Adams, 'I shall file a petition with the courts asking dissolution of the city charter. As owner of the greatest portion of the land included in the corporate limits, both from the standpoint of area and valuation, I understand I have a perfect legal right to do that.'

The mayor gulped, finally brought out some words:

34

'Upon what grounds?' he asked.

'Upon the grounds,' said Adams, 'that there is no further need of it. I do not believe I shall have too hard a time to prove my case.'

'But . . . but . . . that means

'Yeah,' said Gramp, 'you know what it means. It means you are out right on your ear.'

'A park,' said Gramp, waving his arm over the wilderness that once had been the residential section of the city. 'A park so that people can remember how their old folks lived.'

The three of them stood on Tower Hill, with the rusty old water tower looming above them, its sturdy steel legs planted in a sea of waist-high grass.

'Not a park, exactly,' explained Henry Adams. 'A memorial, rather. A memorial to an era of communal life that will be forgotten in another hundred years. A preservation of a number of peculiar types of construction that arose to suit certain conditions and each man's particular tastes. No slavery to any architectural concepts, but an effort made to achieve better living. In another hundred years men will walk through those houses down there with the same feeling of respect and awe they have when they go into a museum today. It will be to them something out of what amounts to a primeval age, a stepping-stone on the way to the better, fuller life. Artists will spend their lives transferring those old houses to their canvases. Writers of historical novels will come here for the breath of authenticity.'

'But you said you meant to restore all the houses, make the lawns and gardens exactly like they were before,' said Webster. 'That will take a fortune. And, after that, another fortune to keep them in shape.'

'I have too much money,' said Adams. 'Entirely too much money. Remember, my grandfather and father got into atomics on the ground floor.'

'Best crap player I ever knew, your granddaddy was,' said Gramp. 'Used to take me for a cleaning every pay day.'

'In the old days,' said Adams, 'when a man had too much

money, there were other things he could do with it. Organized charities, for example. Or medical research or something like that. But there are no organized charities to-day. Not enough business to keep them going. And since the World Committee has hit its stride, there is ample money for all the research, medical or otherwise, anyone might wish to do.

'I didn't plan this thing when I came back to see my grandfather's old house. Just wanted to see it, that was all. He'd told me so much about it. How he planted the tree in the front lawn. And the rose garden he had out back.

'And then I saw it. And it was a mocking ghost. It was something that had been left behind. Something that had meant a lot to someone and had been left behind. Standing there in front of that house with Gramp that day, it came to me that I could do nothing better than preserve for posterity a cross section of the life their ancestors lived.'

A thin blue thread of smoke rose above the trees far below.

Webster pointed to it. 'What about them?'

'The Squatters stay,' said Adams, 'if they want to. There will be plenty of work for them to do. And there'll always be a house or two that they can have to live in.

'There's just one thing that bothers me. I can't be here all the time myself. I'll need someone to manage the project. It'll be a lifelong job.'

He looked at Webster.

'Go ahead, Johnny,' said Gramp.

Webster shook his head. 'Betty's got her heart set on that place out in the country.'

'You wouldn't have to stay here,' said Adams. 'You could fly in every day.'

From the foot of the hill came a hail.

'It's Ole,' yelled Gramp.

He waved his cane. 'Hi, Ole. Come on up.'

They watched Ole striding up the hill, waiting for him, silently.

'Wanted to talk to you, Johnny,' said Ole. 'Got an idea. Waked me out of a sound sleep last night.'

'Go ahead,' said Webster.

Ole glanced at Adams. 'He's all right,' said Webster. 'He's Henry Adams. Maybe you remember his grandfather, old FJ.'

'I remember him,' said Ole. 'Nuts about atomic power, he was. How did he make out?'

'He made out rather well,' said Adams.

'Glad to hear that,' Ole said. 'Guess I was wrong. Said he never would amount to nothing. Day-dreamed all the time.'

'How about that idea?' Webster asked.

'You heard about dude ranches, ain't you?' Ole asked.

Webster nodded.

'Place,' said Ole, 'where people used to go and pretend they were cowboys. Pleased them because they really didn't know all the hard work there was in ranching and figured it was romantic-like to ride horses and—'

'Look,' asked Webster, 'you aren't figuring on turning your farm into a dude ranch, are you?'

'Nope,' said Ole. 'Not a dude ranch. Dude farm, maybe. Folks don't know too much about farms any more, since there ain't hardly no farms. And they'll read about the frost being on the pumpkin and how pretty a—'

Webster stared at Ole. 'They'd go for it, Ole,' he declared. 'They'd kill one another in the rush to spend their vacation on a real, honest-to-God, old-time farm.'

Out of a clump of bushes down the hillside burst a shining thing that chattered and gurgled and screeched, blades flashing, a cranelike arm waving.

'What the—' asked Adams.

'It's that dadburned lawn mower!' yelped Gramp. 'I always knew the day would come when it would strip a gear and go completely off its nut!'

Still alien by all other standards, the second tale strikes a more familiar note than did the first. Here, for the first time, the reader gains an impression that this tale might have been born about a Doggish campfire, a situation unthinkable so far as the first tale is concerned.

Here is voiced some of the high moral and ethical concepts which the Dogs have come to value. Here, too, is a struggle which a Dog can understand, even though the struggle does reveal the mental and moral deterioration of its central character.

For the first time, too, a character emerges which has a familiar ring – the robot. In the robot Jenkins, first introduced in this story, one comes to know a character which for thousands of years has been a puppish favourite. Jenkins is regarded by Tige as the real hero of the legend. In him he sees an extension of Man's influence beyond the day of Man's disappearance, a mechanical device by which human thought continued to guide the Dogs long after Man himself was gone.

We still have our robots, valuable and lovable little contraptions that exist for one purpose only – to furnish us with hands. Throughout the years, however, a Dog's robot has become so much a part of him that no Dog now regards his robot as a thing apart.

Tige's insistence that the robot is an invention of Man, a heritage that our race carries forward from Man, has been sturdily attacked by most other students of the legend.

The idea that the robot may have been fashioned and given

to the Dogs as an aid to the development of their culture, Bounce believes, is an idea which must be summarily ruled out by the very virtue of its romanticism. It is, he contends, a story device on the face of it and as such must necessarily be suspect from the first.

There is no way now of knowing how the Dogs evolved a robot. Those few scholars who have given some time to a study of the development of robotry, point out that the highly specialized use to which the robot is put does indeed argue that it was invented by a Dog. To be so specialized, they argue, the robot must necessarily have been invented and developed by the race for whose particular use it is so singularly fitted. No one other than a Dog, they contend, could have done so good a job on so intricate a tool.

To say that no Dog to-day could build a robot is begging the question. No Dog to-day could build a robot because there is no need to build one, since the robots build themselves. When there was a need, it is quite evident that a Dog did build a robot and, by building a robot endowed with the reproductive urge which resulted in his building others like himself, solved the problem in a typically Doggish manner.

In this story likewise is introduced an idea which runs through the rest of the legend and which for long has puzzled all students and most readers. That is the idea that one may move physically off this world, out into space, crossing it to reach other worlds. While the idea in most part has been regarded as pure fantasy which, of course, has its proper place in any legend, a good deal of study has been devoted to it. Most studies have confirmed the belief that such a thing is impossible. Such a belief would argue that the stars which we see at night are mighty worlds at great distances from our worlds. Everyone knows, of course, that they are only lights hanging in the sky and that most of them are very near to us.

Bounce advances what may be the best explanation for the origin of the across-space world idea. It is, he says, no more than an ancient story-teller's twist on the cobbly worlds, the existence of which the Dogs have known since dim antiquity.

II
Huddling Place

The drizzle sifted from the leaden skies, like smoke drifting through the bare-branched trees. It softened the hedges and hazed the outlines of the buildings and blotted out the distance. It glinted on the metallic skins of the silent robots and silvered the shoulders of the three humans listening to the intonations of the black-garbed man, who read from the book cupped between his hands.

'For I am the Resurrection and the Life—'

The moss-mellowed graven figure that reared above the door of the crypt seemed straining upwards, every crystal of its yearning body reaching towards something that no one else could see. Straining as it had strained since that day of long ago when men had chipped it from the granite to adorn the family tomb with a symbolism that had pleased the first John J. Webster in the last years he held of life.

'And whosoever liveth and believeth in Me—'

Jerome A. Webster felt his son's fingers tighten on his arm, heard the muffled sobbing of his mother, saw the lines of robots standing rigid, heads bowed in respect to the master they had served. The master who now was going home – to the final home of all.

Numbly, Jerome A. Webster wondered if they understood – if they understood life and death – if they understood what it meant that Nelson F. Webster lay there in the casket, that a man with a book intoned words above him.

Nelson F. Webster, fourth of the line of Websters who had lived on these acres, had lived and died here, scarcely leaving, and now was going to his final rest in that place the first of them had prepared for the rest of them – for that long line of shadowy descendants who would live here and cherish the things and the ways and the life that the first John J. Webster had established.

Jerome A. Webster felt his jaw muscles tighten, felt a little tremor run across his body. For a moment his eyes burned and the casket blurred in his sight and the words the man in black was saying were one with the wind that whispered in the pines standing sentinel for the dead. Within his brain remembrance marched – remembrance of a grey-haired man stalking the hills and fields, sniffing the breeze of an early morning, standing, legs braced, before the flaring fireplace with a glass of brandy in his hand.

Pride – the pride of land and life, and the humility and greatness that quiet living breeds within a man. Contentment of casual leisure and surety of purpose. Independence of assured security, comfort of familiar surroundings, freedom of broad acres.

Thomas Webster was joggling his elbow. 'Father,' he was whispering. 'Father.'

The service was over. The black-garbed man had closed his book. Six robots stepped forward, lifted the casket.

Slowly the three followed the casket into the crypt, stood silently as the robots slid it into its receptacle, closed the tiny door and affixed the plate that read:

NELSON F. WEBSTER

2034–2117

That was all. Just the name and dates. And that, Jerome A. Webster found himself thinking, was enough. There was nothing else that needed to be there. That was all those others had. The ones that called the family roll – starting with William Stevens, 1920–1999. Gramp Stevens, they had called him, Webster remembered. Father of the wife of that first John J. Webster, who was here himself – 1951–2020. And after him his son, Charles F. Webster, 1980–2060. And his son, John J. II, 2004–2086. Webster could remember John J. II – a grandfather who had slept beside the fire with his pipe hanging from his mouth, eternally threatening to set his whiskers aflame.

Webster's eyes strayed to another plate, Mary Webster, the mother of the boy here at his side. And yet not a boy. He kept forgetting that Thomas was twenty now, in a week or so would be leaving for Mars, even as in his younger days he, too, had gone to Mars.

All here together, he told himself. The Websters and their wives and children. Here in death together as they had lived together, sleeping in the pride and security of bronze and marble with the pines outside and the symbolic figure above the age-greened door.

The robots were waiting, standing silently, their task fulfilled.

His mother looked at him.

'You're head of the family now, my son,' she told him.

He reached out and hugged her close against his side. Head of the family – what was left of it. Just the three of them now. His mother and his son. And his son would be leaving soon, going out to Mars. But he would come back. Come back with a wife, perhaps, and the family would go on. The family wouldn't stay at three. Most of the big house wouldn't stay closed off, as it now was closed off. There had been a time when it had rung with the life of a dozen units of the family, living in their separate apartments under one big roof. That time, he knew, would come again.

The three of them turned and left the crypt, took the path back to the house, looming like a huge grey shadow in the mist.

A fire blazed in the hearth and the book lay upon his desk. Jerome A. Webster reached out and picked it up, read the title once again:

Martian Physiology, With Especial Reference to the Brain, by Jerome A. Webster, M.D.

Thick and authoritative – the work of a lifetime. Standing

almost alone in its field. Based upon the data gathered during those five plague years on Mars – years when he had labored almost day and night with his fellow colleagues of the World Committee's medical commission, dispatched on an errand of mercy to the neighbouring planet.

A tap sounded on the door.

'Come in,' he called.

The door opened and a robot glided in.

'Your whisky, sir.'

'Thank you, Jenkins,' Webster said.

'The minister, sir,' said Jenkins, 'has left.'

'Oh, yes. I presume that you took care of him.'

'I did, sir. Gave him the usual fee and offered him a drink. He refused the drink.'

'That was a social error,' Webster told him. 'Ministers don't drink.'

'I'm sorry, sir. I didn't know. He asked me to ask you to come to church sometime.'

'Eh?'

'I told him, sir, that you never went anywhere.'

'That was quite right, Jenkins,' said Webster. 'None of us ever go anywhere.'

Jenkins headed for the door, stopped before he got there, turned around. 'If I may say so, sir, that was a touching service at the crypt. Your father was a fine human, the finest ever was. The robots were saying the service was very fitting. Dignified like, sir. He would have liked it had he known.'

'My father,' said Webster, 'would be even more pleased to hear you say that, Jenkins.'

'Thank you, sir,' said Jenkins, and went out.

Webster sat with the whisky and the book and the fire – felt the comfort of the well-known room close in about him, felt the refuge that was in it.

This was home. It had been home for the Websters since that day when the first John J. had come here and built the first unit of the sprawling house. John J. had chosen it because it had a trout stream, or so he always said. But it was something

44

more than that It must have been, Webster told himself, something more than that.

Or perhaps, at first, it had only been the trout stream. The trout stream and the trees and meadows, the rocky ridge where the mist drifted in each morning from the river. Maybe the rest of it had grown, grown gradually through the years, through years of family association until the very soil was soaked with something that approached, but wasn't quite, tradition. Something that made each tree, each rock, each foot of soil a Webster tree or rock or clod of soil. It all belonged.

John J., the first John J., had come after the break-up of the cities, after men had forsaken, once and for all, the twentieth century huddling places, had broken free of the tribal instinct to stick together in one cave or in one clearing against a common foe or a common fear. An instinct that had become outmoded, for there were no fears or foes. Man revolting against the herd instinct economic and social conditions had impressed upon him in ages past. A new security and a new sufficiency had made it possible to break away.

The trend had started back in the twentieth century, more than two hundred years before, when men moved to country homes to get fresh air and elbow room and a graciousness in life that communal existence, in its strictest sense, never had given them.

And here was the end result. A quiet living. A peace that could only come with good things. The sort of life that men had yearned for years to have. A manorial existence, based on old family homes and leisurely acres, with atomics supplying power and robots in place of serfs.

Webster smiled at the fireplace with its blazing wood. That was an anachronism, but a good one – something that Man had brought forward from the caves. Useless, because atomic heating was better – but more pleasant. One couldn't sit and watch atomics and dream and build castles in the flames.

Even the crypt out there, where they had put his father that afternoon. That was family, too. All of a piece with the rest of it. The sombre pride and leisured life and peace. In the old days the dead were buried in vast plots all together, stranger cheek by jowl with stranger—

He never goes anywhere.

That is what Jenkins had told the minister.

And that was right. For what need was there to go anywhere? It all was here. By simply twirling a dial one could talk face to face with anyone one wished, could go, by sense, if not in body, anywhere one wished. Could attend the theatre or hear a concert or browse in a library half-way around the world. Could transact any business one might need to transact without rising from one's chair.

Webster drank the whisky, then swung to the dialled machine beside his desk.

He spun dials from memory without resorting to the log. He knew where he was going.

His finger flipped a toggle and the room melted away – or seemed to melt. There was left the chair within which he sat, part of the desk, part of the machine itself and that was all.

The chair was on a hillside swept with golden grass and dotted with scraggly, wind-twisted trees, a hillside that straggled down to a lake nestling in the grip of purple mountain spurs. The spurs, darkened in long streaks with the bluish-green of distant pine, climbed in staggering stairs, melting into the blue-tinged snow-capped peaks that reared beyond and above them in jagged saw-toothed outline.

The wind talked harshly in the crouching trees and ripped the long grass in sudden gusts. The last rays of the sun struck fire from the distant peaks.

Solitude and grandeur, the long sweep of tumbled land, the cuddled lake, the knife-like shadows on the far-off ranges.

Webster sat easily in his chair, eyes squinting at the peaks.

A voice said almost at his shoulder: 'May I come in?'

A soft, sibilant voice, wholly unhuman. But one that Webster knew.

Webster nodded his head. 'By all means, Juwain.'

He turned slightly and saw the elaborate crouching pedestal, the furry, soft-eyed figure of the Martian squatting on it. Other alien furniture loomed indistinctly beyond the pedestal, half guessed furniture from that dwelling out on Mars.

The Martian flipped a furry hand towards the mountain range.

'You love this,' he said. 'You can understand it. And I can understand how you understand it, but to me there is more terror than beauty in it. It is something we could never have on Mars.'

Webster reached out a hand, but the Martian stopped him.

'Leave it on,' he said. 'I know why you came here. I would not have come at a time like this except I thought perhaps an old friend—'

'It is kind of you,' said Webster. 'I am glad that you have come.'

'Your father,' said Juwain, 'was a great man. I remember how you used to talk to me of him, those years you spent on Mars. You said then you would come back sometime. Why is it you've never come?'

'Why,' said Webster, 'I just never—'

'Do not tell me,' said the Martian. 'I already know.'

'My son,' said Webster, 'is going to Mars in a few days. I shall have him call on you.'

'That would be a pleasure,' said Juwain. 'I shall be expecting him.'

He stirred uneasily on the crouching pedestal. 'Perhaps he carries on tradition.'

'No,' said Webster. 'He is studying engineering. He never cared for surgery.'

'He has a right,' observed the Martian, 'to follow the life that he has chosen. Still, one might be permitted to wish.'

'One could,' Webster agreed. 'But that is over and done with. Perhaps he will be a great engineer. Space structure. Talks of ships out to the stars.'

'Perhaps,' suggested Juwain, 'your family has done enough for medical science. You and your father—'

'And his father,' said Webster, 'before him.'

'Your book,' declared Juwain, 'has put Mars in debt to you.

47

It may focus more attention on Martian specialization. My people do not make good doctors. They have no background for it. Queer how the minds of races run. Queer that Mars never thought of medicine – literally never thought of it. Supplied the need with a cult of fatalism. While even in your early history, when men still lived in caves—'

'There are many things,' said Webster, 'that you thought of and we didn't. Things we wonder now how we ever missed. Abilities that you developed and we do not have. Take your own speciality, philosophy. But different than ours. A science, while ours never was more than ordered fumbling. Yours an orderly, logical development of philosophy, workable, practical, applicable, an actual tool.'

Juwain started to speak, hesitated, then went ahead. 'I am near to something, something that may be new and startling. Something that will be a tool for you humans as well as for the Martians. I've worked on it for years, starting with certain mental concepts that first were suggested to me with arrival of the Earthmen. I have said nothing, for I could not be sure.'

'And now,' suggested Webster, 'you are sure.'

'Not quite,' said Juwain. 'Not positive. But almost.'

They sat in silence, watching the mountains and the lake. A bird came and sat in one of the scraggly trees and sang. Dark clouds piled up behind the mountain ranges and the snow-tipped peaks stood out like graven stone. The sun sank in a lake of crimson, hushed finally to the glow of a fire burned low.

A tap sounded from a door and Webster stirred in his chair, suddenly brought back to the reality of the study, of the chair beneath him.

Juwain was gone. The old philosopher had come and sat an hour of contemplation with his friend and then had quietly slipped away.

The rap came again.

Webster leaned forward, snapped the toggle and the mountains vanished; the room became a room again. Dusk filtered through the high windows and the fire was a rosy flicker in the ashes.

'Come in,' said Webster.

Jenkins opened the door. 'Dinner is served, sir,' he said.

'Thank you,' said Webster. He rose slowly from the chair.

'Your place, sir,' said Jenkins, 'is laid at the head of the table.'

'Ah, yes,' said Webster. 'Thank you, Jenkins. Thank you very much, for reminding me.'

Webster stood on the broad ramp of the space field and watched the shape that dwindled in the sky with faint flickering points of red lancing through the wintry sunlight.

For long minutes after the shape was gone he stood there, hands gripping the railing in front of him, eyes still staring up into the sky.

His lips moved and they said: 'Good-bye, son'; but there was no sound.

Slowly he came alive to his surroundings. Knew that people moved about the ramp, saw that the landing field seemed to stretch interminably to the far horizon, dotted here and there with hump-backed things that were waiting spaceships. Scooting tractors worked near one hangar, clearing away the last of the snowfall of the night before.

Webster shivered and thought that it was queer, for the noonday sun was warm. And shivered again.

Slowly he turned away from the railing and headed for the administration building. And for one brain-wrenching moment he felt a sudden fear – an unreasonable and embarrassing fear of that stretch of concrete that formed the ramp. A fear that left him shaking mentally as he drove his feet towards the waiting door.

A man walked towards him, briefcase swinging in his hand, and Webster, eyeing him, wished fervently that the man would not speak to him.

The man did not speak, passed him with scarcely a glance, and Webster felt relief.

If he were back home, Webster told himself, he would have finished lunch, would now be ready to lie down for his midday nap. The fire would be blazing on the hearth and the flicker of the flames would be reflected from the andirons. Jenkins would bring him a liqueur and would say a word or two – inconsequential conversation.

He hurried towards the door, quickening his step, anxious to get away from the bare-cold expanse of the massive ramp.

Funny how he had felt about Thomas. Natural, of course, that he should have hated to see him go. But entirely unnatural that he should, in those last few minutes, find such horror welling up within him. Horror of the trip through space, horror of the alien land of Mars – although Mars was scarcely alien any longer. For more than a century now Earth-men had known it, had fought it, lived with it; some of them had even grown to love it.

But it had only been utter will power that had prevented him, in those last few seconds before the ship had taken off, from running out into the field, shrieking for Thomas to come back, shrieking for him not to go.

And that, of course, never would have done. It would have been exhibitionism, disgraceful and humiliating – the sort of a thing a Webster could not do.

After all, he told himself, a trip to Mars was no great adventure, not any longer. There had been a day when it had been, but that day was gone for ever. He, himself, in his earlier days had a made a trip to Mars, had stayed there for five long years. That had been – he gasped when he thought of it – that had been almost thirty years ago.

The babble and hum of the lobby hit him in the face as the robot attendant opened the door for him, and in that babble ran a vein of something that was almost terror. For a moment he hesitated, then stepped inside. The door closed softly behind him.

He stayed close to the wall to keep out of people's way, headed for a chair in one corner. He sat down and huddled back, forcing his body deep into the cushions, watching the milling humanity that seethed out in the room.

Shrill people, hurrying people, people with strange, unneighbourly faces. Strangers – every one of them. Not a face he knew. People going places. Heading out for the planets. Anxious to be off. Worried about last details. Rushing here and there.

Out of the crowd loomed a familiar face. Webster hunched forward.

'Jenkins!' he shouted, and then was sorry for the shout, although no one seemed to notice.

The robot moved towards him, stood before him.

'Tell Raymond,' said Webster, 'that I must return immediately. Tell him to bring the 'copter in front at once.'

'I am sorry, sir,' said Jenkins, 'but we cannot leave at once. The mechanics found a flaw in the atomics chamber. They are installing a new one. It will take several hours.'

'Surely,' said Webster, impatiently, 'that could wait until some other time.'

'The mechanic said not, sir,' Jenkins told him. 'It might go at any minute. The entire charge of power—'

'Yes, yes,' agreed Webster, 'I suppose so.'

He fidgeted with his hat. 'I just remembered,' he said, 'something I must do. Something that must be done at once. I must get home. I can't wait several hours.'

He hitched forward to the edge of the chair, eyes staring at the milling crowd.

Faces – faces—

'Perhaps you could televise,' suggested Jenkins. 'One of the robots might be able to do it. There is a booth—'

'Wait, Jenkins,' said Webster. He hesitated a moment. 'There is nothing to do back home. Nothing at all. But I must get there. I can't stay here. If I have to, I'll go crazy. I was frightened, out there on the ramp. I'm bewildered and confused here. I have a feeling – a strange, terrible feeling. Jenkins, I—'

'I understand, sir,' said Jenkins. 'Your father had it, too.'

Webster gasped. 'My father?'

'Yes, sir, that is why he never went anywhere. He was about

51

your age, sir, when he found it out. He tried to make a trip to Europe and he couldn't. He got halfway there and turned back. He had a name for it.'

Webster sat in stricken silence.

'A name for it,' he finally said. 'Of course there's a name for it. My father had it. My grandfather – did he have it, too?'

'I wouldn't know that, sir,' said Jenkins. 'I wasn't created until after your grandfather was an elderly man. But he may have. He never went anywhere, either.'

'You understand, then,' said Webster. 'You know how it is. I feel like I'm going to be sick – physically ill. See if you can charter a 'copter – anything, just so we get home.'

'Yes, sir,' said Jenkins.

He started off and Webster called him back.

'Jenkins, does anyone else know about this? Anyone—'

'No, sir,' said Jenkins. 'Your father never mentioned it and I felt, somehow, that he wouldn't wish me to.'

'Thank you, Jenkins,' said Webster.

Webster huddled back into his chair again, feeling desolate and alone and misplaced. Alone in a humming lobby that pulsed with life – a loneliness that tore at him, that left him limp and weak.

Homesickness. Downright, shameful homesickness, he told himself. Something that boys are supposed to feel when they first leave home, when they first go out to meet the world.

There was a fancy word for it – agoraphobia, the morbid dread of being in the midst of open spaces – from the Greek root for the fear – literally, of the market place.

If he crossed the room to the television booth, he could put in a call, talk with his mother or one of the robots – or, better yet, just sit and look at the place until Jenkins came for him.

He started to rise, then sank back in the chair again. It was no dice. Just talking to someone or looking in on the place wasn't being there. He couldn't smell the pines in the wintry air, or hear familiar snow crunch on the walk beneath his feet or reach out a hand and touch one of the massive oaks that grew along the path. He couldn't feel the heat of the fire or sense the sure, deft touch of belonging, of being one with a tract of ground and the things upon it.

And yet – perhaps it would help. Not much, maybe, but some. He started to rise from the chair again and froze. The few short steps to the booth held terror, a terrible, overwhelming terror. If he crossed them, he would have to run. Run to escape the watching eyes, the unfamiliar sounds, the agonizing nearness of strange faces.

Abruptly he sat down.

A woman's shrill voice cut across the lobby and he shrank away from it. He felt terrible. He felt like hell. He wished Jenkins would get a hustle on.

The first breath of spring came through the window, filling the study with the promise of melting snows, of coming leaves and flowers, of north-bound wedges of waterfowl streaming through the blue, of trout that lurked in pools waiting for the fly.

Webster lifted his eyes from the sheaf of papers on his desk, sniffed the breeze, felt the cool whisper of it on his cheek. His hand reached out for the brandy glass, found it empty, and put it back.

He bent back above the papers once again, picked up a pencil and crossed out a word.

Critically, he read the final paragraphs:

The fact that of the two hundred and fifty men who were invited to visit me, presumably on missions of more than ordinary importance, only three were able to come, does not necessarily prove that all but those three are victims of agoraphobia. Some may have had legitimate reasons for being unable to accept my invitation. But it does indicate a growing unwillingness of men living under the mode of Earth existence set up following the break-up of the cities to move from familiar places, a deepening instinct to stay among the scenes and possessions which in their mind have become associated with contentment and graciousness of life.

What the result of such a trend will be, no one can clearly

indicate since it applies to only a small portion of Earth's population. Among the larger families economic pressure forces some of the sons to seek their fortunes either in other parts of the Earth or on one of the other planets. Many others deliberately seek adventure and opportunity in space while still others become associated with professions or trades which made a sedentary existence impossible.

He flipped the page over, went on to the last one.

It was a good paper, he knew, but it could not be published, not just yet. Perhaps after he had died. No one, so far as he could determine, had ever so much as realized the trend, had taken as matter of course the fact that men seldom left their homes. Why, after all, should they leave their homes?

Certain dangers may be recognized in—

The televisor muttered at his elbow and he reached out to flip the toggle.

The room faded and he was face to face with a man who sat behind a desk, almost as if he sat on the opposite side of Webster's desk. A grey-haired man with sad eyes behind heavy lenses.

For a moment Webster stared, memory tugging at him.

'Could it be—' he asked and the man smiled gravely.

'I have changed,' he said. 'So have you. My name is Clayborne. Remember? The Martian medical commission—'

'Clayborne! I'd often thought of you. You stayed on Mars.'

Clayborne nodded. 'I've read your book, doctor. It is a real contribution. I've often thought one should be written, wanted to myself, but I didn't have the time. Just as well I didn't. You did a better job. Especially on the brain.'

'The Martian brain,' Webster told him, 'always intrigued me. Certain peculiarities. I'm afraid I spent more of those five years taking notes on it than I should have. There was other work to do.'

'A good thing you did,' said Clayborne. 'That's why I'm

54

calling you now. I have a patient – a brain operation. Only you can handle it.'

Webster gasped, his hands trembling. 'You'll bring him here?'

Clayborne shook his head. 'He cannot be moved. You know him, I believe. Juwain, the philosopher.'

'Juwain!' said Webster. 'He's one of my best friends. We talked together just a couple of days ago.'

'The attack was sudden,' said Clayborne. 'He's been asking for you.'

Webster was silent and cold – cold with a chill that crept upon him from some unguessed place. Cold that sent perspiration out upon his forehead, that knotted his fists.

'If you start immediately,' said Clayborne, 'you can be here on time. I've already arranged with the World Committee to have a ship at your disposal instantly. The utmost speed is necessary.'

'But,' said Webster, 'but . . . I cannot come.'

'You can't come!'

'It's impossible,' said Webster. 'I doubt in any case that I am needed. Surely, you yourself—'

'I can't,' said Clayborne. 'No one can but you. No one else has the knowledge. You hold Juwain's life in your hands. If you come, he lives. If you don't, he dies.'

'I can't go into space,' said Webster.

'Anyone can go into space,' snapped Clayborne. 'It's not like it used to be. Conditioning of any sort desired is available.'

'But you don't understand,' pleaded Webster. 'You—'

'No, I don't,' said Clayborne. 'Frankly, I don't. That anyone should refuse to save the life of his friend—'

The two men stared at one another for a long moment neither speaking.

'I shall tell the committee to send the ship straight to your home,' said Clayborne finally. 'I hope by that time you will see your way clear to come.'

Clayborne faded and the wall came into view again – the wall and books, the fireplace and the paintings, the well-loved furniture, the promise of spring that came through the open window.

Webster sat frozen in his chair, staring at the wall in front of him.

Juwain, the furry, wrinkled face, the sibilant whisper, the friendliness and understanding that was his. Juwain, grasping the stuff that dreams are made of and shaping them into logic, into rules of life and conduct. Juwain using philosophy as a tool, as a science, as a stepping stone to better living.

Webster dropped his face into his hands and fought the agony that welled up within him.

Clayborne had not understood. One could not expect him to understand since there was no way for him to know. And even knowing, would he understand? Even he, Webster, would not have understood it in someone else until he had discovered it in himself – the terrible fear of leaving his own fire, his own land, his own possessions, the little symbolisms that he had erected. And yet, not he, himself, alone, but those other Websters as well. Starting with the first John J. Men and women who had set up a cult of Life, a tradition of behaviour.

He, Jerome A. Webster, had gone to Mars when he was a young man, and had not felt or suspected the psychological poison that ran through his veins. Even as Thomas a few months ago had gone to Mars. But thirty years of quiet life here in the retreat that the Websters called a home had brought it forth, had developed it without his even knowing it. There had, in fact, been no opportunity to know it.

It was clear how it had developed – clear as crystal now. Habit and mental pattern and a happiness association with certain things – things that had no actual value in themselves, but had been assigned a value, a definite, concrete value by one family through five generations.

No wonder other places seemed alien, no wonder other horizons held a hint of horror in their sweep.

And there was nothing one could do about it – nothing, that is, unless one cut down every tree and burned the house and

changed the course of waterways. Even that might not do it –
even that—

The televisor purred and Webster lifted his head from his
hands, reached out and thumbed the tumbler.

The room became a flare of white, but there was no image.
A voice said: 'Secret call. Secret call.'

Webster slid back a panel in the machine, spun a pair of
dials, heard the hum of power surge into a screen that blocked
out the room.

'Secrecy established,' he said.

The white flare snapped out and a man sat across the desk
from him. A man he had seen many times before in televized
addresses, in his daily paper.

Henderson, president of the World Committee.

'I have had a call from Clayborne,' said Henderson.

Webster nodded without speaking.

'He tells me you refuse to go to Mars.'

'I have not refused,' said Webster. 'When Clayborne cut off
the question was left open. I had told him it was impossible for
me to go, but he had rejected that, did not seem to understand.'

'Webster, you must go,' said Henderson. 'You are the only
man with the necessary knowledge of the Martian brain to
perform this operation. If it were a simple operation, perhaps
someone else could do it. But not one such as this.'

'That may be true,' said Webster, 'but—'

'It's not just a question of saving a life,' said Henderson.
'Even the life of so distinguished a personage as Juwain. It
involves even more than that. Juwain is a friend of yours.
Perhaps he hinted of something he has found.'

'Yes,' said Webster. 'Yes, he did. A new concept of philosophy.'

'A concept,' declared Henderson, 'that we cannot do without. A concept that will remake the solar system, that will put
mankind ahead a hundred thousand years in the space of two
generations. A new direction of purpose that will aim towards a
goal we heretofore had not suspected, had not even known

existed. A brand new truth, you see. One that never before had occurred to anyone.'

Webster's hands gripped the edge of the desk until his knuckles stood out white.

'If Juwain dies,' said Henderson, 'that concept dies with him. May be lost forever.'

'I'll try,' said Webster. 'I'll try—'

Henderson's eyes were hard. 'Is that the best that you can do?'

'That is the best,' said Webster.

'But man, you must have a reason! Some explanation.'

'None,' said Webster, 'that I would care to give.'

Deliberately he reached out and flipped up the switch.

Webster sat at the desk and held his hands in front of him, staring at them. Hands that had skill, held knowledge. Hands that could save a life if he could get them to Mars. Hands that could save for the solar system, for mankind, for the Martians an idea – a new idea – that would advance them a hundred thousand years in the next two generations.

But hands chained by a phobia that grew out of this quiet life. Decadence – a strangely beautiful – and deadly – decadence.

Man had forsaken the teeming cities, the huddling places, two hundred years ago. He had done with the old foes and the ancient fears that kept him around the common campfire, had left behind the hobgoblins that had walked with him from the caves.

And yet – and yet—

Here was another huddling place. Not a middling place for one's body, but one's mind. A psychological campfire that still held a man within the circle of its light.

Still, Webster knew, he must leave that fire. As the men had done with the cities two centuries before, he must walk off and leave it. And he must not look back.

He had to go to Mars – or at least start for Mars. There was no question there, at all. He had to go.

Whether he would survive the trip, whether he could perform the operation once he had arrived, he did not know. He wondered vaguely, whether agoraphobia could be fatal. In its most exaggerated form, he supposed it could.

He reached out a hand to ring, then hesitated. No use having Jenkins pack. He would do it himself – something to keep him busy until the ship arrived.

From the top shelf of the wardrobe in the bedroom, he took down a bag and saw that it was dusty. He blew on it, but the dust still clung. It had been there for too many years.

As he packed, the room argued with him, talked in that mute tongue with which inanimate but familiar things may converse with a man.

'You can't go,' said the room. 'You can't go off and leave me.'

And Webster argued back, half pleading, half explanatory. 'I have to go. Can't you understand? It's a friend, an old friend. I will be coming back.'

Packing done, Webster returned to the study, slumped into his chair.

He must go and yet he couldn't go. But when the ship arrived, when the time had come, he knew that he would walk out of the house and towards the waiting ship.

He steeled his mind to that, tried to set it in a rigid pattern, tried to blank out everything but the thought that he was leaving.

Things in the room intruded on his brain, as if they were part of a conspiracy to keep them there. Things that he saw as if he were seeing them for the first time. Old, remembered things that suddenly were new. The chronometer that showed both Earthian and Martian time, the days of the month, the phases of the moon. The picture of his dead wife on the desk. The trophy he had won at prep school. The framed short snorter bill that had cost him ten bucks on his trip to Mars.

He stared at them, half unwilling at first, then eagerly, storing up the memory of them in his brain. Seeing them as separate components of a room he had accepted all these years as a finished whole, never realizing what a multitude of things went to make it up.

Dusk was falling, the dusk of early spring, a dusk that smelled of early pussy willows.

The ship should have arrived long ago. He caught himself listening for it, even as he realized that he would not hear it. A ship, driven by atomic motors, was silent except when it gathered speed. Landing and taking off, it floated like thistledown, with not a murmur in it.

It would be here soon. It would have to be here soon or he could never go. Much longer to wait, he knew, and his high-keyed resolution would crumble like a mound of dust in beating rain. Not much longer could he hold his purpose against the pleading of the room, against the flicker of the fire, against the murmur of the land where five generations of Websters had lived their lives and died.

He shut his eyes and fought down the chill that crept across his body. He couldn't let it get him now, he told himself. He had to stick it out. When the ship arrived he still must be able to get up and walk out of the door to the waiting port.

A tap came on the door.

'Come in,' Webster called.

It was Jenkins, the light from the fireplace flickering on his shining metal hide.

'Had you called earlier, sir?' he asked.

Webster shook his head.

'I was afraid you might have,' Jenkins explained, 'and wondered why I didn't come. There was a most extraordinary occurrence, sir. Two men came with a ship and said they wanted you to go to Mars.'

'They are here,' said Webster. 'Why didn't you call me?'

He struggled to his feet.

'I didn't think, sir,' said Jenkins, 'that you would want to be bothered. It was so preposterous. I finally made them understand you could not possibly want to go to Mars.'

Webster stiffened, felt chill fear gripping at his heart. Hands groping for the edge of the desk, he sat down in the chair, sensed the walls of the room closing in about him, a trap that would never let him go.

NOTES ON THE THIRD TALE

To the thousands of readers who love this tale, it is distinguished as the one in which the Dogs first appear. To the student it is much more than that. Basically, it is a tale of guilt and futility. Here the breakdown of the human race continues, with Man assaulted by a sense of guilt and plagued by the instability which results in the human mutants.

The tale attempts to rationalize the mutations, attempts even to explain the Dogs as modifications of the primordial strain. No race, the story says, can become improved if there are no mutations, but there is no word concerning the need of a certain static factor in society to ensure stability. Throughout the legend it becomes abundantly clear that the human race placed little value upon stability.

Tige, who has combed the legend to bolster up contention that the tales actually are human in their origin, believes that no Doggish storyteller would have advanced the theory of mutation, a concept which runs counter to everything in the canine creed. A viewpoint such as this, he claims, must have sprung from some alien mind.

Bounce, however, points out that throughout the legend viewpoints which are diametrically opposed to canine logic often are presented in a favourable light. This, he says, is no more than the mark of a good storyteller – a twisting of values for certain dramatic shock effect.

That Man is presented deliberately as a character who realizes his own shortcomings there can be no doubt at all. In this tale, the human, Grant, talks about a 'groove of logic' and it is apparent that he senses something wrong with human logic. He tells Nathaniel that the human race is always worried. He fastens an almost infantile hope upon the Juwain theory as something which might yet save the human race.

And Grant, in the end, seeing the trend of destruction inherent in his race, passes the destiny of humanity on to Nathaniel.

Of all the characters which appear in the legend, Nathaniel may be the only one having an actual historic basis. In other tales which have come from the racial past, the name Nathaniel is often mentioned. While it is patently impossible that Nathaniel could have accomplished all the deeds which are attributed to him in these tales, it is generally believed that he actually lived and was a figure of importance. The basis of that importance, of course, has been lost in the gulf of time.

The Webster family of humans, which was introduced in the first tale, continues to hold a prominent place throughout the rest of the legend. While this may be another piece of evidence to support Tige's belief, it is possible that the Webster family once again may be no more than a mark of good storytelling, a device used to establish a link of continuity in a series of tales which otherwise are not too closely linked.

To one who reads too literally, the implication that the Dogs are a result of Man's intervention may prove to be somewhat shocking. Rover, who has never seen in the legend anything beyond pure myth, thinks that here we are dealing with an ancient attempt to explain racial origin. To cover up actual lack of knowledge, the tale develops an explanation which amounts to divine intervention. It is an easy and, to the primitive mind, a plausible and satisfactory way to explain something of which nothing at all is known.

III
Census

Richard Grant was resting beside the little spring that gushed out of the hillside and tumbled in a flashing stream across the twisting trail when the squirrel rushed past him and shinnied up a towering hickory tree. Behind the squirrel, in a cyclone of churning autumn-fallen leaves, came the little black dog.

When he saw Grant the dog skidded to a stop, stood watching him, tail wagging, eyes a-dance with fun.

Grant grinned. 'Hello, there,' he said.

'Hi,' said the dog.

Grant jerked out of his easy slouch, jaw hanging limp. The dog laughed back at him, red dish rag of a tongue lolling from its mouth.

Grant jerked a thumb at the hickory. 'Your squirrel's up there.'

'Thanks,' said the dog, 'I know it. I can smell him.'

Startled, Grant looked swiftly around, suspecting a practical joke. Ventriloquism, maybe. But there was no one in sight. The woods were empty except for himself and the dog, the gurgling spring, the squirrel chattering in the tree.

The dog walked closer.

'My name,' he said, 'is Nathaniel.'

The words were there. There was no doubt of it. Almost like human speech, except they were pronounced carefully, as one who was learning the language might pronounce them. And a brogue, an accent that could not be placed, a certain eccentricity of intonation.

'I live over the hill,' declared Nathaniel, 'with the Websters.'

He sat down, beat his tail upon the ground, scattering leaves. He looked extremely happy.

Grant suddenly snapped his fingers.

'Bruce Webster! Now I know. Should have thought of it before. Glad to meet you, Nathaniel.'

'Who are you?' asked Nathaniel.

'Me? I'm Richard Grant, enumerator.'

'What's an enum . . . enumer—'

'An enumerator is someone who counts people,' Grant explained. 'I'm taking a census.'

'There are lots of words,' said Nathaniel, 'that I can't say.'

He got up, walked over to the spring, and lapped noisily. Finished, he plunked himself down beside the man.

'Want to shoot the squirrel?' he asked.

'Want me to?'

'Sure thing,' said Nathaniel.

But the squirrel was gone. Together they circled the tree, searching its almost bare branches. There was no bushy tail sticking out from behind the boll, no beady eyes staring down at them. While they had talked, the squirrel had made his getaway.

Nathaniel looked a bit crestfallen, but he made the best of it.

'Why don't you spend the night with us?' he invited. 'Then, come morning, we could go hunting. Spend all day at it.'

Grant chuckled. 'I wouldn't want to trouble you. I am used to camping out.'

Nathaniel insisted. 'Bruce would be glad to see you. And Grandpa wouldn't mind. He don't know half what goes on, anyway.'

'Who's Grandpa?'

'His real name is Thomas,' said Nathaniel, 'but we all call him Grandpa. He is Bruce's father. Awful old now. Just sits all day and thinks about a thing that happened long ago.'

Grant nodded. 'I know about that, Nathaniel. Juwain.'

'Yeah, that's it,' agreed Nathaniel. 'What does it mean?'

Grant shook his head. 'Wish I could tell you, Nathaniel. Wish I knew.'

He hoisted the pack to his shoulder, stooped and scratched the dog behind the ear. Nathaniel grimaced with delight.

'Thanks,' he said, and started up the path.

Grant followed.

Thomas Webster sat in his wheel chair on the lawn and stared out across the evening hills.

I'll be eighty-six to-morrow, he was thinking. Eighty-six. That's a hell of a long time for a man to live. Maybe too long. Especially when he can't walk any more and his eyes are going bad.

Elsie will have a silly cake for me with lots of candles on it and the robots all will bring me a gift and those dogs of Bruce's will come in and wish me happy returns of the day and wag their tails at me. And there will be a few televisor calls – although not many, perhaps. And I'll pound my chest and say I'm going to live to be a hundred and everyone will grin behind their hands and say 'listen to the old fool'.

Eighty-six years and there were two things I meant to do. One of them I did and the other one I didn't.

A cawing crow skimmed over a distant ridge and slanted down into the valley shadow. From far away, down by the river, came the quacking of a flock of mallards.

Soon the stars would be coming out. Came out early this time of year. He liked to look at them. The stars! He patted the arms of the chair with fierce pride. The stars, by Lord, were his meat. An obsession? Perhaps – but at least something to wipe out that stigma of long ago, a shield to keep the family from the gossip of historic busybodies. And Bruce was helping too. Those dogs of his—

A step sounded in the grass behind him.

'Your whisky, sir,' said Jenkins.

Thomas Webster stared at the robot, took the glass off the tray.

'Thank you, Jenkins,' he said.

He twirled the glass between his fingers. 'How long, Jenkins, have you been lugging drinks to this family?'

'Your father, sir,' said Jenkins. 'And his father before him.'

'Any news?' asked the old man.

Jenkins shook his head. 'No news.'

Thomas Webster sipped the drink. 'That means, then, that they're well beyond the solar system. Too far out even for the Pluto station to relay. Halfway or better to Alpha Centauri. If only I live long enough—'

'You will, sir,' Jenkins told him. 'I feel it in my bones.'

'You,' declared the old man, 'haven't any bones.'

He sipped the drink slowly, tasting it with expert tongue. Watered too much again. But it wouldn't do to say anything. No use flying off the handle at Jenkins. That doctor! Telling Jenkins to water it a bit more. Depriving a man of proper drinking in his final years—

'What's that down there?' he asked, pointing to the path that straggled up the hill.

Jenkins turned to look.

'It appears, sir,' he said, 'that Nathaniel's bringing someone home.'

The dogs had trooped in to say good night, had left again.

Bruce Webster grinned after them.

'Great gang,' he said.

He turned to Grant. 'I imagine Nathaniel gave you quite a start this afternoon.'

Grant lifted the brandy glass, squinted through it at the light.

'He did,' he said. 'Just for a minute. And then I remembered things I'd read about what you're doing here. It isn't in my line, of course, but your work has been popularized, written up in more or less non-technical language.'

'Your line?' asked Webster. 'I thought—'

Grant laughed. 'I see what you mean. A census taker. An enumerator. All of that, I grant you.'

Webster was puzzled, just a bit embarrassed. 'I hope, Mr. Grant, that I haven't—'

'Not at all,' Grant told him. 'I'm used to being regarded as someone who writes down names and ages and then goes on to

68

the next group of human beings. That was the old idea of a census, of course. A nose counting, nothing more. A matter of statistics. After all, the last census was taken more than three hundred years ago. And times have changed.'

'You interest me,' said Webster. 'You make this nose counting of yours sound almost sinister.'

'It isn't sinister,' protested Grant. 'It's logical. It's an evaluation of the human population. Not just how many of them there are, but what are they really like, what are they thinking and doing?'

Webster slouched lower in his chair, stretching his feet out towards the fire upon the hearth. 'Don't tell me, Mr. Grant, that you intend to psycho-analyse me?'

Grant drained the brandy glass, set it on the table. 'I don't need to,' he said. 'The World Committee knows all it needs to know about the folks like you. But it is the others – the ridge runners, you call them here. Up north they're jackpine savages. Farther south they're something else. A hidden population – an almost forgotten population. The ones who took to the woods. The ones who scampered off when the World Committee loosened the strings of government.'

Webster grunted. 'The governmental strings had to be loosened,' he declared. 'History will prove that to anyone. Even before the World Committee came into being the governmental set-up of the world was burdened by ox-cart survivals. There was no more reason for the township government three hundred years ago than there is for a national government to-day.'

'You're absolutely right,' Grant told him, 'and yet when the grip of government was loosened, its hold upon the life of each man was loosened. The man who wanted to slip away and live outside his government, losing its benefits and escaping its obligations, found it an easy thing to do. The World Committee didn't mind. It had more things to worry over than the irresponsibles and malcontents. And there were plenty of them. The farmers, for instance, who lost their way of life with the coming of hydroponics. Many of them found it hard to fit into industrial life. So what? So they slipped away. They reverted to a primitive life. They raised a few crops, they hunted game, they trapped, they cut wood, did a little stealing now and then. Deprived of a livelihood, they went back to the soil, all the way back, and the soil took care of them.'

'That was three hundred years ago,' said Webster. 'The World Committee didn't mind about them then. It did what it could, of course, but, as you say, it didn't really mind if a few slipped through its fingers. So why this sudden interest now?'

'Just, I guess,' Grant told him, 'that they've got around to it.'

He regarded Webster closely, studying the man. Relaxed before the fire, his face held power, the shadows of the leaping flames etching planes upon his features, turning them almost surrealistic.

Grant hunted in his pocket, found his pipe, jammed tobacco in the bowl.

'There is something else,' he said.

'Eh,' asked Webster.

'There is something else about this census. They'd take it anyhow, perhaps, because a picture of Earth's population must always be an asset, a piece of handy knowledge. But that isn't all.'

'Mutants,' said Webster.

Grant nodded. 'That's right. I hardly expected anyone to guess it.'

'I work with mutants,' Webster pointed out. 'My whole life is bound up with mutations.'

'Queer bits of culture have been turning up,' said Grant. 'Stuff that has no precedent. Literary forms which bear the un-mistakable imprint of fresh personalities. Music that has broken away from traditional expression. Art that is like nothing ever seen before. And most of it anonymous or at least hidden under pseudonyms.'

Webster laughed. 'Such a thing, of course, is utter mystery to the World Committee.'

'It isn't that so much as something else,' Grant explained. 'The Committee is not so concerned with art and literature as it is with other things – things that don't show up. If there is a backwoods renaissance taking place, it would first come to notice, naturally, through new art and literary forms. But a renaissance is not concerned entirely with art and literature.'

Webster sank even lower in his chair and cupped his hands beneath his chin.

'I think I see,' he said, 'what you are driving at.'

They sat for long minutes in silence broken only by the crackling of the fire, by the ghostly whisper of an autumn wind in the trees outside.

'There was a chance once,' said Webster, almost as if he were speaking to himself. 'A chance for new viewpoints, for something that might have wiped out the muddle of four thousand years of human thought. A man muffed that chance.'

Grant stirred uncomfortably, then sat rigid, afraid Webster might have seen him move.

'That man,' said Webster, 'was my grandfather.'

Grant knew he must say something, that he could not continue to sit there, unspeaking.

'Juwain may have been wrong,' he said. 'He might not have found a new philosophy.'

'That is a thought,' declared Webster, 'we have used to console ourselves. And yet, it is unlikely. Juwain was a great Martian philosopher, perhaps the greatest Mars had ever known. If he could have lived, there is no doubt in my mind he would have developed that new philosophy. But he didn't live. He didn't live because my grandfather couldn't go to Mars.'

'It wasn't your grandfather's fault,' said Grant. 'He tried to. Agoraphobia is a thing that a man can't fight—'

Webster waved the words aside. 'That is over and done with. It is a thing that cannot be recaptured. We must accept that and go on from there. And since it was my family, since it was grandfather—'

Grant stared, shaken by the thought that occurred to him. 'The dogs! That's why—'

'Yes, the dogs,' said Webster.

From far away, in the river bottoms, came a crying sound, one with the wind that talked in the trees outside.

'A raccoon,' said Webster. 'The dogs will hear him and be rearing to get out.'

The cry came again, closer it seemed, although that must have been imagination.

Webster had straightened in the chair, was leaning forward, staring at the flames.

'After all, why not?' he asked. 'A dog has a personality. You can sense that in every one you meet. No two are exactly alike in mood and temperament. All of them are intelligent, in varying degrees. And that is all that's needed, a conscious personality and some measure of intelligence.

'They didn't get an even break, that's all. They had two handicaps. They couldn't talk and they couldn't walk erect and because they couldn't walk erect they had no chance to develop hands. But for speech and hands, we might be dogs and dogs be men.'

'I'd never thought of it like that,' said Grant. 'Not of your dogs as a thinking race—'

'No,' said Webster, and there was a trace of bitterness running in his words. 'No, of course, you didn't. You thought of them as most of the rest of the world still thinks of them. As curiosities, as sideshow animals, as funny pets. Pets that can talk with you.

'But it's more than that, Grant. I swear to you it is. Thus far Man has come alone. One thinking, intelligent race all by itself. Think of how much farther, how much faster it might have gone had there been two races, two thinking, intelligent races, working together. For, you see, they would not think alike. They'd check their thoughts against one another. What one couldn't think of, the other could. The old story of two heads.

'Think of it, Grant. A *different* mind than the human mind, but one that will work with the human mind. That will see and understand things the human mind cannot, that will develop, if you will, philosophies the human mind could not.'

He spread his hands towards the fire, long fingers with bone-hard, merciless knuckles.

'They couldn't talk and I gave them speech. It was not easy, for a dog's tongue and throat are not designed to speak. But surgery did it . . . an expedient at first . . . surgery and grafting. But now . . . now, I hope, I think . . . it is too soon to say—'

Grant was leaning forward, tensed.

'You mean the dogs are passing on the changes you have made. That there are hereditary evidences of the surgical corrections?'

Webster shook his head. 'It is too soon to say. Another twenty years, maybe I can tell you.'

He lifted the brandy bottle from the table, held it out.

'Thanks,' said Grant.

'I am a poor host,' Webster told him. 'You should have helped yourself.'

He raised the glass against the fire. 'I had good material to work with. A dog is smart. Smarter than you think. The ordinary, run of the mill dog recognizes fifty words or more. A hundred is not unusual. Add another hundred and he has a working vocabulary. You noticed, perhaps, the simple words that Nathaniel used. Almost basic English.'

Grant nodded. 'One and two syllables. He told me there were a lot of words he couldn't say.'

'There is much more to do,' said Webster. 'So much more to do. Reading, for example. A dog doesn't see as you and I do. I have been experimenting with lenses – correcting their eyesight so they can see as we do. And if that fails, there's still another way. Man must visualize the way a dog sees – learn to print books that dogs can read.'

'The dogs,' asked Grant, 'what do they think of it?'

'The dogs?' said Webster. 'Believe it or not, Grant, they're having the time of their merry lives.'

He stared into the fire.

'God bless their hearts,' he said.

*

73

Following Jenkins, Grant climbed the stairs to bed, but as they passed a partially opened door a voice hailed them.

'That you, stranger?'

Grant stopped, jerked around.

Jenkins said, in a whisper, 'That's the old gentleman, sir. Often he cannot sleep.'

'Yes,' called Grant.

'Sleepy?' asked the voice.

'Not very,' Grant told him.

'Come in for a while,' the old man said.

Thomas Webster sat propped up in bed, striped nightcap on his head. He saw Grant staring at it.

'Getting bald,' he rasped. 'Don't feel comfortable unless I got something on. Can't wear my hat to bed.'

He shouted at Jenkins. 'What you standing there for? Don't you see he needs a drink?'

'Yes, sir,' said Jenkins, and disappeared.

'Sit down,' said Thomas Webster. 'Sit down and listen for a while. Talking will help me go to sleep. And, besides we don't see new faces every day.'

Grant sat down.

'What do you think of that son of mine?' the old man asked.

Grant started at the unusual question. 'Why, I think he's splendid. The work he's doing with the dogs—'

The old man chuckled. 'Him and his dogs! Ever tell you about the time Nathaniel tangled with a skunk? Of course, I haven't. Haven't said more than a word or two to you.'

He ran his hands along the bed covering, long fingers picking at the fabric nervously.

'Got another son, you know. Allen. Call him Al. To-night he's the farthest from Earth that Man has ever been. Heading for the stars.'

Grant nodded. 'I know. I read about it. The Alpha Centauri expedition.'

'My father was a surgeon,' said Thomas Webster. 'Wanted me to be one, too. Almost broke his heart, I guess, when I

74

didn't take to it. But if he could know, he'd be proud of us to-night.'

'You mustn't worry about your son,' said Grant. 'He—'

The old man's glare silenced him. 'I built that ship myself. Designed it, watched it grow. If it's just a matter of navigating space, it'll get where it is going. And the kid is good. He can ride that crate through hell itself.'

He hunched himself straighter in the bed, knocking his nightcap askew against the piled-up pillows.

'And I got another reason to think he'll get there and back. Didn't think much about it at the time, but lately I've been recalling it, thinking it over, wondering if it mightn't mean . . . well, if it might not be—'

He gasped a bit for breath. 'Mind you, I'm not super-stitious.'

'Of course you're not,' said Grant.

'You bet I'm not,' said Webster.

'A sign of some sort, perhaps,' suggested Grant. 'A feeling. A hunch.'

'None of those,' declared the old man. 'An almost certain knowledge that destiny must be with me. That I was meant to build a ship that would make the trip. That someone or something decided it was about time Man got out to the stars and took a hand to help him along a bit.'

'You sound as if you're talking about an actual incident,' said Grant, 'As if there were some positive happening that makes you think the expedition will succeed.'

'You bet your boots,' said Webster. 'That's just exactly what I mean. It happened twenty years ago, out on the lawn in front of this very house.'

He pulled himself even straighter, gasped for breath, wheez-ing.

'I was stumped, you understand. The dream was broken. Years spent for nothing. The basic principle I had evolved to get the speed necessary for interstellar flight-simply wouldn't work. And the worst of it was, I knew it was *almost* right. I knew

75

there was just one little thing, one theoretical change that must be made. But I couldn't find it.

'So I was sitting out there on the lawn, feeling sorry for myself, with a sketch of the plan in front of me. I lived with it, you see. I carried it everywhere I went, figuring maybe that by just looking at it, the thing that was wrong would pop into my mind. You know how it does, sometimes.'

Grant nodded.

'While I was sitting there a man came along. One of the ridge runners. You know what a ridge runner is?'

'Sure,' said Grant.

'Well, this fellow came along. Kind of limber-jointed chap, ambling along as if he didn't have a trouble in the world. He stopped and looked over my shoulder and asked me what I had.

' "Spaceship drive," I told him.

'He reached down and took it and I let him have it. After all, what was the use? He couldn't understand a thing about it and it was no good, anyhow.

'And then he handed it back to me and jabbed his finger at one place. "That's your trouble," he said. And then he turned and galloped off and I sat staring after him, too done in to say a single word, to even call him back.'

The old man sat bolt upright in the bed, staring at the wall, nightcap canted crazily. Outside the wind sucked along the eaves with hollow hooting. And in that well-lighted room, there seemed to be shadows, although Grant knew there weren't any.

'Did you ever find him?' asked Grant.

The old man shook his head. 'Hide nor hair,' he said.

Jenkins came through the door with a glass, set it on the bedside table.

'I'll be back sir,' he said to Grant, 'to show you to your room.'

'No need of it,' said Grant. 'Just tell me where it is.'

'If you wish, sir,' said Jenkins. 'It's the third one down. I'll turn on the light and leave the door ajar.'

They sat, listening to the robot's feet go down the hall.

The old man glanced at the glass of whisky and cleared his throat.

'I wish now,' he said, 'I'd had Jenkins bring me one.'

'Why, that's all right,' said Grant. 'Take this one. I don't really need it.'

'Sure you don't?'

'Not at all.'

The old man stretched out his hand, took a sip, sighed gustily.

'Now that's what I call a proper mix,' he said. 'Doctor makes Jenkins water mine.'

There was something in the house that got under one's skin. Something that made one feel like an outsider – uncomfortable and naked in the quiet whisper of its walls.

Sitting on the edge of his bed, Grant slowly unlaced his shoes and dropped them on the carpet.

A robot who had served the family for four generations, who talked of men long dead as if he had brought them a glass of whisky only yesterday. An old man who worried about a ship that slid through the space-darkness beyond the solar system. Another man who dreamed of another race, a race that might go hand in paw with man down the trail of destiny.

And over it all, almost unspoken and yet unmistakable, the shadow of Jerome A. Webster – the man who had failed a friend, a surgeon who had failed his trust.

Juwain, the Martian philosopher, had died, on the eve of a great discovery, because Jerome A. Webster couldn't leave this house, because agoraphobia chained him to a plot a few miles square.

On stockinged feet, Grant crossed to the table where Jenkins had placed his pack. Loosening the straps, he opened it, brought out a thick portfolio. Back at the bed again, he sat down and hauled out sheafs of papers, thumbed through them.

Records, hundreds of sheets of records. The story of hundreds of human lives set down on paper. Not only the things they told him or the questions that they answered, but dozens of other little things – things he had noted down from observation, from sitting and watching, from *living* with them for an hour or day.

For the people that he ferreted out in these tangled hills accepted him. It was his business that they should accept him. They accepted him because he came on foot, briar-scratched and weary, with a pack upon his shoulder. To him clung none of the modernity that would have set him apart from them, made them suspicious of him. It was a tiresome way to make a census, but it was the only way to make the kind the World Committee wanted – and needed.

For somewhere, sometime, studying sheets like these that lay upon the bed, some man like him would find a thing he sought, would find a clue to some life that veered from the human pattern. Some betraying quirk of behaviourism that would set out one life against all the others.

Human mutations were not uncommon, of course. Many of them were known, men who held high position in the world. Most of the World Committee members were mutants, but, like the others, their mutational qualities and abilities had been modified and qualified by the pattern of the world, by unconscious conditioning that had shaped their thoughts and reaction into some conformity with other fellow men.

There had always been mutants, else the race would not have advanced. But until the last hundred years or so they had not been recognized as such. Before that they had merely been great businessmen or great scientists or great crooks. Or perhaps eccentrics who had gained no more than scorn or pity at the hands of a race that would not tolerate divergence from the norm.

Those who had been successful had adapted themselves to the world around them, had bent their greater mental powers into the pattern of acceptable action. And this dulled their usefulness, limited their capacity, hedged their ability with restrictions set up to fit less extraordinary people.

Even as to-day the known mutants' ability was hedged,

unconsciously, by a pattern that had been set – a groove of logic that was a terrible thing.

But somewhere in the world there were dozens, probably hundreds, of other humans who were just a little more than human – persons whose lives had been untouched by the rigidity of complex human life. Their ability would not be hedged, they would know no groove of logic.

From the portfolio Grant brought out a pitifully thin sheaf of papers, clipped together, read the title of the script almost reverently:

'Unfinished Philosophical Proposition and Related Notes of Juwain.'

It would take a mind that knew no groove of logic, a mind unhampered by the pattern of four thousand years of human thought, to carry on the torch the dead hand of the Martian philosopher had momentarily lifted. A torch that lit the way to a new concept of life and purpose, that showed a path that was easier and straighter. A philosophy that would have put mankind ahead a hundred thousand years in two short generations.

Juwain had died and in this very house a man had lived out his haunted years, listening to the voice of his dead friend, shrinking from the censure of a cheated race.

A stealthy scratch came at the door. Startled, Grant stiffened, listened. It came again. Then, a little, silky whine.

Swiftly Grant stuffed the papers back in the portfolio, strode to the door. As he opened it, Nathaniel oozed in, like a sliding black shadow.

'Oscar,' he said, 'doesn't know I'm here. Oscar would give it to me if he knew I was.'

'Who's Oscar?'

'Oscar's the robot that takes care of us.'

Grant grinned at the dog. 'What do you want, Nathaniel?'

'I want to talk to you,' said Nathaniel. 'You've talked to everyone else. To Bruce and Grandpa. But you haven't talked to me and I'm the one that found you.'

'OK,' invited Grant. 'Go ahead and talk.'

'You're worried,' said Nathaniel.

Grant wrinkled his brow. 'That's right, perhaps I am. The human race is always worried. You should know that by now, Nathaniel.'

'You're worrying about Juwain. Just like Grandpa is.'

'Not worrying,' protested Grant. 'Just wondering. And hoping.'

'What's the matter with Juwain?' demanded Nathaniel. 'And who is he and—'

'He's no one, really,' declared Grant. 'That is, he was someone once, but he died years ago. He's just an idea now. A problem. A challenge. Something to think about.'

'I can think,' said Nathaniel triumphantly. 'I think a lot, sometimes. But I mustn't think like human beings. Bruce tells me I mustn't. He says I have to think dog thoughts and let human thoughts alone. He says dog thoughts are just as good as human thoughts, maybe a whole lot better.'

Grant nodded soberly. 'There is something to that, Nathaniel. After all, you must think differently than man. You must—'

'There's lots of things that dogs know that men don't know,' bragged Nathaniel. 'We can see things and hear things that men can't see nor hear. Sometimes we howl at night, and people cuss us out. But if they could see and hear what we do they'd be scared too stiff to move. Bruce says we're . . . we're—'

'Psychic?' asked Grant.

'That's it,' declared Nathaniel. 'I can't remember all them words.'

Grant picked his pyjamas off the table.

'How about spending the night with me, Nathaniel? You can have the foot of the bed.'

Nathaniel stared at him round eyed. 'Gee, you mean you want me to?'

'Sure I do. If we're going to be partners, dogs and men, we better start out on an even footing now.'

'I won't get the bed dirty,' said Nathaniel. 'Honest I won't. Oscar gave me a bath to-night.'

He flipped an ear.

'Except,' he said, 'I think he missed a flea or two.'

Grant stared in perplexity at the atomic gun. A handy thing, it performed a host of services, ranging from cigarette lighter to deadly weapon. Built to last a thousand years, it was foolproof, or so the advertisements said. It never got out of kilter – except now it wouldn't work.

He pointed it at the ground and shook it vigorously and still it didn't work. He tapped it gently on a stone and got no results.

Darkness was dropping on the tumbled hills. Somewhere in the distant river valley an owl laughed irrationally. The first stars, small and quiet, came out in the east and in the west the green-tinged glow that marked the passing of the sun was fading into night.

The pile of twigs was laid before the boulder and other wood lay near at hand to keep the campfire going through the night. But if the gun wouldn't work, there would be no fire.

Grant cursed under his breath, thinking of chilly sleeping and cold rations.

He tapped the gun on the rock again, harder this time. Still no soap.

A twig crunched in the dark and Grant shot bolt upright.

Beside the shadowy trunk of one of the forest giants that towered into the gathering dusk, stood a figure, tall and gangling.

'Hello,' said Grant.

'Something wrong, stranger?'

'My gun—' replied Grant, then cut short the words. No use in letting this shadowy figure know he was unarmed.

The man stepped forward, hand outstretched.

'Won't work, eh?'

Grant felt the gun lifted from his grasp.

The visitor squatted on the ground, making chuckling noises. Grant strained his eyes to see what he was doing, but the creeping darkness made the other's hands an inky blur weaving about the bright metal of the gun.

Metal clicked and scraped. The man sucked in his breath and laughed. Metal scraped again and the man arose, holding out the gun.

'All fixed,' he said. 'Maybe better than it was before.'

A twig crunched again.

'Hey, wait!' yelled Grant, but the man was gone, a black ghost moving among the ghostly trunks.

A chill that was not of the night came seeping from the ground and travelled slowly up Grant's body. A chill that set his teeth on edge, that stirred the short hairs at the base of his skull, that made goose flesh spring out upon his arms.

There was no sound except the talk of water whispering in the dark, the tiny stream that ran just below the campsite.

Shivering, he knelt beside the pile of twigs, pressed the trigger. A thin blue flame lapped out and the twigs burst into flame.

Grant found old Dave Baxter perched on the top rail of the fence, smoke pouring from the short-stemmed pipe almost hidden in his whiskers.

'Howdy, stranger,' said Dave. 'Climb up and squat a while.'

Grant climbed up, stared out over the corn-shocked field, gay with the gold of pumpkins.

'Just walkin'?' asked old Dave. 'Or snoopin'?'

'Snooping,' admitted Grant.

Dave took the pipe out of his mouth, spat put it back in again. The whiskers draped themselves affectionately, and dangerously, about it.

'Diggin'?' asked old Dave.

'Nope,' said Grant.

'Had a feller through here four, five years ago,' said Dave. 'that was worse'n a rabbit dog for diggin'. Found a place where there had been an old town and just purely tore up the place. Pestered the life out of me to tell him about the town, but I didn't rightly remember much. Heard my grandpappy once mention the name of the town, but danged if I ain't forgot it. This here feller had a slew of old maps that he was all the time wavin' around and studying, trying' to figure out what was what but I guess he never did know.'

'Hunting for antiques,' said Grant.

'Mebbe,' old Dave told him. 'Kept out of his way the best I could. But he wasn't no worse'n the one that was tryin' to trace some old road that ran through this way once. He had some maps, too. Left figurin' he'd found it and I didn't have the heart to tell him what he'd found was a path the cows had made.'

He squinted at Grant cagily.

'You ain't huntin' no old roads, be you?'

'Nope,' said Grant. 'I'm a census taker.'

'You're what?'

'Census taker,' explained Grant. 'Take down your name and age and where you live.'

'What for?'

'Government wants to know,' said Grant.

'We don't bother the gov'ment none,' declared old Dave. 'What call's the gov'ment got botherin' us?'

'Government won't bother you any,' Grant told him. 'Might even take a notion to pay you something some day. Never can tell.'

'In that case,' said old Dave, 'it's different.'

They perched on the fence, staring across the fields. Smoke curled up from a chimney hidden in a sunny hollow, yellow with the flame of birches. A creek meandered placidly across a dun autumn-coloured meadow and beyond it climbed the hills, tier on tier of golden maple trees.

Hunched on the rail, Grant felt the heat of the autumn sun soak into his back, smelled the stubbled field.

A good life, he told himself. Good crops, wood to burn, plenty of game to hunt. A happy life.

He glanced at the old man huddled beside him, saw the un-worried wrinkles of kindly age that puckered up his face, tried for a moment to envision a life like this – a simple, pastoral life, akin to the historic days of the old American frontier, with all the frontier's compensations, none of its dangers.

Old Dave took the pipe out of his face, waved it at the field.

'Still lots of work to do,' he announced, 'but it ain't agittin' done. Them kids ain't worth the power to blow 'em up. Huntin' all the time. Fishin' too. Machinery breakin' down. Joe ain't been around for quite a spell. Great hand at machinery, Joe is.'

'Joe your son?'

'No. Crazy feller that lives off in the woods somewhere. Walks in and fixes things up, then walks off and leaves. Scarcely ever talks. Don't wait for a man to thank him. Just up and leaves. Been doin' it for years now. Grandpappy told me how he first came when he was a youngster. Still comin' now.'

Grant gasped. 'Wait a second. It can't be the same man.'

'Now,' said old Dave, 'that's the thing. Won't believe it, stranger, but he ain't a mite older now than when I first saw him. Funny sort of cuss. Lots of wild tales about him. Grandpappy always told about how he fooled around with ants.'

'Ants!'

'Sure. Built a house – glasshouse, you know, over an ant hill and heated it, come winter. That's what grandpappy always said. Claimed he'd seen it. But I don't believe a word of it. Grandpappy was the biggest liar in seven counties. Admitted it hisself.'

A brass-tongued bell clanged from the sunny hollow where the chimney smoked.

The old man climbed down from the fence, tapped out his pipe, squinting at the sun.

The bell boomed again across the autumn stillness.

'That's ma,' said old Dave. 'Dinner's on. Squirrel dumplings, more than likely. Good eatin' as you ever hooked a tooth into. Let's get a hustle on.'

A crazy fellow who came and fixed things and didn't wait for thanks. A man who looked the same as he did a hundred years ago. A chap who built a glasshouse over an ant hill and heated it, come winter.

It didn't make sense and yet old Baxter hadn't been lying. It wasn't another one of those tall yarns that had sprung up and still ran their course out here in the backwoods, amounting now to something that was very close to folklore.

All of the folklore had a familiar ring, a certain similarity, a definite pattern of underlying wit that tagged it for what it was. And this wasn't it. There was nothing humorous, even to the backwoods mind, in housing and heating an ant hill. To qualify for humour a tale like that would have to have a snapper, and this tale didn't have one.

Grant stirred uneasily on the cornshuck mattress, pulling the heavy quilt close around his throat.

Funny, he thought, the places that I sleep in. To-night a cornshuck mattress, last night an open campfire, the night before that a soft mattress and clean sheets in the Webster house.

The wind sucked up the hollow and paused on its way to flap a loose shingle on the house, came back to flap it once again. A mouse skittered somewhere in the darkened place. From the bed across the loft came the sound of regular breathing – two of the Baxter younger fry slept there.

A man who came and fixed things and didn't wait for thanks. That was what had happened with the gun. That was what had been happening for years to the Baxters' haywire farm machinery. A crazy feller by the name of Joe, who didn't age and had a handy bent at tinkering.

A thought came into Grant's head; he shoved it back, repressed it. There was no need of arousing hope. Snoop around some, ask guarded questions, keep your eyes open, Grant. Don't make your questions too pointed or they'll shut up like a clam.

Funny folk, these ridge runners. People who had no part of progress, who wanted no part of it. People who had turned their backs upon civilization, returning to the unhampered life of soil and forest, sun and rain.

Plenty of room for them here on Earth, lots of room for everyone, for Earth's population had dwindled in the last two hundred years, drained by the pioneers who flocked out to settle other planets, to shape the other worlds of the system to the economy of mankind.

Plenty of room and soil and game.

Maybe it was the best way after all. Grant remembered he had often thought that in the months he had tramped these hills. At times like this, with the comfort of the handmade quilt, the rough efficiency of the cornshuck mattress, the whisper of the wind along the shingled roof. Times like when he sat on the top rail of the fence and looked at the groups of golden pumpkins loafing in the sun.

A rustle came to him across the dark, the rustle of the cornshuck mattress where the two boys slept. Then the pad of bare feet coming softly across the boards.

'You asleep, mister?' came the whisper.

'Nope. Want to crawl in with me?'

The youngster ducked under the cover, put cold feet against Grant's stomach.

'Grandpappy tell you about Joe?'

Grant nodded in the dark. 'Said he hadn't been around, lately.'

'Tell you about the ants?'

'Sure did. What do you know about the ants?'

'Me and Bill found them just a little while ago, keeping it a secret. We ain't told anyone but you. But we gotta tell you, I guess. You're from the gov'ment.'

'There really was a glasshouse over the hill?'

'Yes, and . . . and' – the boy's voice gasped with excitement – 'and that ain't all. Them ants had carts and there was chimneys coming out of the hill and smoke comin' from the chimneys. And . . . and—'

'Yes, what else?'

'We didn't wait to see anything else. Bill and me got scared. We ran.'

The boy snuggled deeper into the cornshucks. 'Gee, ever hear of anything like it? Ants pulling carts!'

The ants *were* pulling carts. And there *were* chimneys sticking from the hill, chimneys that belched tiny, acrid puffs of smoke that told of smelting ores.

Head throbbing with excitement, Grant squatted beside the nest, staring at the carts that trundled along the roads leading off into the grass-roots land. Empty carts going out, loaded carts coming back – loaded with seeds and here and there dismembered insect bodies. Tiny carts, moving rapidly, bouncing and jouncing behind the harnessed ants!

The glassite shield that once had covered the nest still was there, but it was broken and had fallen into disrepair, almost as if there were no further use of it, as if it had served a purpose that no longer existed.

The glen was wild, broken land that tumbled down towards the river bluffs, studded with boulders, alternating with tiny patches of meadow and clumps of mighty oaks. A hushed place that one could believe had never heard a voice except the talk of wind in tree-tops and the tiny voices of the wild things that followed secret paths.

A place where ants might live undisturbed by plough or vagrant foot, continuing the millions of years of senseless destiny that dated from a day before there was anything like man – from a day before a single abstract thought had been born on the Earth. A closed and stagnant destiny that had no purpose except that ants might live.

And now someone had uncoiled the angle of that destiny, had set it on another path, had given the ants the secret of the wheel, the secret of working metals – how many other cultural handicaps had been lifted from this ant hill, breaking the bottleneck of progress?

Hunger pressure, perhaps, would be one cultural handicap that would have been lifted for the ants. Providing of abundant food which gave them leisure for other things beyond the continued search for sustenance.

Another race on the road to greatness, developing along the social basis that had been built in that long gone day before the thing called Man had known the stir of greatness.

Where would it lead? What would the ant be like in another million years? Would ant and Man – could ant and Man find any common denominator as dog and Man would find for working out a co-operative destiny?

Grant shook his head. That was something the chances were against. For in dog and Man ran common blood, while ant and Man were things apart, life forms that were never meant to understand the other. They had no common basis such as had been joined in the paleolithic days when dog and Man dozed beside a fire and watched against the eyes that roved out in the night.

Grant sensed rather than heard the rustle of feet in the high grass back of him. Erect, he whirled around and saw the man before him. A gangling man with stooping shoulders and hands that were almost hamlike, but with sensitive fingers that tapered white and smooth.

'You are Joe?' asked Grant.

The man nodded. 'And you are a man who has been hunting me.'

Grant gasped. 'Why perhaps I have. Not you personally, perhaps, but someone like you.'

'Someone different,' said Joe.

'Why didn't you stay the other night?' asked Grant. 'Why did you run off? I wanted to thank you for fixing up the gun.'

Joe merely stared at him, unspeaking, but behind the silent lips Grant sensed amusement, a vast and secret amusement.

'How in the world,' asked Grant, 'did you know the gun was broken? Had you been watching me?'

'I heard you think it was.'

'You heard me think?'

'Yes,' said Joe. 'I hear you thinking now.'

Grant laughed, a bit uneasily. It was disconcerting, but it

was logical. It was the thing that he should have expected – this and more.

He gestured at the hill. 'Those ants are yours?'

Joe nodded and the amusement again was bubbling just behind his lips.

'What are you laughing for?' snapped Grant.

'I am not laughing,' Joe told him and somehow Grant felt rebuked, rebuked and small, like a child that has been slapped for something it should have known better than to do.

'You should publish your notes,' said Grant. 'They might be correlated with the work that Webster's doing.'

Joe shrugged his shoulders. 'I have no notes,' he said.

'No notes!'

The lanky man moved towards the ant hill, stood staring down at it. 'Perhaps,' he declared, 'you've figured out why I did it.'

Grant nodded gravely. 'I might have wondered that. Experimental curiosity, more than likely. Maybe compassion for a lower form of life. A feeling, perhaps, that just because man himself got the head start doesn't give him a monopoly on advancement.'

Joe's eyes glittered in the sunlight. 'Curiosity – maybe. I hadn't thought of that.'

He hunkered down beside the hill. 'Ever wonder why the ant advanced so far and then stood still? Why he built a nearly perfect social organization and let it go at that? What it was that stopped him in his tracks?'

'Hunger pressure, for one thing,' Grant said.

'That and hibernation,' declared the lanky man. 'Hibernation, you see, wiped out the memory pattern from one season to the next. Each spring they started over, began from scratch again. They never were able to benefit from past mistakes, cash in on accumulated knowledge.'

'So you fed them—'

'And heated the hill,' said Joe, 'so they wouldn't have to hibernate. So they wouldn't have to start out fresh with the coming of each spring.'

89

'The carts?'

'I made a couple, left them there. It took ten years, but they finally figured out what they were for.'

Grant nodded at the smokestacks.

'They did that themselves,' Joe told him.

'Anything else?'

Joe lifted his shoulders wearily. 'How should I know?'

'But, man, you watched them. Even if you didn't keep notes, you watched.'

Joe shook his head. 'I haven't laid eyes on them for almost fifteen years. I only came to-day because I heard you here. These ants, you see, don't amuse me any more.'

Grant's mouth opened, then shut tight again. Finally, he said: 'So that's the answer. That's why you did it. Amusement.'

There was no shame on Joe's face, no defence, just a pained expression that said he wished they'd forget all about the ants. His mouth said: 'Sure. Why else?'

'That gun of mine. I suppose that amused you, too.'

'Not the gun,' said Joe.

Not the gun, Grant's brain said. Of course, not the gun, you dumb-bell, but you yourself. You're the one that amused him. And you're amusing him right now.

Fixing up old Dave Baxter's farm machinery, then walking off without a word, doubtless had been a screaming joke. And probably he'd hugged himself and rocked for days with silent mirth after that time up at the Webster house when he'd pointed out the thing that was wrong with old Thomas Webster's space drive.

Like a smart-Aleck playing tricks on an awkward puppy.

Joe's voice broke his thoughts.

'You're an enumerator, aren't you? Why don't you ask me the questions? Now that you've found me you can't go off and not get it down on paper. My age especially. I'm one hundred and sixty-three and I'm scarcely adolescent. Another thousand years at least.'

He hugged his knobby knees against his chest and rocked

slowly back and forth. 'Another thousand years and if I take good care of myself—'

'But that isn't all of it,' Grant told him, trying to keep his voice calm. 'There is something more. Something that you must do for us.'

'For us?'

'For society,' said Grant. 'For the human race.'

'Why?'

Grant stared. 'You mean that you don't care.'

Joe shook his head and in the gesture there was no bravado, no defiance of convention. It was just blunt statement of the fact.

'Money?' suggested Grant.

Joe waved his hands at the hills about them, at the spreading river valley. 'I have this,' he said. 'I have no need of money.'

'Fame, perhaps?'

Joe did not spit, but his face looked like he had.

'The gratitude of the human race?'

'It doesn't last,' said Joe and the old mockery was in his words, the vast amusement just behind his lips.

'Look, Joe,' said Grant and, hard as he tried to keep it out, there was pleading in his voice, 'this thing I have for you to do is important . . . important to generations yet to come, important to the human race, a milestone in our destiny—'

'And why should I,' asked Joe, 'do something for someone who isn't even born yet? Why should I look beyond the years of my own life? When I die, I die, and all the shouting and the glory, all the banners and the bugles will be nothing to me. I will not know whether I lived a great life or a very poor one.'

'The race,' said Grant.

Joe laughed, a shout of laughter. 'Race preservation, race advancement. That's what you're getting at. Why should you be concerned with that? Or I?'

The laughter lines smoothed out around his mouth and he shook a finger in mock admonishment. 'Race preservation is a myth . . . a myth that you all have lived by – a sordid thing that has arisen out of your social structure. The race ends every day.

91

When a man dies the race ends for him – so far as he's concerned there is no longer any race.'

'You just don't care,' said Grant.

'That,' declared Joe, 'is what I've been telling you.'

He squinted at the pack upon the ground and a flicker of a smile wove about his lips. 'Perhaps,' he suggested, 'if it interested me—'

Grant opened up the pack, brought out the portfolio. Almost reluctantly he pulled out the thin sheaf of papers, glanced at the title:

'Unfinished Philosophical—'

He handed it across, sat watching as Joe read swiftly and even as he watched he felt the sickening wrench of terrible failure closing on his brain.

Back in the Webster house he had thought of a mind that knew no groove of logic, a mind unhampered by four thousand years of mouldy human thought. That, he had told himself, might do the trick.

And here it was. But it still was not enough. There was something lacking – something he had never thought of, something the men in Geneva had never thought of, either. Something, a part of the human make-up that everyone, up to this moment, had taken for granted.

Social pressure was the thing that had held the human race together through all millennia – held the human race together as a unit just as hunger pressure had held the ants enslaved to a social pattern.

The need of one human being for the approval of his fellow humans, the need for a certain cult of fellowship – a psychological, almost physiological need for approval of one's thought and action. A force that kept men from going off at unsocial tangents, a force that made for social security and human solidarity, for the working together of the human family.

Men died for that approval, sacrificed for that approval, lived lives they loathed for that approval. For without it a man was on his own, an outcast, an animal that had been driven from the pack.

It had led to terrible things, of course – to mob psychology, to racial persecution, to mass atrocities in the name of patriotism or religion. But likewise it had been the sizing that held the race together, the thing that from the very start had made human society possible.

And Joe didn't have it. Joe didn't give a damn. He didn't care what anyone thought of him. He didn't care whether anyone approved or not.

Grant felt the sun hot upon his back, heard the whisper of the wind that walked in the trees above him. And in some thicket a bird struck up a song.

Was this the trend of mutancy? This sloughing off of the basic instinct that made man a member of the race?

Had this man in front of him, reading the legacy of Juwain, found within himself, through his mutancy, a life so full that he could dispense with the necessity for the approval of his fellows? Had he, finally, after all these years, reached that stage of civilization where a man stood independent, disdaining all the artificiality of society?

Joe looked up.

'Very interesting,' he said. 'Why didn't he go ahead and finish it?'

'He died,' said Grant.

Joe clucked his tongue inside his cheek. 'He was wrong in one place.' He flipped the pages, jabbed with a finger. 'Right here. That's where the error cropped up. That's what bogged him down.'

Grant stammered. 'But . . . but there shouldn't be an error. He died, that's all. He died before he finished it.'

Joe folded the manuscript neatly, tucked it in his pocket.

'Just as well,' he said. 'He probably would have botched it.'

'Then you can finish it? You can—'

There was, Grant knew, no use of going on. He read the answer in Joe's eyes.

'You really think,' said Joe and his words were terse and measured, 'that I'd turn this over to you squalling humans?'

Grant shrugged in defeat. 'I suppose not. I suppose I should have known. A man like you—'

'I,' said Joe, 'can use this thing myself.'

He rose slowly, idly swung his foot, ploughing a furrow through the ant hill, toppling the smoking chimneys, burying the toiling carts.

With a cry, Grant leaped to his feet, blind anger gripping him, blind anger driving the hand that snatched out his gun.

'Hold it!' said Joe.

Grant's arm halted with the gun still pointing towards the ground.

'Take it easy, little man,' said Joe. 'I know you'd like to kill me, but I can't let you do it. For I have plans, you see. And, after all, you wouldn't be killing me for the reason that you think.'

'What difference would it make why I killed you?' rasped Grant. 'You'd be dead, wouldn't you? You wouldn't be loose with Juwain's philosophy.'

'But,' Joe told him, almost gently, 'that's not why you would kill me. You'd do it because you're sore at me for mussing up the ant hill.'

'That might have been the reason first,' said Grant. 'But not now—'

'Don't try it,' said Joe. 'Before you ever pressed the trigger you'd be meat yourself.'

Grant hesitated.

'If you think I'm bluffing,' Joe taunted him, 'go ahead and call me.'

For a long moment the two stood face to face, the gun still pointing at the ground.

'Why can't you throw in with us?' asked Grant. 'We need a man like you. You were the one that showed old Tom Webster how to build a space drive. The work you've done with ants—'

Joe was stepping forward, swiftly, and Grant heaved up the gun. He saw the fist coming at him, a hamlike, powerful fist that fairly whistled with its vicious speed.

A fist that was faster than his finger on the trigger.

Something wet and hot was rasping across Grant's face and he lifted a hand and tried to brush it off.

But it went on, licking across his face.

He opened his eyes and Nathaniel did a jig in front of them.

'You're all right,' said Nathaniel 'I was so afraid—'

'Nathaniel!' croaked Grant. 'What are you doing here?'

'I ran away,' Nathaniel told him. 'I want to go with you.'

Grant shook his head. 'You can't go with me. I have far to go. I have a job to do.'

He got to his hands and knees and felt along the ground. When his hand touched cold metal, he picked it up and slid it in the holster.

'I let him get away,' he said, 'and I can't let him go. I gave him something that belonged to all mankind and I can't let him use it.'

'I can track,' Nathaniel told him. 'I track squirrels like everything.'

'You have more important things to do than tracking,' Grant told the dog. 'You see, I found out something to-day. Got a glimpse of a certain trend – a trend that all mankind may follow. Not to-day nor to-morrow, nor even a thousand years from now. Maybe never, but it's a thing we can't overlook. Joe may be just a little farther along the path than the rest of us and we may be following faster than we think. We may all end up like Joe. And if that is what is happening, if that is where it all will end, you dogs have a job ahead of you.'

Nathaniel stared up at him, worried wrinkles on his face.

'I don't understand,' he pleaded. 'You use words I can't make out.'

'Look, Nathaniel. Men may not always be the way they are to-day. They may change. And, if they do, you have to carry on; you have to take the dream and keep it going. You'll have to pretend that you are men.'

'Us dogs,' Nathaniel pledged, 'will do it.'

'It won't come for thousands and thousands of years,' said

Grant. 'You will have time to get ready. But you must know. You must pass the word along. You must not forget.'

'I know,' said Nathaniel. 'Us dogs will tell the pups and the pups will tell their pups.'

'That's the idea,' said Grant.

He stooped and scratched Nathaniel's ear and the dog, tail wagging to a stop, stood and watched him climb the hill.

NOTES ON THE FOURTH TALE

Of all the tales this is the one which has occasioned the most anguish on the part of those who would seek some explanation and significance in the legend.

That it must be entirely myth and nothing else even Tige will admit. But if it is myth, what does it mean? If this tale is myth, are not all the others myth as well?

Jupiter, where the action takes place, is supposed to be one of the other worlds which may be found by crossing space. The scientific impossibility of the existence of such worlds has been noted elsewhere. And, if we are to accept Bounce's theory that the other worlds dealt with in the legend are none other than our own multiple worlds, it seems reasonable to suppose that such a world as the one described would have been located by this date. That there are certain of the cobbly worlds which are closed is common knowledge, but the reason for their closure is well known and none of them is closed because of conditions such as those described in this fourth tale.

Some scholars believe that the fourth tale is an interloper, that it has no business in the legend, that it is something which was picked up and inserted bodily. It is hard to accept this conclusion since the tale does tie in with the legend, furnishing one of the principal story pivots upon which the legend turns.

The character of Towser in this tale has been cited on many occasions as inconsistent with the essential dignity of our race.

Yet, while Towser may be distasteful to certain squeamish readers, he serves well as a foil for the human in the story. It is Towser, not the human, who is first ready to accept the situation which develops; Towser, not the human, who is the first to understand. And Towser's mind, once it is freed from human domination, is shown to be at least the equal of the human's.

Towser, flea-bitten as he may be, is a character one need not be ashamed of.

Short as it is, this fourth tale probably is the most rewarding of the eight. It is one that recommends itself for thoughtful, careful reading.

IV
Desertion

Four men, two by two, had gone into the howling maelstrom that was Jupiter and had not returned. They had walked into the keening gale – or rather, they had loped, bellies low against the ground, wet sides gleaming in the rain.

For they did not go in the shape of men.

Now the fifth man stood before the desk of Kent Fowler, head of Dome No. 3, Jovian Survey Commission.

Under Fowler's desk, old Towser scratched a flea, then settled down to sleep again.

Harold Allen, Fowler saw with a sudden pang, was young – too young. He had the easy confidence of youth, the face of one who never had known fear. And that was strange. For men in the domes of Jupiter did know fear – fear and humility. It was hard for Man to reconcile his puny self with the mighty forces of the monstrous planet.

'You understand,' said Fowler, 'that you need not do this. You understand that you need not go.'

It was formula, of course. The other four had been told the same thing, but they had gone. This fifth one, Fowler knew, would go as well. But suddenly he felt a dull hope stir within him that Allen wouldn't go.

'When do I start?' asked Allen.

There had been a time when Fowler might have taken quiet pride in that answer, but not now. He frowned briefly.

'Within the hour,' he said.

Allen stood waiting, quietly.

'Four other men have gone out and have not returned,' said

Fowler. 'You know that, of course. We want you to return. We don't want you going off on any heroic rescue expedition. The main thing, the only thing, is that you come back, that you prove man can live in a Jovian form. Go to the first survey stake, no farther, then come back. Don't take any chances. Don't investigate anything. Just come back.'

Allen nodded. 'I understand all that.'

'Miss Stanley will operate the converter,' Fowler went on. 'You need have no fear on that particular score. The other men were converted without mishap. They left the converter in apparently perfect condition. You will be in thoroughly competent hands. Miss Stanley is the best qualified conversion operator in the Solar System. She has had experience on most of the other planets. That is why she's here.'

Allen grinned at the woman and Fowler saw something flicker across Miss Stanley's face – something that might have been pity, or rage – or just plain fear. But it was gone again and she was smiling back at the youth who stood before the desk. Smiling in that prim, school-teacherish way she had of smiling, almost as if she hated herself for doing it.

'I shall be looking forward,' said Allen, 'to my conversion.'

And the way he said it, he made it all a joke, a vast ironic joke.

But it was no joke.

It was serious business, deadly serious. Upon these tests, Fowler knew, depended the fate of men on Jupiter. If the tests succeeded, the resources of the giant planet would be thrown open. Man would take over Jupiter as he already had taken over the other smaller planets. And if they failed—

If they failed, Man would continue to be chained and hampered by the terrific pressure, the greater force of gravity, the weird chemistry of the planet. He would continue to be shut within the domes, unable to set actual foot upon the planet, unable to see it with direct, unaided vision, forced to rely upon the awkward tractors and the televisor, forced to work with clumsy tools and mechanisms or through the medium of robots that themselves were clumsy.

For Man, unprotected and in his natural form, would be blotted out by Jupiter's terrific pressure of fifteen thousand pounds per square inch, pressure that made terrestrial sea bottoms seem a vacuum by comparison.

Even the strongest metal Earthmen could devise couldn't exist under pressure such as that, under the pressure and the alkaline rains that forever swept the planet. It grew brittle and flaky, crumbling like clay, or it ran away in little streams and puddles of ammonia salts. Only by stepping up the toughness and strength of that metal, by increasing its electronic tension, could it be made to withstand the weight of thousands of miles of swirling, choking gases that made up the atmosphere. And even when that was done, everything had to be coated with tough quartz to keep away the rain – the liquid ammonia that fell as bitter rain.

Fowler sat listening to the engines in the sub-floor of the dome – engines that ran on endlessly, the dome never quiet of them. They had to run and keep on running, for if they stopped the power flowing into the metal walls of the dome would stop, the electronic tension would ease up and that would be the end of everything.

Towser roused himself under Fowler's desk and scratched another flea, his leg thumping hard against the floor.

'Is there anything else?' asked Allen.

Fowler shook his head. 'Perhaps there's something you want to do,' he said. 'Perhaps you—'

He had meant to say write a letter and he was glad he caught himself quick enough so he didn't say it.

Allen looked at his watch. 'I'll be there on time,' he said. He swung around and headed for the door.

Fowler knew Miss Stanley was watching him and he didn't want to turn and meet her eyes. He fumbled with a sheaf of papers on the desk before him.

'How long are you going to keep this up?' asked Miss Stanley and she bit off each word with a vicious snap.

He swung around in his chair and faced her then. Her lips

were drawn into a straight, thin line, her hair seemed skinned back from her forehead tighter than ever, giving her face that queer, almost startling death-mask quality.

He tried to make his voice cool and level. 'As long as there's any need of it,' he said. 'As long as there's any hope.'

'You're going to keep on sentencing them to death,' she said. 'You're going to keep marching them out face to face with Jupiter. You're going to sit in here safe and comfortable and send them out to die.'

'There is no room for sentimentality, Miss Stanley,' Fowler said, trying to keep the note of anger from his voice. 'You know as well as I do why we're doing this. You realize that Man in his own form simply cannot cope with Jupiter. The only answer is to turn men into the sort of things that can cope with it. We've done it on the other planets.

'If a few men die, but we finally succeed, the price is small. Through the ages men have thrown away their lives on foolish things, for foolish reasons. Why should we hesitate, then, at a little death in a thing as great as this?'

Miss Stanley sat stiff and straight, hands folded in her lap, the lights shining on her greying hair and Fowler, watching her, tried to imagine what she might feel, what she might be thinking. He wasn't exactly afraid of her, but he didn't feel quite comfortable when she was around. Those sharp blue eyes saw too much, her hands looked far too competent. She should be somebody's Aunt sitting in a rocking chair with her knitting needles. But she wasn't. She was the top-notch conversion unit operator in the Solar System and she didn't like the way he was doing things.

'There is something wrong, Mr. Fowler,' she declared.

'Precisely,' agreed Fowler. 'That's why I'm sending young Allen out alone. He may find out what it is.'

'And if he doesn't?'

'I'll send someone else.'

She rose slowly from her chair, started towards the door, then stopped before his desk.

'Some day,' she said, 'you will be a great man. You never let a chance go by. This is your chance. You knew it was when this dome was picked for the tests. If you put it through, you'll go up a notch or two. No matter how many men may die you'll go up a notch or two.'

'Miss Stanley,' he said and his voice was curt, 'young Allen is going out soon. Please be sure that your machine—'

'My machine,' she told him icily, 'is not to blame. It operates along the co-ordinates the biologists set up.'

He sat hunched at his desk, listening to her footsteps go down the corridor.

What she said was true, of course. The biologists had set up the co-ordinates. But the biologists could be wrong. Just a hair-breadth of difference, one iota of digression and the converter would be sending out something that wasn't the thing they meant to send. A mutant that might crack up, go haywire, come unstuck under some condition or stress of circumstance wholly unsuspected.

For Man didn't know much about what was going on outside. Only what his instruments told him was going on. And the samplings of those happenings furnished by those instruments and mechanisms had been no more than sam-plings, for Jupiter was unbelievably large and the domes were very few.

Even the work of the biologists in getting the data on the Lopers, apparently the highest form of Jovian life, had involved more than three years of intensive study and after that two years of checking to make sure. Work that could have been done on Earth in a week or two. But work that, in this case, couldn't be done on Earth at all, for one couldn't take a Jovian life form to Earth. The pressure here on Jupiter couldn't be duplicated outside of Jupiter and at Earth pressure and tem-perature the Lopers would simply have disappeared in a puff of gas.

Yet it was work that had to be done if Man ever hoped to go about Jupiter in the life form of the Lopers. For before the converter could change a man to another life form, every detailed physical characteristic of that life form must be known – surely and positively, with no chance of mistake.

Allen did not come back.

The tractors, combing the nearby terrain, found no trace of him, unless the skulking thing reported by one of the drivers had been the missing Earthman in Loper form.

The biologists sneered their most accomplished academic sneers when Fowler suggested the co-ordinates might be wrong. Carefully they pointed out, the co-ordinates worked. When a man was put into the converter and the switch was thrown, the man became a Loper. He left the machine and moved away, out of sight, into the soupy atmosphere.

Some quirk, Fowler had suggested; some tiny deviation from the thing a Loper should be, some minor defect. If there were, the biologists said, it would take years to find it.

And Fowler knew that they were right.

So there were five men now instead of four and Harold Allen had walked out into Jupiter for nothing at all. It was as if he'd never gone so far as knowledge was concerned.

Fowler reached across his desk and picked up the personnel file, a thin sheaf of paper neatly clipped together. It was a thing he dreaded but a thing he had to do. Somehow the reason for these strange disappearances must be found. And there was no other way than to send out more men.

He sat for a moment listening to the howling of the wind above the dome, the everlasting thundering gale that swept across the planet in boiling, twisting wrath.

Was there some threat out there, he asked himself? Some danger they did not know about? Something that lay in wait and gobbled up the Lopers, making no distinction between Lopers that were *bona fide* and Lopers that were men? To the gobblers, of course, it would make no difference.

Or had there been a basic fault in selecting the Lopers as the type of life best fitted for existence on the surface of the planet? The evident intelligence of the Lopers, he knew, had been one factor in that determination. For if the thing Man became did not have capacity for intelligence, Man could not for long retain his own intelligence in such a guise.

Had the biologists let that one factor weigh too heavily, using it to offset some other factor that might be unsatisfactory, even disastrous? It didn't seem likely. Stiffnecked as they might be, the biologists knew their business.

Or was the whole thing impossible, doomed from the very start? Conversion to other life forms had worked on other planets, but that did not necessarily mean it would work on Jupiter. Perhaps Man's intelligence could not function correctly through the sensory apparatus provided by Jovian life. Perhaps the Lopers were so alien there was no common ground for human knowledge and the Jovian conception of existence to meet and work together.

Or the fault might lie with Man, be inherent with the race. Some mental aberration which, coupled with what they found outside, wouldn't let them come back. Although it might not be an aberration, not in the human sense. Perhaps just one ordinary human mental trait, accepted as commonplace on Earth, would be so violently at odds with Jovian existence that it would blast human sanity.

Claws rattled and clicked down the corridor. Listening to them, Fowler smiled wanly. It was Towser coming back from the kitchen, where he had gone to see his friend, the cook.

Towser came into the room, carrying a bone. He wagged his tail at Fowler and flopped down beside the desk, bone between his paws. For a long moment his rheumy old eyes regarded his master and Fowler reached down a hand to ruffle a ragged ear.

'You still like me, Towser?' Fowler asked and Towser thumped his tail.

'You're the only one,' said Fowler.

He straightened and swung back to the desk. His hand reached out and picked up the file.

Bennett? Bennett had a girl waiting for him back on Earth.

Andrews? Andrews was planning on going back to March

Tech just as soon as he earned enough to see him through a year.

Olson? Olson was nearing pension age. All the time telling the boys how he was going to settle down and grow roses.

Carefully, Fowler laid the file back on the desk.

Sentencing men to death. Miss Stanley had said that, her pale lips scarcely moving in her parchment face. Marching men out to die while he, Fowler, sat here safe and comfortable.

They were saying it all through the dome, no doubt, especially since Allen had failed to return. They wouldn't say it to his face, of course. Even the man or men he called before this desk and told they were the next to go, wouldn't say it to him.

But he would see it in their eyes.

He picked up the file again. Bennett, Andrews, Olson. There were others, but there was no use in going on.

Kent Fowler knew that he couldn't do it, couldn't face them, couldn't send more men out to die.

He leaned forward and flipped up the toggle on the inter-communicator.

'Yes, Mr. Fowler.'

'Miss Stanley, please.'

He waited for Miss Stanley, listening to Towser chewing half-heartedly on the bone. Towser's teeth were getting bad.

'Miss Stanley,' said Miss Stanley's voice.

'Just wanted to tell you, Miss Stanley, to get ready for two more.'

'Aren't you afraid,' asked Miss Stanley, 'that you'll run out of them? Sending out one at a time, they'd last longer, give you twice the satisfaction.'

'One of them,' said Fowler, 'will be a dog.'

'A dog!'

'Yes, Towser.'

He heard the quick, cold rage that iced her voice. 'Your own dog! He's been with you all these years—'

'That's the point,' said Fowler. 'Towser would be unhappy if I left him behind.'

106

It was not the Jupiter he had known through the televisor. He had expected it to be different, but not like this. He had expected a hell of ammonia rain and stinking fumes and the deafening, thundering tumult of the storm. He had expected swirling clouds and fog and the snarling flicker of monstrous thunderbolts.

He had not expected the lashing downpour would be reduced to drifting purple mist that moved like fleeing shadows over a red and purple sward. He had not even guessed the snaking bolts of lightning would be flares of pure ecstasy across a painted sky.

Waiting for Towser, Fowler flexed the muscles of his body, amazed at the smooth, sleek strength he found. Not a bad body, he decided, and grimaced at remembering how he had pitied the Lopers when he glimpsed them through the television screen.

For it had been hard to imagine a living organism based upon ammonia and hydrogen rather than upon water and oxygen, hard to believe that such a form of life could know the same quick thrill of life that humankind could know. Hard to conceive of life out in the soupy maelstrom that was Jupiter, not knowing, of course, that through Jovian eyes it was no soupy maelstrom at all.

The wind brushed against him with what seemed gentle fingers and he remembered with a start that by Earth standards the wind was a roaring gale, a two-hundred-mile an hour howler laden with deadly gases.

Pleasant scents seeped into his body. And yet scarcely scents, for it was not the sense of smell as he remembered it. It was as if his whole being was soaking up the sensation of lavender – and yet not lavender. It was something, he knew, for which he had no word, undoubtedly the first of many enigmas in terminology. For the words he knew, the thought symbols that served him as an Earthman would not serve him as a Jovian.

The lock in the side of the dome opened and Towser came tumbling out – at least he thought it must be Towser.

He started to call to the dog, his mind shaping the words he meant to say. But he couldn't say them. There was no way to say them. He had nothing to say them with.

For a moment his mind swirled in muddy terror, a blind fear that eddied in little puffs of panic through his brain.

How did Jovians talk? How—

Suddenly he was aware of Towser, intensely aware of the bumbling, eager friendliness of the shaggy animal that had followed him from Earth to many planets. As if the thing that was Towser had reached out and for a moment sat within his brain.

And out of the bubbling welcome that he sensed, came words.

'Hiya, pal.'

Not words, really, better than words. Thought symbols in his brain, communicated thought symbols that had shades of meaning words could never have.

'Hiya, Towser,' he said.

'I feel good,' said Towser. 'Like I was a pup. Lately I've been feeling pretty punk. Legs stiffening up on me and teeth wearing down to almost nothing. Hard to mumble a bone with teeth like that. Besides, the fleas give me hell. Used to be I never paid much attention to them. A couple of fleas more or less never meant much in my early days.'

'But . . . but—' Fowler's thoughts tumbled awkwardly. 'You're talking to me!'

'Sure thing,' said Towser. 'I always talked to you, but you couldn't hear me. I tried to say things to you, but I couldn't make the grade.'

'I understood you sometimes,' Fowler said.

'Not very well,' said Towser. 'You knew when I wanted food and when I wanted a drink and when I wanted out, but that's about all you ever managed.'

'I'm sorry,' Fowler said.

'Forget it,' Towser told him. 'I'll race you to the cliff.'

For the first time, Fowler saw the cliff, apparently many miles away, but with a strange crystalline beauty that sparkled in the shadow of the many-coloured clouds.

Fowler hesitated. 'It's a long way—'

'Ah, come on,' said Towser and even as he said it he started for the cliff.

Fowler followed, testing his legs, testing the strength in that new body of his, a bit doubtful at first, amazed a moment later, then running with a sheer joyousness that was one with the red and purple sward, with the drifting smoke of the rain across the land.

As he ran the consciousness of music came to him, a music that beat into his body, that surged throughout his being, that lifted him on wings of silver speed. Music like bells might make from some steeple on a sunny, springtime hill.

As the cliff drew nearer the music deepened and filled the universe with a spray of magic sound. And he knew the music came from the tumbling waterfall that feathered down the face of the shining cliff.

Only, he knew, it was no waterfall, but an ammonia-fall and the cliff was white because it was oxygen, solidified.

He skidded to a stop beside Towser where the waterfall broke into a glittering rainbow of many hundred colours. Literally many hundred, for here, he saw, was no shading of one primary to another as human beings saw, but a clear-cut selectivity that broke the prism down to its last ultimate classification.

'The music,' said Towser.

'Yes, what about it?'

'The music,' said Towser, 'is vibrations. Vibrations of water falling.'

'But, Towser, you don't know about vibrations.'

'Yes, I do,' contended Towser. 'It just popped into my head.'

Fowler gulped mentally. 'Just popped!'

And suddenly, within his own head, he held a formula – the formula for a process that would make metal to withstand the pressure of Jupiter.

He stared, astounded, at the waterfall and swiftly his mind took the many colours and placed them in their exact sequence in the spectrum. Just like that. Just out of blue sky. Out of nothing, for he knew nothing either of metals or of colours.

'Towser,' he cried. 'Towser, something's happening to us!'

'Yeah, I know,' said Towser.

'It's our brains,' said Fowler. 'We're using them, all of them, down to the last hidden corner. Using them to figure out things we should have known all the time. Maybe the brains of Earth things naturally are slow and foggy. Maybe we are the morons of the universe. Maybe we are fixed so we have to do things the hard way.'

And, in the new sharp clarity of thought that seemed to grip him, he knew that it would not only be the matter of colours in a waterfall or metals that would resist the pressure of Jupiter. He sensed other things, things not yet quite clear. A vague whispering that hinted of greater things, of mysteries beyond the pale of human thought, beyond even the pale of human imagination. Mysteries, fact, logic built on reasoning. Things that any brain should know if it used all its reasoning power.

'We're still mostly Earth,' he said, 'We're just beginning to learn a few of the things we are to know – a few of the things that were kept from us as human beings, perhaps because we Were human beings. Because our human bodies were poor bodies. Poorly equipped for thinking, poorly equipped in certain senses that one has to have to know. Perhaps even lacking in certain senses that are necessary to true knowledge.'

He stared back at the dome, a tiny black thing dwarfed by the distance.

Back there were men who couldn't see the beauty that was Jupiter. Men who thought that swirling clouds and lashing rain obscured the planet's face. Unseeing human eyes. Poor eyes. Eyes that could not see the beauty in the clouds, that could not see through the storm. Bodies that could not feel the thrill of trilling music stemming from the rush of broken water.

Men who walked alone, in terrible loneliness, talking with their tongue like Boy Scouts wigwagging out their messages, unable to reach out and touch one another's mind as he could reach out and touch Towser's mind. Shut off forever from that personal, intimate contact with other living things.

He, Fowler, had expected terror inspired by alien things out here on the surface, had expected to cower before the threat of unknown things, had steeled himself against disgust of a situation that was not of Earth.

But instead he had found something greater than Man had ever known. A swifter, surer body. A sense of exhilaration, a deeper sense of life. A sharper mind. A world of beauty that even the dreamers of the Earth had not yet imagined.

'Let's get going,' Towser urged.

'Where do you want to go?'

'Anywhere,' said Towser. 'Just start going and see where we end up. I have a feeling . . . well, a feeling—'

'Yes, I know,' said Fowler.

For he had the feeling, too. The feeling of high destiny. A certain sense of greatness. A knowledge that somewhere off beyond the horizons lay adventure and things greater than adventure.

Those other five had felt it, too. Had felt the urge to go and see, the compelling sense that here lay a life of fullness and of knowledge.

That, he knew, was why they had not returned.

'I won't go back,' said Towser.

'We can't let them down,' said Fowler.

Fowler took a step or two, back towards the dome, then stopped.

Back to the dome. Back to that aching, poison-laden body he had left. It hadn't seemed aching before, but now he knew it was.

Back to the fuzzy brain. Back to muddled thinking. Back to the flapping mouths that formed signals others understood. Back to eyes that now would be worse than no sight at all. Back to squalor, back to crawling, back to ignorance.

'Perhaps some day,' he said, muttering to himself.

'We got a lot to do and a lot to see,' said Towser. 'We got a lot to learn. We'll find things—'

Yes, they could find things. Civilizations, perhaps. Civilizations that would make the civilization of Man seem puny by comparison. Beauty and, more important, an understanding of that beauty. And a comradeship no one had ever known before – that no man, no dog had ever known before.

And life. The quickness of life after what seemed a drugged existence.

'I can't go back,' said Towser.

'Nor I,' said Fowler.

'They would turn me back into a dog,' said Towser.

'And me,' said Fowler, 'back into a man.'

Bit by bit, as the legend unfolds, the reader gets a more accurate picture of the human race. By degrees, one gains the conviction that here is a race which can be little more than pure fantasy. It is not the kind of race which could rise from humble beginnings to the eminence of culture with which it is gifted in these tales. Its equipment is too poor.

So far its lack of stability has become apparent. Its pre-occupation with a mechanical civilization rather than with a culture based on some of the sounder, more worthwhile concepts of life indicates a lack of basic character.

And now, in this tale, we learn of the limited communications which it possessed, a situation which certainly is not conducive to advancement. Man's inability to understand and appreciate the thought and the viewpoint of another man would be a stumbling block which no amount of mechanical ability could overcome.

That Man himself realized this is quite apparent in his anxiety to obtain the Juwain philosophy, but it will be noted that he did not wish it for the understanding that it might give him, but for the power and glory and the knowledge that it might make possible. The philosophy was seen by Man as something which would advance him a hundred thousand years in the space of two short generations.

Throughout these tales it becomes clear that Man was running a race, if not with himself, then with some imagined follower who pressed close upon his heels, breathing on his back. Man was engaged in a mad scramble for power and knowledge, but nowhere is there any hint of what he meant to do with it once he had attained it.

He has, according to the legend, come from the caves a million years before. And yet, only a little over a hundred years before the time of this tale, has he been able to eliminate killing as a basic part of his way of life. Here, then, is the true measure of his savagery: After a million years he has rid himself of killing and he regards it as a great accomplishment.

To most readers it will be easy, after reading this tale, to accept Rover's theory that Man is set up deliberately as the antithesis of everything the Dogs stand for, a sort of mythical strawman, a sociological fable.

This is underlined by the recurring evidence of Man's aimlessness, his constant running hither and yon, his grasping at a way of life which continually eludes him, possibly because he never knows exactly what he wants.

V
Paradise

The dome was a squatted, alien shape that did not belong beneath the purple mist of Jupiter, a huddled, frightened structure that seemed to cower against the massive planet.

The creature that had been Kent Fowler stood spraddling on its thick-set legs.

An alien thing, he thought. That's how far I've left the human race. For it's not alien at all. Not alien to me. It is the place I lived in, dreamed in, planned in. It is the place I left – afraid. And it is the place I come back to – driven and afraid.

Driven by the memory of the people who were like me before I became the thing I am, before I knew the aliveness and the fitness and the pleasure that is possible if one is not a human being.

Towser stirred beside him and Fowler sensed the bumbling friendliness of the one-time dog, the *expressed* friendliness and comradeship and love that had existed all the time, perhaps, but was never known so long as they were man and dog.

The dog's thoughts seeped into his brain. 'You can't do it, pal,' said Towser.

Fowler's answer was almost a wail. 'But I have to, Towser. That's what I went out for. To find what Jupiter really is like. And now I can tell them, now I can bring them word.'

You should have done it long ago, said a voice deep inside of him, a faint, far-off human voice that struggled up through his Jovian self. *But you were a coward and you put it off – and put it off. You ran away because you were afraid to go back. Afraid to be turned into a man again.*

'I'll be lonesome,' said Towser, and yet he did not say it. At least there were no words – rather a feeling of loneliness, a heart-wrench cry at parting. As if, for the moment, Fowler had moved over and shared Towser's mind.

Fowler stood silent, revulsion growing in him. Revulsion at the thought of being turned back into a man – into the inadequacy that was the human body and the human mind.

'I'd come with you,' Towser told him, 'but I couldn't stand it. I might die before I could get back. I was nearly done for, you remember, I was old and full of fleas. My teeth were wore right down to nubbins and my digestion was all shot. And I had terrible dreams. Used to chase rabbits when I was a pup, but towards the last it was the rabbits that were chasing me.'

'You stay here,' said Fowler. 'I'll be coming back.'

If I can make them understand, he thought. *If only I can. If I can explain.*

He lifted his massive head and stared at the lift of hills which swelled to mountain peaks shrouded in the rose and purple mist. A lightning bolt snaked across the sky and the clouds and mist were lighted with a fire of ecstasy.

He shambled forwards, slowly, reluctantly. A whiff of scent came down the breeze and his body drank it in – like a cat rolling in catnip. And yet it wasn't scent – although that was the closest he could come to it, the nearest word he had. In years to come the human race would develop a new terminology.

How could one, he wondered, explain the mist that drifted on the land and the scent that was pure delight. Other things they'd understand, he knew. That one never had to eat, that one never slept, that one was done with the whole range of depressive neurosis of which Man was victim. Those things they would understand, because they were things that could be told in simple terms, things which could be explained in existent language.

But what about the other things – the factors that called for a new vocabulary? The emotions that Man had never known. The abilities that Man had never dreamed of. The clarity of mind and the understanding – the ability to use one's brain down to the ultimate cell. The things one knew and could do instinctively that Man could never do because his body did not carry the senses with which they could be done.

'I'll write it down,' he told himself. 'I'll take my time and write it down.'

But the written word, he realized, was a sorry tool.

A televisor port bulged out of the crystalline hide of the dome and he shambled towards it. Rivulets of condensed mist ran down across it and he reared up to stare straight into the port.

Not that he could see anything, but the men inside would see him. The men who always watched, staring out at the brutality of Jupiter, the roaring gales and ammonia rains, the drifting clouds of deadly methane scudding past. For that was the way that men saw Jupiter.

He lifted a forepaw and wrote swiftly in the wetness on the port – printing backwards.

They had to know who it was, so there would be no mistake. They had to know what co-ordinates to use. Otherwise they might convert him back into the wrong body, use the wrong matrix and he would come out somebody else – young Allen, maybe, or Smith, or Pelletier. And that might well be fatal.

The ammonia ran down and blurred the printing, wiped it out. He wrote the name again.

They would understand that name. They would know that one of the men who had been converted into a Loper had come back to report.

He dropped to the ground and whirled around, staring at the door which led into the converter unit. The door moved slowly, swinging outwards.

'Good-bye, Towser,' said Fowler softly.

A warning cry rose in his brain: *It's not too late. You aren't in there yet. You still can change your mind. You still can turn and run.*

He plodded on, determined, gritting mental teeth. He felt the metal floor underneath his pads, sensed the closing of the door behind him. He caught one last, fragmentary thought from Towser and then there was only darkness.

The conversion chamber lay just ahead and he moved up the sloping ramp to reach it.

A man and dog went out, he thought, and now the man comes back.

The press conference had gone well. There had been satisfactory things to report.

Yes, Tyler Webster told the newsmen, the trouble on Venus had been all smoothed out. Just a matter of the parties involved sitting down and talking. The life experiments out in the cold laboratories of Pluto were progressing satisfactorily. The expedition for Centauri would leave as scheduled, despite reports it was all balled up. The trade commission soon would issue new monetary schedules on various interplanetary products, ironing out a few inequalities.

Nothing sensational. Nothing to make headlines. Nothing to lead off the newscast.

'And Jon Culver tells me,' said Webster, 'to remind you gentlemen that to-day is the one hundred and twenty-fifth anniversary of the last murder committed in the Solar System. One hundred and twenty-five years without a death by premeditated violence.'

He leaned back in the chair and grinned at them, masking the thing he dreaded, the question that he knew would come.

But they were not ready to ask it yet – there was a custom to be observed – a very pleasant custom.

Burly Stephen Andrews, press chief for *Interplanetary News*, clearing his throat as if about to make an important announcement, asked with what amounted to mock gravity:

'And how's the boy?'

A smile broke across Webster's face. 'I'm going home for the week end,' he said. 'I bought my son a toy.'

He reached out, lifted the little tube from off the desk.

'An old-fashioned toy,' he said. 'Guaranteed old-fashioned. A company just started putting them out. You put it up to your eye and turn it and you see pretty pictures. Coloured glass falling into place. There's a name for it—'

'Kaleidoscope,' said one of the newsmen quickly. 'I've read about them. In an old history on the manners and customs of the early twentieth, century.'

'Have you tried it, Mr Chairman?' asked Andrews.

'No,' said Webster. 'To tell the truth, I haven't. I just got it this afternoon and I've been too busy.'

'Where'd you get it, Mr Chairman?' asked a voice. 'I got to get one of those for my own kid.'

'At the shop just around the corner. The toy shop, you know. They just came in to-day.'

Now, Webster knew, was the time for them to go. A little bit of pleasant, friendly banter and they'd get up and leave.

But they weren't leaving – and he knew they weren't. He knew it by the sudden hush and the papers that rattled quickly to cover up the hush.

Then Stephen Andrews was asking the question that Webster had dreaded. For a moment Webster was grateful that Andrews should be the one to ask it. Andrews had been friendly, generally speaking, and *Interplanetary Press* dealt in objective news, with none of the sly slanting of words employed by interpretative writers.

'Mr Chairman,' said Andrews, 'we understand a man who was converted on Jupiter has come back to Earth. We would like to ask you if the report is true?'

'It is true,' said Webster, stiffly.

They waited and Webster waited, unmoving in his chair.

'Would you wish to comment?' asked Andrews, finally.

'No,' said Webster.

Webster glanced around the room, ticking off the faces. Tensed faces, sensing some of the truth beneath his flat refusal to discuss the matter. Amused faces, masking brains that even now were thinking how they might twist the few words he had spoken. Angry faces that would write outraged interpretative pieces about the people's right to know.

'I am sorry, gentlemen,' said Webster.

Andrews rose heavily from the chair. 'Thank you, Mr Chairman,' he said.

Webster sat in his chair and watched them go, felt the coldness and emptiness of the room when they were gone.

They'll crucify me, he thought. *They'll nail me to the barn door and I haven't got a comeback. Not a single one.*

He rose from the chair and walked across the room, stood staring out of the window at the garden in the sun of afternoon.

Yet you simply couldn't tell them.

Paradise! Heaven for the asking! And the end of humanity! The end of all the ideals and all the dreams of mankind, the end of the race itself.

The green light on his desk flashed and chirped and he strode back across the room.

'What is it?' he asked.

The tiny screen flashed and a face was there.

'The dogs just reported, sir, that Joe, the mutant, went to your residence and Jenkins let him in.'

'Joe! You're sure?'

'That's what the dogs said. And the dogs are never wrong.'

'No,' said Webster slowly, 'no, they never are.'

The face faded from the screen and Webster sat down heavily.

He reached with numbed fingers for the control panel on his desk, twirled the combination without looking.

The house loomed on the screen, the house in North America that crouched on the windy hilltop. A structure that had stood for almost a thousand years. A place where a long line of Websters had lived and dreamed and died.

Far in the blue above the house a crow was flying and Webster heard, or imagined that he heard, the wind-blown *caw* of the soaring bird.

Everything was all right – or seemed to be. The house drowsed in the morning light and the statue still stood upon the sweep of lawn – the statue of that long-gone ancestor who had vanished on the star-path. Allen Webster, who had been the first to leave the Solar System, heading for Centauri – even as the expedition now on Mars would head out in a day or two.

There was no stir about the house, no sign of any moving thing.

Webster's hand moved out and flipped a toggle. The screen went dead.

Jenkins can handle things, he thought. *Probably better than a man could handle them. After all, he's got almost a thousand years of wisdom packed in that metal hide of his. He'll be calling in before long to let me know what it's all about.*

His hand reached out, set up another combination.

He waited for long seconds before the face came on the screen.

'What is it, Tyler?' asked the face.

'Just got a report that Joe—'

Jon Culver nodded. 'I just got it, too. I'm checking up.'

'What do you make of it?'

The face of the World Security chief crinkled quizzically. 'Softening up, maybe. We've been pushing Joe and the other mutants pretty hard. The dogs have done a top-notch job.'

'But there have been no signs of it,' protested Webster. 'Nothing in the records to indicate any trend that way.'

'Look,' said Culver. 'They haven't drawn a breath for more than a hundred years we haven't known about. Got everything they've done down on tape in black and white. Every move they've made, we've blocked. At first they figured it was just tough luck, but now they know it isn't. Maybe they've up and decided they are licked.'

'I don't think so,' said Webster, solemnly. 'Whenever those babies figure they're licked, you better start looking for a place that's soft to light.'

'I'll keep on top of it,' Culver told him. 'I'll keep you posted.'

The plate faded and was a square of glass. Webster stared at it moodily.

The mutants weren't licked – not by a long shot. He knew that, and so did Culver. And yet—

Why had Joe gone to Jenkins? Why hadn't he contacted the

government here in Geneva? Face saving, maybe. Dealing through a robot. After all, Joe had known Jenkins for a long, long time.

Unaccountably, Webster felt a surge of pride. Pride that if such were the case, Joe had gone to Jenkins. For Jenkins, despite his metal hide, was a Webster, too.

Pride, thought Webster. *Accomplishment and mistake. But always counting for something. Each of them down the years. Jerome, who had lost the world the Juwain philosophy. And Thomas, who had given the world the space-drive principle that now had been perfected. And Thomas' son, Allen, who had tried for the stars and failed. And Bruce, who had first conceived the twin civilization of man and dog. Now, finally, himself – Tyler Webster, chairman, of the World Committee.*

Sitting at the desk, he clasped his hands in front of him, stared at the evening light pouring through the window.

Waiting, he confessed. Waiting for the snicker of the signal that would tell him Jenkins was calling to report on Joe. If only—

If only an understanding could be reached. If only mutants and men could work together. If they could forget this half-hidden war of stalemate, they could go far, the three of them together – man and dog and mutant.

Webster shook his head. It was too much to expect. The difference was too great, the breach too wide. Suspicion on the part of men and a tolerant amusement on the part of the mutants would keep the two apart. For the mutants were a different race, an offshoot that had jumped too far ahead. Men who had become true individuals with no need of society, no need of human approval, utterly lacking in the herd instinct that had held the race together, immune to social pressures.

And because of the mutants the little group of mutated dogs so far had been of little practical use to their older brother, Man. For the dogs had watched for more than a hundred years, had been the police force that kept the human mutants under observation.

Webster slid back his chair, opened a desk drawer, took out a sheaf of papers.

One eye on the televisor plate, he snapped over the toggle that called his secretary.

'Yes, Mr Webster.'

'I'm going to call on Mr Fowler,' said Webster. 'If a call comes through—'

The secretary's voice shook just a little. 'If one does, sir, I'll contact you right away.'

'Thanks,' said Webster.

He snapped the toggle back.

They've heard of it already, he thought. *Everyone in the whole building is standing around with their tongues hanging out, waiting for the news.*

Kent Fowler lounged in a chair in the garden outside his room, watching the little black terrier dig frantically after an imagined rabbit.

'You know, Rover,' said Fowler, 'you aren't fooling me.'

The dog stopped digging, looked over his shoulder with grinning teeth, barked excitedly. Then went back to digging.

'You'll slip up one of these days,' Fowler told him, 'and say a word or two and I'll have you dead to rights.'

Rover went on digging.

Foxy little devil, thought Fowler. *Smarter than a whip. Webster sicked him on me and he's played the part, all right. He's dug for rabbits and he's been disrespectful to the shrubs and he's scratched for fleas – the perfect picture of a perfect dog. But I'm on to him. I'm on to all of them.*

A foot crunched in the grass and Fowler looked up.

'Good evening,' said Tyler Webster.

'I've been wondering when you'd come,' said Fowler shortly. 'Sit down and give it to me – straight. You don't believe me, do you?'

Webster eased himself into the second chair, laid the sheaf of papers in his lap.

'I can understand how you feel,' he said.

'I doubt if you can,' snapped Fowler. 'I came here, bringing news that I thought was important. A report that has cost me more than you can imagine.'

He hunched forward in his chair. 'I wonder if you can realize that every hour I've spent as a human being has been mental torture.'

'I'm sorry,' said Webster. 'But we had to be sure. We had to check your reports.'

'And make certain tests?'

Webster nodded.

'Like Rover over there?'

'His name isn't Rover,' said Webster, gently. 'If you've been calling him that, you've hurt his feelings. All the dogs have human names. This one's Elmer.'

Elmer had stopped his digging, was trotting towards them. He sat down beside Webster's chair, scrubbed at his dirt-filled whiskers with a clay-smeared paw.

'What about it, Elmer?' asked Webster.

'He's human, all right,' said the dog, 'but not all human. Not a mutant you know. But something else. Something alien.'

'That's to be expected,' said Fowler. 'I was a Loper for five years.'

Webster nodded. 'You'd retain part of the personality. That's understandable. And the dog would spot it. They're sensitive to things like that. Psychic, almost. That's why we put them on the mutants. They can sniff one out no matter where he is.'

'You mean that you believe me?'

Webster rustled the papers in his lap, smoothed them out with a careful hand. 'I'm afraid I do,'

'Why afraid?'

'Because,' Webster told him, 'you're the greatest threat mankind's ever faced.'

'Threat! Man, don't you understand? I'm offering you . . . offering you—'

'Yes, I know,' said Webster. 'The word is Paradise.'

'And you're afraid of that?'

'Terrified,' said Webster. 'Just try to envision what it would mean if we told the people and the people all believed. Everyone would want to go to Jupiter and become a Loper. The very fact that the Lopers apparently have life spans running into thousands of years would be reason enough if there were no others.

'We would be faced by a system-wide demand that everyone immediately be sent to Jupiter. No one would want to remain human. In the end there would be no humans – all the humans would be Lopers. Had you thought of that?'

Fowler licked his lips with a nervous tongue. 'Certainly. That is what I had expected.'

'The human race would disappear,' said Webster, speaking evenly. 'It would be wiped out. It would junk all the progress it has made over thousands of years. It would disappear just when it is on the verge of its greatest advancement.'

'But you don't know,' protested Fowler. 'You can't know. You've never been a Loper. I have.' He tapped his chest. 'I know what it is like.'

Webster shook his head. 'I'm not arguing on that score. I'm ready to concede that it may be better to be a Loper than a human. What I can't concede is that we would be justified in wiping out the human race – that we should trade what the human race has done and will do for what the Lopers might do. The human race is going places. Maybe not so pleasantly nor so clear-headedly nor as brilliantly as your Lopers, but in the long run I have a feeling that it will go much farther. We have a racial heritage and a racial destiny that we can't throw away.'

Fowler leaned forward in his chair. 'Look,' he said, 'I've played this fair. I came straight to you and the World Committee. I could have told the press and radio and forced your hand, but I didn't do it.'

'What you're getting at,' suggested Webster, 'is that the World Committee doesn't have the right to decide this thing themselves. You're suggesting that the people have their say about it.'

Fowler nodded, tight-lipped.

'Frankly,' said Webster, 'I don't trust the people. You'd get mob reaction. Selfish response. Not a one of them would think about the race, but only of themselves.'

'Are you telling me,' asked Fowler, 'that I'm right, but you can't do a thing about it?'

'Not exactly. We'll have to work out something. Maybe Jupiter could be made a sort of old folks' home. After a man had lived out a useful life—'

Fowler made a tearing sound of disgust deep inside his throat. 'A reward,' he snapped. 'Turning an old horse out to pasture. Paradise by special dispensation.'

'That way,' Webster pointed out, 'we'd save the human race and still have Jupiter.'

Fowler came to his feet in a swift, lithe motion. 'I'm sick of it,' he shouted. 'I brought you a thing you wanted to know. A thing you spent billions of dollars and, so far as you knew, hundreds of lives, to find out. You set up reconversion stations all over Jupiter and you sent out men by dozens and they never came back and you thought that they were dead and still you sent out others. And none of them came back – because they didn't want to come back, because they couldn't come back, because they couldn't stomach being men again. Then I came back and what does it amount to? A lot of high-flown talk . . . a lot of quibbling . . . questioning me and doubting me. Then finally saying I am all right, but that I made a mistake in coming back at all.'

He let his arms fall to his side and his shoulders drooped.

'I'm free, I suppose,' he said. 'I don't need to stay here.'

Webster nodded slowly. 'Certainly, you are free. You were free all the time. I only asked that you stay until I could check.'

'I could go back to Jupiter?'

'In the light of the situation,' said Webster, 'that might be a good idea.'

'I'm surprised you didn't suggest it,' said Fowler, bitterly. 'It would be an out for you. You could file away the report and forget about it and go on running the Solar System like a child's game played on a parlour floor. Your family has blundered its way through centuries and the people let you come back for more. One of your ancestors lost the world the Juwain philosophy and another blocked the effort of the humans to co-operate with the mutants—'

Webster spoke sharply. 'Leave me and my family out of this, Fowler! It is a thing that's bigger—'

But Fowler was shouting, drowning out his words. 'And I'm not going to let you bungle this. The world has lost enough because of you Websters. Now the world's going to get a break. I'm going to tell the people about Jupiter. I'll tell the press and radio. I'll yell it from the housetops. I'll—'

His voice broke and his shoulders shook.

Webster's voice was cold with sudden rage. 'I'll fight you, Fowler. I'll go on the beam against you. I can't let you do a thing like this.'

Fowler had swung around, was striding towards the garden gate.

Webster, frozen in his chair, felt the paw clawing at his leg.

'Shall I get him, Boss?' asked Elmer. 'Shall I go and get him?'

Webster shook his head. 'Let him go,' he said. 'He has as much right as I have to do the thing he wishes.'

A chill wind came across the garden wall and rustled the cape about Webster's shoulders.

Words beat in his brain – words that had been spoken here in this garden scant seconds ago, but words that came from centuries away. *One of your ancestors lost the Juwain philosophy. One of your ancestors—*

Webster clenched his fists until the nails dug into his palms.

A jinx, thought Webster. *That's what we are. A jinx upon humanity. The Juwain philosophy. And the mutants. But the mutants had had the Juwain philosophy for centuries now and they had never used it. Joe had stolen it from Grant and Grant had spent his life trying to get it back. But he never had.*

Maybe, thought Webster, trying to console himself, *it really didn't amount to much. If it had, the mutants would have used it. Or maybe – just maybe – the mutants had been bluffing. Maybe they didn't know any more about it than the humans did.*

A metallic voice coughed softly and Webster looked up. A small grey robot stood just outside the doorway.

'The call, sir,' said the robot. 'The call you've been expecting.'

Jenkins' face came into the plate – an old face, obsolete and ugly. Not the smooth, lifelike face boasted by the latest model robots.

'I'm sorry to disturb you, sir,' he said, 'but it is most unusual Joe came up and asked to use our visor to put in a call to you. Won't tell me what he wants, sir. Says it's just a friendly call to an old-time neighbour.'

'Put him on,' said Webster.

'He went at it most unusual, sir,' persisted Jenkins. 'He came up and sat around and chewed the fat for an hour or more before he asked to use it I'd say, if you'd pardon me, that it's most peculiar.'

'I know,' said Webster. 'Joe is peculiar, in a lot of ways.'

Jenkins' face faded from the screen and another face came in – that of Joe, the mutant It was a strong face with a wrinkled, leathery skin and blue-grey eyes that twinkled, hair that was just turning salt and pepper at the temples.

'Jenkins doesn't trust me, Tyler,' said Joe and Webster felt his hackles rising at the laughter that lurked behind the words.

'For that matter,' he told him bluntly, 'neither do I.'

Joe clucked with his tongue. 'Why, Tyler, we've never given you a single minute's trouble. Not a single one of us. You've watched us and you've worried and fretted about us, but we've never hurt you. You've had so many of the dogs spying on us that we stumble over them everywhere we turn and you've kept files on us and studied us and talked us up and down until you must be sick to death of it.'

'We know you,' said Webster grimly. 'We know more about you than you know about yourselves. We know how many there are of you and we know each of you personally. Want to know what any one of you were doing at any given moment in the last hundred years or so? Ask us and we'll tell you.'

Butter wouldn't have melted in Joe's mouth. 'And all the time,' he said, 'we were thinking kindly of you. Figuring out how sometime we might want to help you.'

'Why didn't you do it, then?' snapped Webster. 'We were ready to work with you at first. Even after you stole the Juwain philosophy from Grant—'

'Stole it?' asked Joe. 'Surely, Tyler, you must have that wrong. We only took it so we could work it out. It was all botched up, you know.'

'You probably figured it out the day after you had your hands on it,' Webster told him, flatly. 'What were you waiting for? Any time you had offered that to us we'd known that you were with us and we'd have worked with you. We'd have called off the dogs, we'd have accepted you.'

'Funny thing,' said Joe. 'We never seemed to care about being accepted.'

And the old laughter was back again, the laughter of a man who was sufficient to himself, who saw the whole fabric of the human community of effort as a vast, ironic joke. A man who walked alone and liked it. A man who saw the human race as something that was funny and probably just a little dangerous – but funnier than ever because it was dangerous. A man who felt no need of the brotherhood of man, who rejected that brotherhood as a thing as utterly provincial and pathetic as the twentieth century booster clubs.

'OK,' said Webster sharply. 'If that's the way you want it. I'd hoped that maybe you had a deal to offer – some chance of conciliation. We don't like things as they are – we'd rather they were different. But the move is up to you.'

'Now, Tyler,' protested Joe, 'no use in flying off the handle. I was thinking maybe you'd ought to know about the Juwain philosophy. You've sort of forgotten about it now, but there was a time when the System was all stirred up about it.'

'All right,' said Webster, 'go ahead and tell me.' The tone of his voice said he knew Joe wouldn't.

'Basically,' said Joe, 'you humans are a lonely lot of folks. You never have known your fellow-man. You can't know him because you haven't the common touch of understanding that makes it possible to know him. You have friendships, sure, but those friendships are based on pure emotions, never on real understanding. You get along together, sure. But you get along by tolerance rather than by understanding. You work out your problems by agreement, but that agreement is simply a matter of the stronger-minded among you beating down the opposition of the weaker ones.'

'What's that got to do with it?'

'Why, everything,' Joe told him. 'With the Juwain philosophy you'd actually understand.'

'Telepathy?' asked Webster.

'Not exactly,' said Joe. 'We mutants have telepathy. But this is something different. The Juwain philosophy provides an ability to sense the viewpoint of another. It won't necessarily make you agree with that viewpoint, but it does make you recognize it. You not only know what the other fellow is talking about but how he feels about it. With Juwain's philosophy you have to accept the validity of another man's ideas and knowledge, not just the words he says, but the thought back of the words.'

'Semantics,' said Webster.

'If you insist on the term,' Joe told him. 'What it really means is that you understand not only the intrinsic meaning, but the implied meaning of what someone else is saying. Almost telepathy, but not quite. A whole lot better, some ways.'

'And, Joe, how do you go about it? How do you—'

The laughter was back again. 'You think about it a while, Tyler . . . find out how bad you want it. Then maybe we can talk.'

'Horse trading,' said Webster.

Joe nodded.

'Booby-trapped, too, I suppose,' said Webster.

'Couple of them,' said Joe. 'You find them and we'll talk about that, too.'

'What are you fellows going to want?'

'Plenty,' Joe told him, 'but maybe it'll be worth it.'

The screen went dead and Webster sat staring at it with unseeing eyes. Booby-trapped? Of course it was. Clear up to the hilt.

Webster screwed his eyes shut and felt the blood pounding in his brain.

What was it that had been claimed for the Juwain philosophy in that far-gone day when it had been lost? That it would have put mankind a hundred thousand years ahead in two short generations. Something like that.

Maybe stretching it a bit – but not too much. A little justified exaggeration, that was all.

Men understanding one another, accepting one another's ideas at face value, each man seeing behind the words, seeing the thing as someone else would see it and accepting that concept as if it were his own. Making it, in fact, part of his own knowledge that could be brought to bear upon the subject at hand. No misunderstanding, no prejudice, no bias, no jangling – but a clear, complete grasp of all the conflicting angles of any human problem. Applicable to any thing, to any type of human endeavour. To sociology, to psychology, to engineering, to all the various facets of a complex civilization. No more bungling, no more quarrelling, but honest and sincere appraisal of the facts and the ideas at hand.

A hundred thousand years in two generations? Perhaps not too far off, at that.

But booby-trapped? Or was it? Did the mutants really mean to part with it? For any kind of prize? Just another bait dangled in front of mankind's eyes while around the corner the mutants rolled with laughter.

The mutants hadn't used it. Of course, they hadn't, for they had no real need of it. They already had telepathy and that would serve the purpose as far as the mutants were concerned. Individualists would have little use for a device which would make them understand one another, for they would not care whether they understood one another. The mutants got along together, apparently, tolerating whatever contact was necessary to safeguard their interests. But that was all. They'd work together to save their skins, but they found no pleasure in it.

An honest offer? A bait, a lure to hold man's attention in one quarter while a dirty deal was being pulled off in another? A mere ironic joke? Or an offer that had a stinger in it?

Webster shook his head. There was no telling. No way to gauge a mutant's motives or his reason.

Soft, glowing light had crept into the walls and ceiling of the office with the departing of the day, the automatic, hidden light growing stronger as the darkness fell. Webster glanced at the window, saw that it was an oblong of blackness, dotted by the few advertising signs that flared and flickered on the city's skyline.

He reached out, thumbed over a tumbler, spoke to the secretary in the outer office.

'I'm sorry I kept you so long. I forgot the time.'

'That's all right, sir,' said the secretary. 'There's a visitor to see you, Mr Fowler.'

'Fowler?'

'Yes, the gentleman from Jupiter.'

'I know,' said Webster wearily. 'Ask him to come in.'

He had almost forgotten Fowler and the threat the man had made.

He stared absent-mindedly at his desk, saw the kaleidoscope lying where he'd left it. *Funny toy*, he thought. *Quaint idea. A simple thing for the simple minds of long ago. But the kid will get a boot out of it.*

He reached out a hand and grasped it, lifted it to his eyes. The transmitted light wove a pattern of crazy colour, a geometric nightmare. He twirled the tube a bit and the pattern changed. And yet again—

His brain wrenched with a sudden sickness and the colour burned itself into his mind in a single flare of soul-twisting torture.

The tube dropped and clattered on the desk. Webster reached out with both hands and clutched at the desk edge.

And through his brain went the thought of horror: *What a toy for a kid!*

The sickness faded and he sat stock-still, brain clear again, breath coming regularly.

Funny, he thought. *Funny that it should do a thing like that. Or could it have been something else and not the kaleidoscope at all. A seizure of some sort. Heart acting up. A bit too young for that and he'd been checked just recently.*

The door clicked and Webster looked up.

Fowler came across the room with measured step, slowly, until he stood across from the desk.

'Yes, Fowler?'

'I left in anger,' Fowler said, 'and I didn't want it that way. You might have understood, but again you might not have. It was just that I was upset, you see. I came from Jupiter, feeling that finally all the years I'd spend there in the domes had been justified, that all the anguish I had felt when I saw the men go out somehow had paid off. I was bringing news, you understand, news that the world awaited. To me it was the most wonderful thing that could have happened and I thought you'd see it, too. I thought the people would see it. It was as if I had been bringing them word that Paradise was just around the corner. For that is what it is, Webster . . . that is what it is.'

He put his hands flat upon the desk and leaned forward, whispering.

'You see how it is, don't you, Webster? You understand a bit.'

Webster's hands were shaking and he laid them in his lap, clenched them together until the fingers hurt.

'Yes,' he whispered back. 'Yes, I think I know.'

For he did know.

Knew more than the words had told him. Knew the anguish and the pleading and bitter disappointment that lay behind the words. Knew them almost as if he'd said the words himself – almost as if he were Fowler.

Fowler's voice broke in alarm. 'What's the matter, Webster? What's the trouble with you?'

Webster tried to speak and the words were dust. His throat tightened until there was a knot of pain above his Adam's apple.

He tried again and the words were low and forced. 'Tell me, Fowler. You learned a lot of things out there. Things that men don't know or know imperfectly. Like high grade telepathy, maybe . . . or . . . or—'

'Yes,' said Fowler, 'a lot of things. But I didn't bring them back with me. When I became a man again, that was all I was. Just a man, that's all. None of it came back. Most of it just hazy memories and a . . . well, you might call it yearning.'

'You mean that you haven't one of the abilities you had when you were a Loper?'

'Not a single one.'

'You couldn't, by chance, be able to *make* me understand a thing you wanted me to know. Make me feel the way you feel.'

'Not a chance,' said Fowler.

Webster reached out a hand, pushed the kaleidoscope gently with his finger. It rolled forwards, then came to rest again.

'What did you come back for?' asked Webster.

'To square myself with you,' said Fowler. 'To let you know I wasn't really sore. To try to make you understand that I had a side, too. Just a difference of opinion, that's all. I thought maybe we might shake on it.'

'I see. And you're still determined to go out and tell the people?'

Fowler nodded. 'I have to, Webster. You must surely know that. It's . . . it's . . . well, almost a religion with me. It's something I believe in. I have to tell the rest of them that there's a better world and a better life. I have to lead them to it.'

'A messiah,' said Webster.

Fowler straightened. 'That's one thing I was afraid of. Scoffing isn't—'

'I wasn't scoffing,' Webster told him, almost gently.

He picked up the kaleidoscope, polishing its tube with the

palm of his hand, considering. *Not yet*, he thought. *Not yet. Have to think it out. Do I want him to understand me as well as I understand him?*

'Look, Fowler,' he said, 'lay off a day or two. Wait a bit. Just a day or two. Then let us talk again.'

'I've waited long enough already.'

'But I want you to think this over: A million years ago man first came into being – just an animal. Since that time he has inched his way up a cultural ladder. Bit by painful bit he has developed a way of life, a philosophy, a way of doing things. His progress has been geometrical. To-day he does much more than he did yesterday. To-morrow he'll do even more than he did to-day. For the first time in human history, Man is really beginning to hit the ball. He's just got a good start, the first stride, you might say. He's going a lot farther in a lot less time than he's come already.

'Maybe it isn't as pleasant as Jupiter, maybe not the same at all. Maybe humankind is drab compared with the life forms of Jupiter. But it's man's life. It's the thing he's fought for. It's the thing he's made himself. It's a destiny he has shaped.

'I hate to think, Fowler, that just when we're going good we'll swap our destiny for one we don't know about, for one we can't be sure about.'

'I'll wait,' said Fowler. 'Just a day or two. But I'm warning you. You can't put me off. You can't change my mind.'

'That's all I ask,' said Webster. He rose and held out his hand. 'Shake on it?' he asked.

But even as he shook Fowler's hand, Webster knew it wasn't any good. Juwain philosophy or not, mankind was heading for a showdown. A showdown that would be even worse because of the Juwain philosophy. For the mutants wouldn't miss a bet. If this was to be their joke, if this was their way of getting rid of the human race, they wouldn't overlook a thing. By to-morrow morning every man, woman and child somehow or other would have managed to look through a kaleidoscope. Or something else. Lord only knew how many other ways there were.

He watched until Fowler had closed the door behind him, then walked to the window and stared out. Flashing on the skyline of the city was a new advertising sign – one that had not been there before. A crazy sign that made crazy coloured patterns in the night. Flashing on and off as if one were turning a kaleidoscope.

Webster stared at it, tight-lipped.

He should have expected it.

He thought of Joe with a flare of murderous fury surging through his brain. For that call had been a cackling chortle behind a covering hand, a smart-Aleck gesture designed to let man know what it was all about, to let him know after he was behind the eight-ball and couldn't do a thing about it.

We should have killed them off, thought Webster, and was surprised at the calm coldness of the thought. *We should have stamped them out like we would a dangerous disease.*

But man had forsaken violence as a world and individual policy. Not for one hundred and twenty-five years had one group been arrayed against another group in violence.

When Joe had called, the Juwain philosophy had lain on the desk. I had only to reach out my hand and touch it, Webster thought.

He stiffened with the realization of it. I had only to reach out my hand and touch it. *And I did just that!*

Something more than telepathy, something more than guessing. Joe knew he would pick up the kaleidoscope – must have known it. Foresight – an ability to roll back the future. Just an hour or so, perhaps, but that would be enough.

Joe – and the other mutants, of course – had known about Fowler. Their probing, telepathic minds could have told them all that they wished to know. But this was something else, something different.

He stood at the window, staring at the sign. Thousands of people, he knew, were seeing it. Seeing it and feeling that sudden sick impact in their mind.

Webster frowned, wondering about the shifting pattern of

the lights. Some physiological impact upon a certain centre of the human brain, perhaps. A portion of the brain that had not been used before – a portion of the brain that in due course of human development might naturally have come into its proper function. A function now that was being forced.

The Juwain philosophy, at last! Something for which men had sought for centuries, now finally come to pass. Given man at a time when he'd have been better off without it.

Fowler had written in his report: *I cannot give a factual account because there are no words for the facts that I want to tell.* He still didn't have the words, of course, but he had something else that was even better – an audience that could understand the sincerity and the greatness which lay beneath the words he did have. An audience with a new-found sense which would enable them to grasp some of the mighty scope of the thing Fowler had to tell.

Joe had planned it that way. Had waited for this moment. Had used the Juwain philosophy as a weapon against the human race.

For with the Juwain philosophy, man would go to Jupiter. Faced by all the logic in the world, he still would go to Jupiter. For better or for worse, he would go to Jupiter.

The only chance there had ever been of winning against Fowler had been Fowler's inability to describe what he saw, to tell what he felt, to reach the people with a clear exposition of the message that he brought. With mere human words that message would have been vague and fuzzy and while the people at first might have believed, they would have been shaky in their belief, would have listened to other argument.

But now that chance was gone, for the words would be no longer vague and fuzzy. The people would know, as clearly and as vibrantly as Fowler knew himself, what Jupiter was like.

The people would go to Jupiter, would enter upon a life other than the human life.

And the Solar System, the entire Solar System, with the exception of Jupiter, would lie open for the new race of mutants to take over, to develop any kind of culture that they might wish – a culture that would scarcely follow the civilization of the parent race.

Webster swung away from the window, strode back to the desk. He stooped and pulled out a drawer; reached inside. His hand came out clutching something that he had never dreamed of using – a relic, a museum piece he had tossed there years before.

With a handkerchief, he polished the metal of the gun, tested its mechanism with trembling fingers.

Fowler was the key. With Fowler dead—

With Fowler dead and the Jupiter stations dismantled and abandoned, the mutants would be licked. Man would have the Juwain philosophy and would retain his destiny. The Centauri expedition would blast off for the stars. The life experiments would continue on Pluto. Man would march along the course that his culture plotted.

Faster than ever before. Faster than anyone could dream.

Two great strides. The renunciation of violence as a human policy – the understanding that came with the Juwain philosophy. The two great things that would speed man along the road to wherever he was going.

The renunciation of the violence and the—

Webster stared at the gun clutched in his hand and heard the roar of winds tumbling through his head.

Two great strides – and he was about to toss away the first.

For one hundred and twenty-five years no man had killed another – for more than a thousand years killing had been obsolete as a factor in the determination of human affairs.

A thousand years of peace and one death might undo the work. One shot in the night might collapse the structure, might hurl man back to the old bestial thinking.

Webster killed – why can't I? After all, there are some men who should be killed. Webster did right, but he shouldn't have stopped with only one. I don't see why they're hanging him; he'd ought to get a medal. We ought to start on the mutants first. If it hadn't been for them—

That was the way they'd talk.

That, thought Webster, *is the wind that's roaring in my brain.*

The flashing of the crazy coloured sign made a ghostly flicker along the walls and floor.

Fowler is seeing that, thought Webster. *He is looking at it and, even if he isn't, I still have the kaleidoscope.*

He'll be coming in and we'll sit down and talk. We'll sit down and talk—

He tossed the gun back into the drawer, walked towards the door.

NOTES ON THE SIXTH TALE

If there has been any doubt concerning the origin of the other tales in the legend, there can be no doubt in this. Here, in the sixth tale, we have unmistakably the hallmarks of Doggish story telling. It has the deeper emotional value, the close attention to ethical matters which are stressed in all other Doggish myths.

And yet, strangely enough, it is in this particular tale that Tige finds his weightiest evidence of the actuality of the human race. Here, he points out, we have evidence that the Dogs told these self-same tales before the blazing fire when they sat and talked of Man buried in Geneva or gone to Jupiter. Here, he says, we are given an account of the Dogs' first probing into the cobbly worlds, their first step towards the development of an animal brotherhood.

Here, too, he thinks, we have evidence that Man was another contemporary race which went part way down the path of culture with the Dogs. Whether or not the disaster which is portrayed in this tale is the one which actually overwhelmed Man, Tige says, we cannot be sure. He admits that through the centuries the tale as we know it to-day has been embellished and embroidered. But it does provide, he contends, good and substantial evidence that some disaster was visited upon the human race.

Rover, who does not admit to the factual evidence seen by Tige, believes that the storyteller in this tale brings to a logical conclusion a culture such as Man developed. Without at least broad purpose, without certain implanted stability, no culture can survive, and this is the lesson, Rover believes, the tale is meant to spell.

Man, in this story, is treated with a certain tenderness which is not accorded him in any of the other tales. He is at once a lonely and pitiful creature, and yet somehow glorious. It is entirely typical of him that in the end he should make a grand gesture, that he should purchase godhood by self-immolation.

Yet the worship which is accorded him by Ebenezer has certain disturbing overtones which have become the source of particularly bitter dispute among the legend's students.

Bounce, in his book, *The Myth of Man*, asks this question: If Man had taken a different path, might he not, in time to come, have been as great as Dog?

It is a question, perhaps, that many readers of the legend have stopped to ask themselves.

VI
Hobbies

The rabbit ducked around a bush and the little black dog zipped after him, then dug in his heels and skidded. In the pathway stood a wolf, the rabbit's twitching, bloody body hanging from his jaws.

Ebenezer stood very still and panted, red rag of a tongue lolling out, a little faint and sick at the sight before him.

It had been such a nice rabbit!

Feet pattered on the trail behind him and Shadow whizzed around the bush, slid to a stop alongside Ebenezer.

The wolf flicked his glare from the dog to the pint-size robot, then back to the dog again. The yellow light of wildness slowly faded from his eyes.

'You shouldn't have done that, Wolf,' said Ebenezer softly. 'The rabbit knew I wouldn't hurt him and it was all in fun. But he ran straight into you and you snapped him up.'

'There's no use talking to him,' Shadow hissed out of the corner of his mouth. 'He doesn't know a word you're saying. Next thing you know, he'll be gulping you.'

'Not with you around, he won't,' said Ebenezer. 'And, anyhow, he knows me. He remembers last winter. He was one of the pack we fed.'

The wolf paced forward slowly, step by cautious step, until less than two feet separated him from the little dog. Then, very slowly, very carefully, he laid the rabbit on the ground, nudged it forward with his nose.

Shadow made a tiny sound that was almost a gasp. 'He's giving it to you!'

'I know,' said Ebenezer calmly. 'I told you he remembered. He's the one that had a frozen ear and Jenkins fixed it up.'

The dog advanced a step, tail wagging, nose outstretched. The wolf stiffened momentarily, then lowered his ugly head and sniffed. For a second the two noses almost rubbed together, then the wolf stepped back.

'Let's get out of here,' urged Shadow. 'You high-tail it down the trail and I'll bring up the rear. If he tries anything—'

'He won't try anything,' snapped Ebenezer. 'He's a friend of ours. It's not his fault about the rabbit. He doesn't understand. It's the way he lives. To him a rabbit is just a piece of meat.'

Even, he thought, *as it once was for us. As it was for us before the first dog came to sit with a man before a cave-mouth fire – and for a long time after that. Even now a rabbit sometimes—*

Moving slowly, almost apologetically, the wolf reached forward, gathered up the rabbit in his gaping jaws. His tail moved – not quite a wag, but almost.

'You see!' cried Ebenezer and the wolf was gone. His feet moved and there was a blur of grey fading through the trees – a shadow drifting in the forest.

'He took it back,' fumed Shadow. 'Why, the dirty—'

'But he gave it to me,' said Ebenezer triumphantly. 'Only he was so hungry he couldn't make it stick. He did something a wolf has never done before. For a moment he was more than an animal.'

'Indian giver,' snapped Shadow.

Ebenezer shook his head. 'He was ashamed when he took it back. You saw him wag his tail. That was explaining to me – explaining he was hungry and he needed it. Worse than I needed it.'

The dog stared down the green aisles of the fairy forest, smelled the scent of decaying leaves, the heady perfume of hepatica and bloodrot and spidery windflower, the quick, sharp odour of the new leaf, of the woods in early spring.

'Maybe some day—' he said.

'Yeah, I know,' said Shadow. 'Maybe some day the wolves

will be civilized, too. And the rabbits and squirrels and all the other wild things. The way you dogs go mooning around—'

'It isn't mooning,' Ebenezer told him. 'Dreaming, maybe. Men used to dream. They used to sit around and think up things. That's how we happened. A man named Webster thought us up. He messed around with us. He fixed up our throats so we could talk. He rigged up contact lenses so that we could read. He—'

'A lot of good it did men for all their dreaming,' said Shadow, peevishly.

And that, thought Ebenezer, *is the solemn truth. Not many men left now. Just the mutants squatting in their towers and doing no one knows what and the little colony of real men still living in Geneva. The others, long ago, had gone to Jupiter. Had gone to Jupiter and changed themselves into things that were not human.*

Slowly, tail drooping, Ebenezer swung around, clumped slowly up the path.

Too bad about the rabbit, he thought. *It had been such a nice rabbit. It had run so well. And it really wasn't scared. He had chased it lots of times and it knew he wouldn't catch it.*

But even at that, Ebenezer couldn't bring himself to blame the wolf. To a wolf a rabbit wasn't just something that was fun to chase. For the wolf had no herds for meat and milk, no fields of grain for meal to make dog biscuits.

'What I ought to do,' grumbled the remorseless Shadow, treading at his heels, 'is tell Jenkins that you ran out. You know that you should be listening.'

Ebenezer did not answer, kept on trudging up the trail. For what Shadow said was true. Instead of rabbit-chasing, he should have been sitting up at Webster House listening-listening for the things that came to one – sounds and scents and *awareness* of something that was near. Like listening on one side of a wall to the things that were happening on the other, only they were faint and sometimes far away and hard to catch. Even harder, most times, to understand.

It's the animal in me, thought Ebenezer. *The old flea-scratching,*

*bone-chewing, gopher-digging dog that will not let me be – that sends me
sneaking out to chase a rabbit when I should be listening, out prowling
the forest when I should be reading the old books from the shelves that line
the study wall.*

Too fast, he told himself. *We came up too fast. Had to come up too
fast.*

*It took Man thousands of years to turn his grunts into the rudiments of
speech. Thousands of years to discover fire and thousands more of years to
invent the bow and arrow – thousands of years to learn to till the soil and
harvest food, thousands of years to forsake the cave for a house he built
himself.*

*But in a little more than a thousand years from the day we learned to
talk we were on our own – our own, that is, except for Jenkins.*

The forest thinned out into gnarled, scattered oaks that
straggled up the hill, like hobbling old men who had wandered
off the path.

The house stood on the hilltop, a huddled structure that had
taken root and crouched close against the earth. So old that it
was the colour of the things around it, of grass and flowers and
trees, of sky and wind and weather. A house built by men who
loved it and the surrounding acres even as the dogs now loved
them. Built and lived in and died in by a legendary family that
had left a meteoric trail across centuries of time. Men who lent
their shadows to the stories that were told around the blazing
fireplace of stormy nights when the wind sucked along the
eaves. Stories of Bruce Webster and the first dog, Nathaniel; of
a man named Grant who had given Nathaniel a word to pass
along; of another man who had tried to reach the stars and of
the old man who had sat waiting for him in the wheelchair on
the lawn. And other stories of the ogre mutants the dogs had
watched for years.

And now the men had gone and the family was a name and
the dogs carried on as Grant had told Nathaniel that far-gone
day they must.

As if you were men, as if the dog were man. Those were the words
that had been handed down for ten full centuries – and at last
the time had come.

The dogs had come home when the men had gone, come from the far corners of the earth back to the place where the first dog had spoken the first word, where the first dog had read the first line of print – back to Webster House where a man, long ago, had dreamed of a dual civilization, of man and dog going down the ages, hand in paw.

'We've done the best we could,' said Ebenezer, almost as if he were speaking to someone. 'We still are doing it.'

From the other side of the hill came the tinkle of a cow bell, a burst of frantic barking. The pups were bringing in the cows for the evening milking.

The dust of centuries lay within the vault, a grey, powdery dust that was not an alien thing, but a part of the place itself – the part that had died in the passing of the years.

Jon Webster smelled the acrid scent of the dust cutting through the mustiness of the room, heard the silence humming like a song within his head. One dim radium bulb glowed above the panel with its switch and wheel and half a dozen dials.

Fearful of disturbing the sleeping silence, Webster moved forward quietly, half awed by the weight of time that seemed to press down from the ceiling. He reached out a finger and touched the open switch, as if he had expected it might not be there, as if he must feel the pressure of it against his fingertip to know that it was there.

And it was there. It and the wheel and dials, with the single light above them. And that was all. There was nothing else. In all that small, bare vault there was nothing else.

Exactly as the old map had said that it would be.

Jon Webster shook his head, thinking: I might have known that it would have been. The map was right. The map remembered. We were the ones that had forgotten – forgotten or never known or never cared. And he knew that more than likely it was the last that would be right. Never cared.

Although it was probable that very few had ever known about this vault. Had never known because it was best that only a few should know. That it never had been used was no factor in its secrecy. There might have been a day—

He stared at the panel, wondering. Slowly his hand reached out again and then he jerked it back. Better not, he told himself, better not. For the map had given no clue to the purpose of the vault, to the mechanics of the switch.

'Defence,' the map had said, and that was all.

Defence! Of course, there would have been defence back in that day of a thousand years ago. A defence that never had been needed, but a defence that had to be there, a defence against the emergency of uncertainty. For the brotherhood of peoples even then was a shaky thing that a single word or act might have thrown out of kilter. Even after ten centuries of peace, the memory of war would have been a living thing – an ever-present possibility in the mind of the World Committee, something to be circumvented, something to be ready for.

Webster stood stiff and straight, listening to the pulse of history beating in the room. History that had run its course and ended. History that had come to a dead end – a stream that suddenly had flowed into the backwater of a few hundred futile human lives and now was a stagnant pool unrelieved by the eddying of human struggle and achievement.

He reached out a hand, put it flat against the masonry, felt the slimy cold, the rough crawl of dust beneath his palm.

The foundation of empire, he thought. The sub-cellar of empire. The nethermost stone of the towering structure that soared in proud strength on the surface far above – a great building that in olden times had hummed with the business of a solar system, an empire not in the sense of conquest but an empire of orderly human relations based on mutual respect and tolerant understanding.

A seat of human government lent an easy confidence by the psychological fact of an adequate and foolproof defence. For it would have been both adequate and foolproof, it would have had to be. The men of that day took no chances, overlooked no bets. They had come up through the hard school and they knew their way around.

148

Slowly, Webster swung about, stared at the trail his feet had left across the dust. Silently, stepping carefully, following the trail he'd made, he left the vault, closed the massive door behind him and spun the lock that held its secret fast.

Climbing the tunnelled stairs, he thought: *Now I can write my history. My notes are almost complete and I know how it should go. It will be brilliant and exhaustive and it might be interesting if anyone should read it.*

But he knew that no one would. No one would take the time or care.

For a long moment, Webster stood on the broad marble steps before his house, looking down the street. A pretty street, he told himself, the prettiest street in all Geneva, with its boulevard of trees, its carefully tended flower beds, the walks that glistened with the scrub and polish of ever-working robots.

No one moved along the street and it wasn't strange. The robots had finished their work early in the day and there were few people.

From some high tree-top a bird sang and the song was one with the sun and flowers, a gladsome song that strained at the bursting throat, a song that tripped and skipped with boundless joy.

A neat street drowsing in the sun and a great, proud city that had lost its purpose. A street that should be filled with laughing children and strolling lovers and old men resting in the sun. And a city, the last city on Earth, the only city on Earth, that should be filled with noise and business.

A bird sang and a man stood on the steps and looked and the tulips nodded blissfully in the tiny fragrant breeze that wafted down the street.

Webster turned to the door, fumbled it open, walked across the threshold.

The room was hushed and solemn, cathedral-like with its stained glass windows and soft carpeting. Old wood glowed with the patina of age and silver and brass winked briefly in the light that fell from the slender windows. Over the fireplace hung a massive canvas, done in subdued colouring – a house upon a hill, a house that had grown roots and clung against the land with a jealous grip. Smoke came from the chimney, a wind-whipped, tenuous smoke that smudged across a storm-grey sky.

Webster walked across the room and there was no sound of walking. *The rugs*, he thought, *the rugs protect the quietness of the place. Randall wanted to do this one over, too, but I wouldn't let him touch it and I'm glad I didn't. A man must keep something that is old, something he can cling to, something that is a heritage and a legacy and promise.*

He reached his desk, thumbed a tumbler and the light came on above it. Slowly, he let himself into a chair, reached out for the portfolio of notes. He flipped the cover open and stared at the title page: '*A Study of the Functional Development of the City of Geneva.*'

A brave title. Dignified and erudite. And a lot of work. Twenty years of work. Twenty years of digging among old dusty records, twenty years of reading and comparing, of evaluating the weight and words of those who had gone before, sifting and rejecting and working out the facts, tracing the trend not only of the city but of men. No hero worship, no legends, but facts. And facts are hard to come by.

Something rustled. No footstep, but a rustle, a sense that someone was near. Webster twisted in his chair. A robot stood just outside the circle of the desk light.

'Beg pardon, sir,' the robot said, 'but I was supposed to tell you. Miss Sara is waiting in the Seashore.'

Webster started slightly. 'Miss Sara, eh? It's been a long time since she's been here.'

'Yes, sir,' said the robot. 'It seemed almost like old times, sir, when she walked in the door.'

'Thank you, Oscar, for telling me,' said Webster. 'I'll go right out. You will bring some drinks.'

'She brought her own drinks, sir,' said Oscar. 'Something that Mr Ballentree fixed up.'

'Ballentree!' exclaimed Webster. 'I hope it isn't poison.'

'I've been observing her,' Oscar told him, 'and she's been drinking it and she's still all right.'

Webster rose from his chair, crossed the room and went down the hall. He pushed open the door and the sound of the surf came to him. He blinked in the light that shone on the hot sand beach, stretching like a straight line white to either horizon. Before him the ocean was a sun-washed blue tipped with the white of foaming waves.

Sand gritted underneath his feet as he walked forward, eyes adjusting themselves to the blaze of sunlight.

Sara, he saw, was sitting in one of the bright canvas chairs underneath the palm trees and beside the chair was a pastel, very ladylike jug.

The air had a tang of salt and the wind off the water was cool in the sun-warm air.

The woman heard him and stood up and waited for him, with her hands outstretched. He hurried forward, clasped the out-stretched hands and looked at her.

'Not a minute older,' he said. 'As pretty as the day I saw you first.'

She smiled at him, eyes very bright. 'And you, Jon. A little grey around the temples. A little handsomer. That is all.'

He laughed. 'I'm almost sixty, Sara. Middle age is creeping up.'

'I brought something,' said Sara. 'One of Ballentree's latest masterpieces. It will cut your age in half.'

He grunted. 'Wonder Ballentree hasn't killed off half Geneva, the drinks that he cooks up.'

'This one is really good.'

It was. It went down smooth and it had a strange, half metallic, half ecstatic taste.

Webster pulled another chair close to Sara's, sat down and looked at her.

'You have such a nice place here,' said Sara. 'Randall did it, didn't he?'

Webster nodded. 'He had more fun than a circus, I had to

beat him off with a club. And those robots of his! They're crazier than he is.'

'But he does wonderful things. He did a Martian room for Quentin and it's simply *unworldly*.'

'I know,' said Webster. 'Was set on a deep-space one for here. Said it would be just the place to sit and think. Got sore at me when I wouldn't let him do it.'

He rubbed the back of his left hand with his right thumb, staring off at the blue haze above the ocean. Sara leaned forward, pulled his thumb away.

'You still have the warts,' she said.

He grinned. 'Yes. Could have had them taken off, but never got around to it. Too busy, I guess. Part of me by now.'

She released the thumb and he went back to rubbing the warts absent-mindedly.

'You've been busy,' she said. 'Haven't seen you around much. How is the book coming?'

'Ready to write,' said Webster. 'Outlining it by chapters now. Checked on the last thing to-day. Have to make sure, you know. Place way down under the old Solar Administration Building. Some sort of a defence set-up. Control room. You push a lever and—'

'And what?'

'I don't know,' said Webster. 'Something effective, I suppose. Should try to find out, but can't find the heart to do it. Been digging around in too much dust these last twenty years to face any more.'

'You sound discouraged, Jon. Tired. You shouldn't get tired. There's no reason for it. You should get around. Have another drink?'

He shook his head. 'No, Sara, thanks. Not in the mood, I guess. I'm afraid, Sara – afraid.'

'Afraid?'

'This room,' said Webster. 'Illusion. Mirrors that give an illusion of distance. Fans that blow the air through a salt spray, pumps that stir up the waves. A synthetic sun. And if I don't like the sun, all I have to do is snap a switch and I have a moon.'

'Illusion,' said Sara.

'That's it,' said Webster. 'That is all we have. No real work, no real job. Nothing that we're working for, no place we're going. I've worked for twenty years and I'll write a book and not a soul will read it. All they'd have to do would be spend the time to read it, but they won't take the time. They won't care. All they'd have to do would be come and ask me for a copy – and if they didn't want to do that I'd be so glad someone was going to read it that I'd take it to them. But no one will. It will go on the shelves with all the other books that have been written. And what do I get out of it? Wait . . . I'll tell you. Twenty years of work, twenty years of fooling myself, twenty years of sanity.'

'I know,' said Sara softly. 'I know, Jon. The last three paintings—'

He looked up quickly. 'But, Sara—'

She shook her head. 'No, Jon. No one wanted them. They're out of style. Naturalistic stuff is passê. Impressionalism now.' Daubs—'

'We are too rich,' said Webster. 'We have too much. Everything was left for us – everything and nothing. When Mankind went out to Jupiter the few that were left behind inherited the Earth and it was too big for them. They couldn't handle it. They couldn't manage it. They thought they owned it, but they were the ones that were owned. Owned and dominated and awed by the things that had gone before.' She reached out a hand and touched his arm.

'Poor Jon,' she said.

'We can't flinch away from it,' he said. 'Some day some of us must face the truth, must start over again – from scratch.'

'I—'

'Yes, what is it, Sara?'

'I came here to say good-bye.'

'Good-bye?'

153

'I'm going to take the Sleep.'

He came to his feet, swiftly, horrified. 'No, Sara!'

She laughed and the laugh was strained. 'Why don't you come with me, Jon. A few hundred years. Maybe it will all be different when we awake.'

'Just because no one wants your canvases. Just because—'

'Because of what you said just a while ago. Illusion, Jon. I knew it, felt it, but I couldn't think it out.'

'But the Sleep is illusion, too.'

'I know. But you don't know it's illusion.' You think it's real. You have no inhibitions and you have no fears except the fears that are planned deliberately. It's natural, Jon – more natural than life. I went up to the Temple and it was all explained to me.'

'And when you awake?'

'You're adjusted. Adjusted to whatever life is like in whatever era you awake. Almost as if you belonged, even from the first. And it might be better. Who knows? It might be better.'

'It won't be,' Jon told her grimly. 'Until, or unless, someone does something about it. And a people that run to the Sleep to hide are not going to bestir themselves.'

She shrank back in the chair and suddenly he felt ashamed.

'I'm sorry, Sara. I didn't mean you. Nor any one person. Just the lot of us.'

The palms whispered harshly, fronds rasping. Little pools of water, left by the surging tide, sparkled in the sun.

'I won't try to dissuade you,' Webster said. 'You've thought it out, you know what it is you want.'

It hadn't always been like that with the human race, he thought. *There would have been a day, a thousand years ago, when a man would have argued about a thing like this. But Juwainism had ended all the petty quarrels. Juwainism had ended a lot of things.*

'I've always thought,' Sara told him softly, 'if we could have stayed together—'

He made a gesture of impatience. 'It's just another thing we've lost, another thing that the human race let loose. Come

154

to think it over, we lost a lot of things. Family ties and business, work and purpose.'

He turned to face her squarely. 'If you want to come back, Sara—'

She shook her head. 'It wouldn't work, Jon. It's been too many years.'

He nodded. There was no use denying it.

She rose and held out her hand. 'If you ever decide to take the Sleep, find out my date. I'll have them reserve a place right next to me.'

'I don't think I ever shall,' he told her.

'All right, then. Good-bye, Jon.'

'Wait a second, Sara. You haven't said a word about our son. I used to see him often, but—'

She laughed brightly. 'Tom's almost a grown man now, Jon. And it's the strangest thing. He—'

'I haven't seen him for so long,' Webster said again.

'No wonder. He's scarcely in the city. It's his hobby. Something he inherited from you, I guess. Pioneering in a way. I don't know what else you'd call it.'

'You mean some new research. Something unusual.'

'Unusual, yes, but not research. Just goes out in the woods and lives by himself. He and a few of his friends. A bag of salt, a bow and arrows— Yes, it's queer,' Sara admitted, 'but he has a lot of fun. Claims he's learning something. And he does look healthy. Like a wolf. Strong and lean and a look about his eyes.'

She swung around and moved away.

'I'll see you to the door,' said Webster.

She shook her head. 'No. I'd rather that you wouldn't.'

'You're forgetting the jug.'

'You keep it, Jon. I won't need it where I'm going.'

Webster put on the plastic 'thinking cap', snapped the button of the writer on his desk.

Chapter Twenty-six, he thought and the writer clicked and chuckled and wrote 'Chapter XXVI'.

For a moment Webster held his mind clear, assembling his

data, arranging his outline, then he began again. The writer clicked and gurgled, hummed into steady work:

The machines ran on, tended by the robots as they had been before, producing all the things they had produced before.

And the robots worked as they knew it was their right to work, their right and duty, doing the things they had been made to do.

The machines went on and the robots went on, producing wealth as if there were men to use it, as if there were millions of men instead of a bare five thousand.

And the five thousand who had stayed behind or who had been left behind suddenly found themselves the masters of a world that had been geared to the millions, found themselves possessed of the wealth and services that only months before had been the wealth and services that had been due the millions.

There was no government, but there was no need of government, for all the crimes and abuses that government had held in check were as effectively held in check by the sudden wealth the five thousand had inherited. No man will steal when he can pick up what he wants without the bother of thievery. No man will contest with his neighbour over real estate when the entire world is real estate for the simple taking. Property rights almost overnight became a phrase that had no meaning in a world where there was more than enough for all.

Crimes of violence long before had been virtually eliminated from human society and with the economic pressure eased to a point where property rights ceased to be a point of friction, there was no need of government. No need, in fact, of many of the encumbrances of custom and convenience which man had carried forward from the beginnings of commerce. There was no need of currency, for exchange had no meaning in a world where to get a thing one need but ask for it or take it.

Relieved of economic pressure, the social pressures lessened, too. A man no longer found it necessary to conform to the standards and the acts of custom which had played so large a part in the post-Jovian world as an indication of commercial character.

Religion, which had been losing ground for centuries, entirely disappeared. The family unit, held together by tradition and by the economic necessity of a provider and protector, fell apart. Men and women lived together as they wished, parted when they wished. For there was no economic reason, no social reason why they shouldn't.

Webster cleared his mind and the machine purred softly at him. He put up his hands, took off the cap, re-read the last paragraph of the outline.

There, he thought, *there is the root of it. If the families had stayed together. If Sara and I stayed together.*

He rubbed the warts on the back of his hand, wondering: *Wonder if Tom goes by my name or hers. Usually they take their mother's name. I know I did at first until my mother asked me to change it. Said it would please my father and she didn't mind. Said he was proud of the name he bore and I was his only child. And she had others.*

If only we had stayed together. Then there'd be something worth living for. If we'd stayed together, Sara wouldn't be taking the Sleep, wouldn't be lying in a tank of fluid in suspended animation with the 'dream cap' on her head.

Wonder what kind of dream she chose – what kind of synthetic life she picked out to live. I wanted to ask her, but I didn't dare. It's not the kind of thing, after all, that one can ask.

He reached out and picked up the cap again, put it on his head, marshalled his thoughts anew. The writer clicked into sudden life:

Man was bewildered. But not for long. Man tried. But not for long.

For the five thousand could not carry on the work of the millions who had gone to Jupiter to enter upon a better life in alien bodies. The five thousand did not have the skill, nor the dreams, nor the incentive.

And there were the psychological factors. The psychological

factor of tradition which bore like a weight upon the minds of the men who had been left behind. The psychological factor of Juwainism which forced men to be honest with themselves and others, which forced men to perceive at last the hopelessness of the things they sought to do. Juwainism left no room for false courage. And false, foolhardy courage that didn't know what it was going up against was the one thing the five thousand needed most.

What they did suffered by comparison with what had been done before and at last they came to know that the human dream of millions was too vast a thing for five thousand to attempt.

Life was good. 'Why worry? There was food and clothes and shelter, human companionship and luxury and entertainment – there was everything that one could ever wish.

Man gave up trying. Man enjoyed himself. Human achievement became a zero factor and human life a senseless paradise.

Webster took off the cap again, reached out and clicked off the writer.

If someone would only read it once I get it done, he thought. *If someone would read and understand. If someone could realize where human life is going.*

I could tell them, of course. I could go out and buttonhole them one by one and hold them fast until I told them what I thought. And they would understand, for Juwainism would make them understand. But they wouldn't pay attention. They'd tuck it all away in the backs of their brains somewhere for future reference and they'd never have the time or take the trouble to drag it out again.

They'd go on doing the foolish things they're doing, following the footless hobbies they have taken up in lieu of work. Randall with his crew of zany robots going around begging to be allowed to re-design his neighbours' homes. Ballentree spending hours on end figuring out new alcoholic mixtures. Yes, and Jon Webster wasting twenty years digging into the history of a single city.

*

158

A door creaked faintly and Webster swung around. The robot cat-footed into the room.

'Yes, what is it, Oscar?'

The robot halted, a dim figure in the half-light of the dusk-filled room.

'It's time for dinner, sir. I came to see—'

'Whatever you can think up,' said Webster. 'And, Oscar, you can lay the fire.'

'The fire is laid, sir.'

Oscar stalked across the room, bent above the fireplace. Flame flickered in his hand and the kindling caught.

Webster, slouched in his chair staring at the flames crawling up the wood, heard the first, faint hiss and crackle of the wood, the suction mumble at the fireplace throat.

'It's pretty, sir,' said Oscar.

'You like it, too?'

'Indeed I do.'

'Ancestral memories,' said Webster soberly. 'Remembrance of the forge that made you.'

'You think so, sir?' asked Oscar.

'No, Oscar, I was joking. Anachronisms, that's what you and I are. Not many people have fires these days. No need for them. But there's something about them, something that is clean and comforting.'

He stared at the canvas above the mantelpiece, lighted now by the flare of burning wood. Oscar saw his stare.

'Too bad about Miss Sara, sir.'

Webster shook his head. 'No, Oscar, it was something that she wanted. Like turning off one life and starting on another. She will lie up there in the Temple, asleep for years, and she will live another life. And this one, Oscar, will be a happy life. For she would have it planned that way.'

His mind went back to other days in this very room.

'She painted that picture, Oscar,' he said. 'Spent a long time at it, being very careful to catch the thing she wanted to express. She used to laugh at me and tell me I was in the painting, too.'

'I don't see you, sir,' said Oscar.

'No. I'm not. And yet, perhaps, I am. Or part of me. Part of what and where I came from. That house in the painting, Oscar, is the Webster House in North America. And I am a Webster. But a long ways from the house – a long ways from the men who built that house.'

'North America's not so far, sir.'

'No,' Webster told him. 'Not so far in distance. But far in other ways.'

He felt the warmth of the fire steal across the room and touch him.

Far. Too far – and in the wrong direction.

The robot moved softly, feet padding on the rug, leaving the room.

She worked a long time, being very careful to catch the thing she wanted to express.

And what was that thing? He had never asked her and she had never told him. He had always thought, he remembered, that it probably had been the way the smoke streamed, wind-whipped across the sky, the way the house crouched against the ground, blending in with the trees and grass, huddled against the storm that walked above the land.

But it may have been something else. Some symbolism. Something that made the house synonymous with the kind of men who built it.

He got up and walked closer, stood before the fire with head tilted back. The brush strokes were there and the painting looked less a painting than when viewed from the proper distance. A thing of technique, now. The basic strokes and shadings the brushes had achieved to create illusion.

Security. Security by the way the house stood foursquare and solid. Tenacity by the way it was a part of the land itself. Sternness, stubbornness and a certain bleakness of the spirit.

She had sat for days on end with the visor beamed on the house, sketching carefully, painting slowly, often sitting and watching and doing nothing at all. There had been dogs, she said, and robots, but she had not put them in, because all she wanted was the house. One of the few houses left standing in the open country. Through centuries of neglect, the others had fallen in, had given the land back to the wilderness.

But there were dogs and robots in this one. One big robot, she had said, and a lot of little ones.

Webster had paid no attention – he had been too busy.

He swung around, went back to the desk again.

Queer thing, once you came to think of it. Robots and dogs living together. A Webster once had messed around with dogs, trying to put them on the road to a culture of their own, trying to develop a dual civilization of man and dog.

Bits of remembrance came to him – tiny fragments, half recalled, of the legends that had come down the years about the Webster House. There had been a robot named Jenkins who had served the family from the very first. There had been an old man sitting in a wheel chair on the front lawn, staring at the stars and waiting for a son who never came. And a curse had hung above the house, the curse of having lost to the world the philosophy of Juwain.

The visor was in one corner of the room, an almost forgotten piece of furniture, something that was scarcely used. There was no need to use it. All the world was here in the city of Geneva.

Webster rose, moved towards it, stopped and thought. The dial settings were listed in the log book, but where was the log book? More than likely somewhere in his desk.

He went back to the desk, started going through the drawers. Excited now, he pawed furiously, like a terrier digging for a bone.

Jenkins, the ancient robot, scrubbed his metallic chin with metallic fingers. It was a thing he did when he was deep in thought, a meaningless, irritating gesture he had picked up from long association with the human race.

His eyes went back to the little black dog sitting on the floor beside him.

'So the wolf was friendly,' said Jenkins. 'Offered you the rabbit.'

Ebenezer jigged excitedly upon his bottom. 'He was one of them we fed last winter. The pack that came up to the house and we tried to tame them.'

'Would you know the wolf again?'

Ebenezer nodded. 'I got his scent,' he said. 'I'd remember him.'

Shadow shuffled his feet against the floor. 'Look, Jenkins, ain't you going to smack him one? He should have been listening and he ran away. He had no business chasing rabbits—'

Jenkins spoke sternly. 'You're the one that should get the smacking, Shadow. For your attitude. You are assigned to Ebenezer, you should be part of him. You aren't an individual. You're just Ebenezer's hands. If he had hands, he'd have no need of you. You aren't his mentor nor his conscience. Just his hands. Remember that.'

Shadow shuffled his feet rebelliousIy. 'I'll run away,' he said.

'Join the wild robots, I suppose,' said Jenkins.

Shadow nodded. 'They'd be glad to have me. They're doing things. They need all the help that they can get.'

'They'd bust you up for scrap,' Jenkins told him sourly. 'You have no training, no abilities that would make you one of them.'

He turned to Ebenezer. 'We have other robots.'

Ebenezer shook his head. 'Shadow is all right. I can handle him. We know one another. He keeps me from getting lazy, keeps me on my toes.'

'That's fine,' said Jenkins. 'You two run along. And if you ever happen to be out chasing rabbits, Ebenezer, and run into this wolf again, try to cultivate him.'

The rays of the westering sun were streaming through the windows, touching the age-old room with the warmth of a late spring evening.

Jenkins sat quietly in the chair, listening to the sounds that came from outside – the tinkle of cowbells, the yapping of the puppies, the ringing thud of an axe splitting fireplace logs.

Poor little fellow, thought Jenkins. *Sneaking out to chase a rabbit when he should have been listening. Too far – too fast. Have to watch that. Have to keep them from breaking down. Come fall and we'll knock off work for a week or two and have some coon hunts. Do them a world of good.*

Although there'd come a day when there'd be no coon hunts, no rabbit chasing – the day when the dogs finally had tamed everything, when all the wild things would be thinking, talking, working beings. A wild dream and a far one – but, thought Jenkins, *no wilder and no farther than some of the dreams of man.*

Maybe even better than the dreams of man, for they held none of the ruthlessness that the human race had planned, aimed at none of the mechanistic brutality the human race had spawned.

A new civilization, a new culture, a new way of thought. Mystic, perhaps, and visionary, but so had man been visionary. Probing into mysteries that man had brushed by as unworthy of his time, as mere superstition that could have no scientific basis.

Things that go bump in the night. Things that prowl around a house and the dogs get up and growl and there are no tracks in the snow. Dogs howling when someone dies.

The dogs knew. The dogs had known long before they had been given tongues to talk, contact lenses to read. They had not come along the road as far as men – they were not cynical and sceptic. They believed the things they heard and sensed. They did not invent superstition as a form of wishful thinking, as a shield against the things unseen.

Jenkins turned back to the desk again, picked up the pen, bent above the note-book in front of him. The pen screeched as he pushed it along.

Ebenezer reports friendliness in wolf. Recommend council detach Ebenezer from listening and assign him to contact the wolf.

Wolves, mused Jenkins, *would be good friends to have. They'd make splendid scouts. Better than the dogs. Tougher, faster, sneaky. They could watch the wild robots across the river and relieve the dogs. Could keep an eye on the mutant castles.*

Jenkins shook his head. *Couldn't trust anyone these days. The robots seemed to be all right. Were friendly, dropped in at times, helped out now and then. Real neighbourly, in fact. But you never knew. And they were building machines.*

The mutants never bothered anyone, were scarcely seen, in fact. But they had to be watched, too. Never knew what devilment they might be up to. Remember what they'd done to man. That dirty trick with Juwainism, handing it over at a time when it would doom the race.

Men. They were gods to us and now they're gone. Left us on our own. A few in Geneva, of course, but they can't be bothered, have no interest in us.

He sat in the twilight, thinking of the whiskies he had carried, of the errands he had run, of the days when Websters had lived and died within these walls.

And now – father confessor to the dogs. Cute little devils and bright and smart – and trying hard.

A bell buzzed softly and Jenkins jerked upright in his seat. It buzzed again and a green light winked on the televisor. Jenkins came to his feet, stood unbelieving, staring at the winking light.

Someone calling!

Someone calling after almost a thousand years!

He staggered forward, dropped into the chair, reached put with fumbling fingers to the toggle, tripped it over.

The wall before him melted away and he sat facing a man across a desk. Behind the man the flames of a fireplace lighted up a room with high, stained-glass windows.

'You're Jenkins,' said the man and there was something in his face that jerked a cry from Jenkins.

'You . . . you—'

'I'm Jon Webster,' said the man.

Jenkins pressed his hands flat against the top of the televisor, sat straight and stiff, afraid of the unrobotlike emotions that welled within his metal being.

'I would have known you anywhere,' said Jenkins. 'You

have the look of them. I should recognize one of you. I worked for you long enough. Carried drinks and . . . and—'

'Yes, I know,' said Webster. 'Your name has come down with us. We remembered you.'

'You are in Geneva, Jon?' And then Jenkins remembered. 'I meant, sir.'

'No need of it,' said Webster. 'I'd rather have it Jon. And, yes, I'm in Geneva. But I'd like to see you. I wonder if I might.'

'You mean come out here?'

Webster nodded.

'But the place is overrun with dogs, sir.'

Webster grinned. 'The talking dogs?' he asked.

'Yes,' said Jenkins, 'and they'll be glad to see you. They know all about the family. They sit around at night and talk themselves to sleep with stories from the old days and . . . and—'

'What is it, Jenkins?'

'I'll be glad to see you, too. It has been so lonesome!'

God had come.

Ebenezer shivered at the thought, crouching in the dark. *If Jenkins knew I was here*, he thought, *he'd whale my hide for fair. Jenkins said we were to leave him alone, for a while, at least.*

Ebenezer crept forward on fur-soft pads, sniffed at the study door. And the door was open – open by the barest crack!

He crouched on his belly, listening, and there was not a thing to hear. Just a scent, an unfamiliar, tangy scent that made the hair crawl along his back in swift, almost unbearable ecstasy.

He glanced quickly over his shoulder, but there was no movement. Jenkins was out in the dining-room, telling the dogs how they must behave, and Shadow was off somewhere tending to some robot business.

Softly, carefully, Ebenezer pushed at the door with his nose and the door swung wider. Another push and it was half open.

The man sat in front of the fireplace, in the easy-chair, long legs crossed, hands clasped across his stomach.

Ebenezer crouched tighter against the floor, a low involuntary whimper, in his throat.

At the sound Jon Webster jerked erect.

'Who's there?' he asked

Ebenezer froze against the floor, felt the pumping of his heart jerking at his body.

'Who's there?' Webster asked once more and then he saw the dog.

His voice was softer when he spoke again. 'Come in, feller. Come on in.'

Ebenezer did not stir.

Webster snapped his fingers at him. 'I won't hurt you. Come on in. Where are all the others?'

Ebenezer tried to rise, tried to crawl along the floor, but his bones were rubber and his blood was water. And the man was striding towards him, coming in long strides across the floor.

He saw the man bending over him, felt strong hands beneath his body, knew that he was being lifted up. And the scent that he had smelled at the open door – the overpowering god-scent – was strong within his nostrils.

The hands held him tight against the strange fabric the man wore instead of fur and a voice crooned at him – not words, but comforting.

'So you came to see me,' said Jon Webster. 'You sneaked away and you came to see me.'

Ebenezer nodded weakly. 'You aren't angry, are you? You aren't going to tell Jenkins?'

Webster shook his head. 'No, I won't tell Jenkins.'

He sat down and Ebenezer sat in his lap, staring at his face – a strong, lined face with the lines deepened by the flare of the flames within the fireplace.

Webster's hand came up and stroked Ebenezer's head and Ebenezer whimpered with doggish happiness.

'It's like coming home,' said Webster and he wasn't talking to the dog. 'It's like you've been away for a long, long time and then you come home again. And it's so long you don't recognize the place. Don't know the furniture, don't recognize the floor plan. But you know by the feel of it that it's an old familiar place and you are glad you came.'

'I like it here,' said Ebenezer and he meant Webster's lap, but the man misunderstood.

'Of course, you do,' he said. 'It's your home as well as mine. More your home, in fact, for you stayed here and took care of it while I forgot about it.'

He patted Ebenezer's head and pulled Ebenezer's ears.

'What's your name?' he asked.

'Ebenezer.'

'And what do you do, Ebenezer?'

'I listen.'

'You listen?'

'Sure, that's my job. I listen for the cobblies.'

'And you hear the cobblies?'

'Sometimes. I'm not very good at it. I think about chasing rabbits and I don't pay attention.'

'What do cobblies sound like?'

'Different things. Sometimes they walk and other times they just go bump. And once in a while they talk. Although oftener, they think.'

'Look here, Ebenezer, I don't seem to place these cobblies.'

'They aren't any place,' said Ebenezer. 'Not on this earth, at least.'

'I don't understand.'

'Like there was a big house,' said Ebenezer. 'A big house with lots of rooms. And doors between the rooms. And if you're in one room, you can hear whoever's in the other rooms, but you can't get to them.'

'Sure you can,' said Webster. 'All you have to do is go through the door.'

'But you can't open the door,' said Ebenezer. 'You don't even know about the door. You think this one room you're in is the only room in all the house. Even if you did know about the door you couldn't open it.'

'You're talking about dimensions.'

Ebenezer wrinkled his forehead in worried thought. 'I don't

know that word you said, Dimensions. What I told you was the way Jenkins told it to us. He said it wasn't really a house and it wasn't really rooms and the things we heard probably weren't like us.'

Webster nodded to himself. That was the way one would have to do. Have to take it easy. Take it slow. Don't confuse them with big names. Let them get the idea first and then bring in the more exact and scientific terminology. And more than likely it would be a manufactured terminology. Already there was a coined word. Cobblies – the things behind the wall, the things that one hears and cannot identify – the dwellers in the next room.

Cobblies.

The cobblies will get you if you don't watch out.

That would be the human way. Can't understand a thing. Can't see it. Can't test it. Can't analyse it. OK, it isn't there. It doesn't exist. It's a ghost, a goblin, a cobbly.

The cobblies will get you—

It's simpler that way, more comfortable. Scared? Sure, but you forget it in the light. And it doesn't plague you, haunt you. Think hard enough and you wish it away. Make it a ghost or goblin and you can laugh at it – in the daylight.

A hot, wet tongue rasped across Webster's chin and Ebenezer wriggled with delight.

'I like you,' said Ebenezer. 'Jenkins never held me this way. No one's ever held me this way.'

'Jenkins is busy,' said Webster.

'He sure is,' agreed Ebenezer. 'He writes things down in a book. Things that us dogs hear when we are listening and things that we should do.'

'You've heard about the Websters?' asked the man.

'Sure. We know all about them. You're a Webster. We didn't think there were any more of them.'

'Yes, there is,' said Webster. 'There's been one here all the time. Jenkins is a Webster.'

'He never told us that.'

168

'He wouldn't.'

The fire had died down and the room had darkened. The sputtering flames chased feeble flickers across the walls and floor.

And something else. Faint rustlings, faint whisperings, as if the very walls were talking. An old house with long memories and a lot of living tucked within its structure. Two thousand years of living. Built to last and it had lasted. Built to be a home and it still was a home – a solid place that put its arms around one and held one close and warm, claimed one for its own.

Footsteps walked across his brain – footsteps from the long ago, footsteps that had been silenced to the final echo centuries before. The walking of the Websters. Of the ones that went before me, the ones that Jenkins waited on from their day of birth to the hour of death.

History. Here is history. History stirring in the drapes and creeping on the floor, sitting in the corners, watching from the wall. Living history that a man can feel in the bones of him and against his shoulder blades – the impact of the long dead eyes that come back from the night.

Another Webster, eh? Doesn't look like much. Worthless. The breed's played out. Not like we were in our day. Just about the last of them.

Jon Webster stirred. 'No, not the last of them,' he said. 'I have a son.'

Well, it doesn't make much difference. He says he has a son. But he can't amount to much—

Webster started from the chair, Ebenezer slipping from his lap.

'That's not true,' cried Webster. 'My son—'

And then sat down again.

His son out in the woods with bow and arrows, playing a game, having fun.

A hobby, Sara had said before she climbed the hill to take a hundred years of dreams.

A hobby. Not a business. Not a way of life. Not necessity.

A hobby.

An artificial thing. A thing that had no beginning and no

end. A thing a man could drop at any minute and no one would ever notice.

Like cooking up recipes for different kinds of drinks.

Like painting pictures no one wanted.

Like going around with a crew of crazy robots begging people to let you redecorate their homes.

Like writing history no one cares about.

Like playing Indian or caveman or pioneer with bow and arrows.

Like thinking up centuries-long dreams for men and women who are tired of life and yearn for fantasy.

The man sat in the chair, staring at the nothingness that spread before his eyes, the dread and awful nothingness that became to-morrow and to-morrow.

Absent-mindedly his hands came together and the right thumb stroked the back of the left hand.

Ebenezer crept forward through the fire-flared darkness, put his front paws on the man's knee and looked into his face.

'Hurt your hand?' he asked.

'Eh?'

'Hurt your hand? You're rubbing it.'

Webster laughed shortly. 'No, just warts.' He showed them to the dog.

'Gee, warts!' said Ebenezer. 'You don't want them, do you?'

'No,' Webster hesitated. 'No, I guess I don't. Never got around to having them taken off.'

Ebenezer dropped his nose and nuzzled the back of Webster's hand.

'There you are,' he announced triumphantly.

'There I'm what?'

'Look at the warts,' invited Ebenezer.

A log fell in the fire and Webster lifted his hand, looked at it in the flare of light.

The warts were gone. The skin was smooth and clean.

Jenkins stood in the darkness and listened to the silence, the soft sleeping silence that left the house to shadows, to the half-forgotten footsteps, the phrase spoken long ago, the tongues that murmured in the walls and rustled in the drapes.

By a single thought the night could have been as day, a simple adjustment in his lenses would have done the trick, but the ancient robot left his sight unchanged. For this was the way he liked it, this was the hour of meditation, the treasured time when the present sloughed away and the past came back and lived.

The others slept, but Jenkins did not sleep. For robots never sleep. Two thousand years of consciousness, twenty centuries of full time unbroken by a single moment of unawareness.

A long time, thought Jenkins. *A long time, even for a robot. For even before man had gone to Jupiter most of the older robots had been deactivated, had been sent to their death in favour of the newer models. The newer models that looked more like men, that were smoother and more sightly, with better speech and quicker responses within their metal brains.*

But Jenkins had stayed on because he was an old and faithful servant, because Webster House would not have been home without him.

'They loved me,' said Jenkins to himself. And the three words held deep comfort – comfort in a world where there was little comfort, a world where a servant had become a leader and longed to be a servant once again.

He stood at the window and stared out across the patio to the night-dark clumps of oaks that staggered down the hill. Darkness. No light anywhere. There had been a time when there had been lights. Windows that shone like friendly beams in the vast land that lay across the river.

But man had gone and there were no lights. The robots needed no lights, for they could see in darkness, even as Jenkins could have seen, had he but chosen to do so. And the castles of the mutants were as dark by night as they were fearsome by day.

Now man had come again, one man. Had come, but he probably wouldn't stay. He'd sleep for a few nights in the great master bedroom on the second floor, then go back to Geneva. He'd walk the old forgotten acres and stare across the river and rummage through the books that lined the study wall, then he would up and leave.

Jenkins swung around. *Ought to see how he is*, he thought. *Ought to find if he needs anything. Maybe take him up a drink, although I'm afraid the whisky is all spoiled. A thousand years is a long time for a bottle of good whisky.*

He moved across the room and a warm peace came upon him, the close and intimate peacefulness of the old days when he had trotted, happy as a terrier, on his many errands.

He hummed a snatch of tune in minor key as he headed for the stairway.

He'd just look in and if Jon Webster were asleep, he'd leave, but if he wasn't, he'd say: 'Are you comfortable, sir? Is there anything you wish? A hot toddy, perhaps?'

And he took two stairs at the time.

For he was doing for a Webster once again.

Jon Webster lay propped in bed, with the pillows piled behind him. The bed was hard and uncomfortable and the room was close and stuffy – not like his own bedroom back in Geneva, where one lay on the grassy bank of a murmuring stream and stared at the artificial stars that glittered in an artificial sky. And smelled the artificial scent of artificial lilacs that would go on blooming longer than a man would live. No murmur of a hidden waterfall, no flickering of captive fireflies – but a bed and room that were functional.

Webster spread his hands flat on his blanket covered thighs and flexed his fingers, thinking.

Ebenezer had merely touched the warts and the warts were gone. And it had been no happenstance – it had been intentional. It had been no miracle, but a conscious power. For miracles sometimes fail to happen, and Ebenezer had been sure.

A power, perhaps, that had been gathered from the room beyond, a power that had been stolen from the cobblies Ebenezer listened to.

A laying-on of hands, a power of healing that involved no

drugs, no surgery, but just a *certain* knowledge, a very special knowledge.

In the old dark ages certain men had claimed the power to make warts disappear, had bought them for a penny, or had traded them for something or had performed other mumbo jumbo – and in due time, sometimes, the warts would disappear.

Had these queer men listened to the cobblies, too?

The door creaked just a little and Webster straightened suddenly.

A voice came out of the darkness: 'Are you comfortable, sir? Is there anything you wish?'

'Jenkins?' asked Webster.

'Yes, sir,' said Jenkins.

The dark form padded softly through the door.

'Yes, there's something I want,' said Webster. 'I want to talk to you.'

He stared at the dark, metallic figure that stood beside the bed.

'About the dogs,' said Webster.

'They try so hard,' said Jenkins. 'And it's hard for them. For they have no one, you see. Not a single soul.'

'They have you.'

Jenkins shook his head. 'But I'm not enough, you see. I'm just . . . well, just a sort of mentor. It is men they want. The need of men is ingrown in them. For thousands of years it has been man and dog. Man and dog, hunting together. Man and dog, watching the herds together. Man and dog, fighting their enemies together. The dog watching while the man slept and the man dividing the last bit of food, going hungry himself so that his dog might eat.'

Webster nodded. 'Yes, I suppose that is the way it is.'

'They talk about men every night,' said Jenkins, 'before they go to bed. They sit around together and one of the old ones tells one of the stories that have been handed down and they sit and wonder, sit and hope.'

'But where are they going? What are they trying to do? Have they got a plan?'

'I can detect one,' said Jenkins. 'Just a faint glimmer of what may happen. They are psychic, you see. Always have been. They have no mechanical sense, which is understandable, for they have no hands. Where man would follow metal, the dogs will follow ghosts.'

'Ghosts?'

'The things you men call ghosts. But they aren't ghosts. I'm sure of that. They're something in the next room. Some other form of life on another plane.'

'You mean there may be many planes of life co-existing simultaneously upon Earth?'

Jenkins nodded. 'I'm beginning to believe so, sir. I have a note-book full of things the dogs have heard and seen and now, after all these many years, they begin to make a pattern.'

He hurried on. 'I may be mistaken, sir. You understand I have no training. I was just a servant in the old days, sir. I tried to pick up things after . . . after Jupiter, but it was hard for me. Another robot helped me make the first little robots for the dogs and now the little ones produce their own kind in the workshop when there are in need of more.'

'But the dogs – they just sit and listen.'

'Oh, no, sir, they do many other things. They try to make friends with the animals and they watch the wild robots and the mutants—'

'These wild robots? There are many of them.'

Jenkins nodded. 'Many, sir. Scattered all over the world in little camps. The ones that were left behind, sir. The ones man had no further use for when he went to Jupiter. They have banded together and they work—'

'Work. What at?'

'I don't know, sir. Building machines, mostly. Mechanical, you know. I wonder what they'll do with all the machines they have. What they plan to use them for.'

'So do I,' said Webster.

And he stared into the darkness and wondered – wondered

how man, cooped up in Geneva, should have lost touch with the world. How man should not have known about what the dogs were doing, about the little camps of busy robots, about the castles of the feared and hated mutants.

We lost touch, Webster thought. *We locked the world outside. We created ourselves a little niche and we huddled in it – in the last city in the world. And we didn't know what was happening outside the city – we could have known, we should have known, but we didn't care.*

It's time, he thought, *that we took a hand again.*

We were lost and awed and at first we tried, but finally we just threw in the hand.

For the first time the few that were left realized the greatness of the race, saw for the first time the mighty works the hand of man had reared. And they tried to keep it going and they couldn't do it. And they rationalized – as man rationalizes almost everything. Fooling himself that there really are no ghosts, calling things that go bumping in the night the first suave, sleek word of explanation that comes into his mind.

We couldn't keep it going and so we rationalized, we took refuge in a screen of words and Juwainism helped us do it. We came close to ancestor worship. We sought to glorify the race of man. We couldn't carry on the work of man and so we tried to glorify it, attempted to enthrone the men who had. As we attempt to glorify and enthrone all good things that die.

We became a race of historians and we dug with grubby fingers in the ruins of the race, clutching each irrelevant little fact to our breast as if it were a priceless gem. And that was the first phase, the hobby that bore us up when we knew ourselves for what we really were – the dregs in the tilted cup of humanity.

But we got over it. Oh, sure, we got over it. In about one generation. Man is an adaptable creature – he can survive anything. So we couldn't build great spaceships. So we couldn't reach the stars. So we couldn't puzzle out the secret of life. So what?

We were the inheritors, we had been left the legacy, we were better off than any race had ever been or could hope to be again. And so we rationalized once more and we forgot about the glory of the race, for while it was a shining thing, it was a toilsome and humiliating concept.

'Jenkins,' said Webster soberly, 'we've wasted ten whole centuries.'

'Not wasted, sir,' said Jenkins. 'Just resting, perhaps. But now, maybe, you can come out again. Come back to us.'

'You want us?'

'The dogs need you,' Jenkins told him. 'And the robots, too. For both of them were never anything other than the servants of man. They are lost without you. The dogs are building a civilization, but it is building slowly.'

'Perhaps a better civilization than we built ourselves,' said Webster. 'Perhaps a more successful one. For ours was not successful, Jenkins.'

'A kinder one,' Jenkins admitted, 'but not too practical. A civilization based on the brotherhood of animals – on the psychic understanding and perhaps eventual communication and intercourse with interlocking worlds. A civilization of the mind and of understanding, but not too positive. No actual goals, limited mechanics – just a groping after truth, and the groping is in a direction that man passed by without a second glance.'

'And you think that man could help?'

'Man could give leadership,' said Jenkins.

'The right kind of leadership?'

'That is hard to answer.'

Webster lay in the darkness, rubbed his suddenly sweating hands along the blankets that covered his body.

'Tell me the truth,' he said and his words were grim. 'Man could give leadership, you say. But man also could take over once again. Could discard the things the dogs are doing as impractical. Could round the robots up and use their mechanical ability in the old, old pattern. Both the dogs and robots would knuckle down to man.'

'Of course,' said Jenkins. 'For they were servants once. But man is wise – man knows best.'

'Thank you, Jenkins,' said Webster. 'Thank you very much.'

He stared into the darkness and the truth was written there.

His track still lay across the floor and the smell of dust was a sharpness in the air. The radium bulb glowed above the panel and the switch and wheel and dials were waiting, waiting against the day when there would be need of them.

Webster stood in the doorway, smelling the dampness of the stone through the dusty bitterness.

Defence, he thought, staring at the switch. *Defence – a thing to keep one out, a device to seal off a place against all the real or imagined weapons that a hypothetical enemy might bring to bear.*

And undoubtedly the same defence that would keep an enemy out would keep the defended in. Not necessarily, of course, but—

He strode across the room and stood before the switch and his hand went out and grasped it, moved it slowly, and knew that it would work.

Then his arm moved quickly and the switch shot home. From far below came a low, soft hissing as machines went into action. The dial needles flickered and stood out from the pins.

Webster touched the wheel with hesitant fingertips, stirred it on its shaft and the needles flickered again and crawled across the glass. With a swift, sure hand, Webster spun the wheel and the needles slammed against the farthest pins.

He turned abruptly on his heel, marched out of the vault, closed the door behind him, climbed the crumbling steps.

Now if it only works, he thought. *If it only works*. His feet quickened on the steps and the blood hammered in his head.

If it only works!

He remembered the hum of machines far below as he had slammed the switch. That meant that the defence mechanism – or at least part of it – still worked.

But even if it worked, would it do the trick? What if it kept the enemy out, but failed to keep men in?

What if—

When he reached the street, he saw that the sky had changed. A grey, metallic overcast had blotted out the sun and the city lay in twilight, only half relieved by the automatic street lights. A faint breeze wafted at his cheek.

*

The crinkly grey ash of the burned notes and the map that he had found still lay in the fireplace and Webster strode across the room, seized the poker, stirred the ashes viciously until there was no hint of what they once had been.

Gone, he thought. *The last clue gone. Without the map, without the knowledge of the city that it had taken him twenty years to ferret out, no one would ever find that hidden room with the switch and wheel and dials beneath the single lamp.*

No one would know exactly what had happened. And even if one guessed, there'd be no way to make sure. And even if one were sure, there'd be nothing that could be done about it.

A thousand years before it would not have been that way. For in that day man, given the faintest hint, would have puzzled out any given problem.

But man had changed. He had lost the old knowledge and old skills. His mind had become a flaccid thing. He lived from one day to the next without any shining goal. But he still kept the old vices – the vices that had become virtues from his own viewpoint and raised him by his own bootstraps. He kept the unwavering belief that his was the only kind, the only life that mattered – the smug egoism that made him the self-appointed lord of all creation.

Running feet went past the house on the street outside and Webster swung away from the fireplace, faced the blind panes of the high and narrow windows.

I got them stirred up, he thought. *Got them running now. Excited. Wondering what it's all about. For centuries they haven't stirred outside the city, but now that they can't get out – they're foaming at the mouth to do it.*

His smile widened.

Maybe they'll be so stirred up, they'll do something about it. Rats in a trap will do some funny things – if they don't go crazy first.

And if they do get out – well, it's their right to do so. If they do get out, they've earned their right to take over once again.

He crossed the room, stood in the doorway for a moment, staring at the painting that hung above the mantel. Awkwardly, he raised his hand to it, a fumbling salute, a haggard goodbye. Then he let himself out into the street and climbed the hill – the route that Sara had walked only days before.

The Temple robots were kind and considerate, soft-footed and dignified. They took him to the place where Sara lay and showed him the next compartment that she had reserved for him.

'You will want to choose a dream,' said the spokesman of the robots. 'We can show you many samples. We can blend them to your taste. We can—'

'Thank you,' said Webster. 'I do not want a dream.'

The robot nodded, understanding. 'I see, sir. You only want to wait, to pass away the time.'

'Yes,' said Webster. 'I guess you'd call it that.'

'For about how long?'

'How long?'

'Yes. How long do you want to wait?'

'Oh, I see,' said Webster. 'How about forever?'

'Forever!'

'Forever is the word, I think,' said Webster. 'I might have said eternity, but it doesn't make much difference. There is no use of quibbling over two words that mean about the same.'

'Yes, sir,' said the robot.

No use of quibbling. No, of course, there wasn't. For he couldn't take the chance. He could have said a thousand years, but then he might have relented and gone down and flipped the switch.

And that was the one thing that must not happen. The dogs had to have their chance. Had to be left unhampered to try for success where the human race had failed. And so long as there was a human element they would not have that chance. For man would take over, would step in and spoil things, would laugh at the cobblies that talked behind a wall, would object to the taming and civilizing of the wild things of the earth.

A new pattern – a new way of thought and life – a new approach to the age-old social problem. And it must not be tainted by the stale breath of man's thinking.

The dogs would sit around at night when the work was done

and they would talk of man. They would spin the old, old story and tell the old, old tales and man would be a god.

And it was better that way.

For a god can do no wrong.

NOTES ON THE SEVENTH TALE

Several years ago an ancient literary fragment came to light. Apparently at one time it had been an extensive body of writing and although only a small part of it was discovered, the few tales that it contained were enough to indicate that it was a group of fables concerning the various members of the animal brotherhood. The tales are archaic and the viewpoints and manner of their telling sound strange to us to-day. A number of scholars who have studied the fragments agree with Tige that they may very well be of non-Doggish origin.

Their title is Aesop. The title of this tale likewise is Aesop and the tale's title has come down intact with the tale itself from dim antiquity.

What, ask the scholars, is the significance of this? Tige, quite naturally, believes it is yet another link in his theory that the present legend is human in its origin. Most of the other students fail to agree, but so far have advanced no explanation which would serve instead.

Tige points, too, to this seventh tale as proof that if there is no historic evidence of Man's existence it is because he was forgotten deliberately, because his memory was wiped out to assure the continuance of the canine culture in its purest form.

In this tale the Dogs have forgotten Man. In the few members of the human race existing among them they do not recognize Man, but call these queer creatures by the old family name of Webster. But the word, Webster, has become a common instead of a proper noun. The Dogs think of men as websters, while Jenkins still thinks of them with the capital W.

'What's men?' Lupus asks and Bruin, when he tries to explain, can't tell him.

Jenkins says, in the tale, that the Dogs must never know about Man. He outlines for us, in the body of the story, the steps that he has taken to wipe away the memory of Man.

The old fireside tales are gone, says Jenkins. And in this Tige sees a deliberate conspiracy of forgetfulness, perhaps not so altruistic as Jenkins makes it sound, to save Doggish dignity. The tales are gone, says Jenkins, and must stay gone. But apparently they weren't gone. Somewhere, in some far corner of the world, they still were told, and so to-day we have them with us yet.

But if the tales persisted, Man himself was gone, or nearly so. The wild robots still existed, but even they, if they ever were more than pure imagination, are gone now, too. The Mutants were gone and they are of a piece with Man. If Man existed, the Mutants probably existed too.

The entire controversy surrounding the legend can be boiled down to one question: Did Man exist? If, in reading these tales, the reader finds himself confused, he is in excellent company. The experts and scholars themselves, who have spent their lives in the study of the legend, may have more data, but are just as confused as you are.

VII
Aesop

The grey shadow slid along the rocky ledge, heading for the den, mewing to itself in frustration and bitter disappointment – for the Words had failed.

The slanting sun of early afternoon picked out a face and head and body, indistinct and murky, like a haze of morning mist rising from a gully.

Suddenly the ledge pinched off and the shadow stopped, bewildered, crouched against the rocky wall – for there was no den. The ledge pinched off before it reached the den!

It whirled around like a snapping whip, stared back across the valley. And the river was all wrong. It flowed closer to the bluffs than it had flowed before. There was a swallow's nest on the rocky wall and there'd never been a swallow's nest before.

The shadow stiffened and the tufted tentacles upon its ears came up and searched the air.

There was life! The scent of it lay faint upon the air, the feel of it vibrated across the empty notches of the marching hills.

The shadow stirred, came out of its crouch, flowed along the ledge.

There was no den and the river was different and there was a swallow's nest plastered on the cliff.

The shadow quivered, drooling mentally.

The Words had been right. They had not failed. This was a different world.

A different world – different in more ways than one. A world so full of life that it hummed in the very air. Life, perhaps, that could not run so fast nor hide so well.

The wolf and bear met beneath the great oak tree and stopped to pass the time of day.

'I hear,' said Lupus, 'there's been killing going on.'

Bruin grunted. 'A funny kind of killing, brother. Dead, but not eaten.'

'Symbolic killing,' said the wolf.

Bruin shook his head. 'You can't tell me there's such a thing as symbolic killing. This new psychology the Dogs are teaching us is going just a bit too far. When there's killing going on, it's for either hate or hunger. You wouldn't catch me killing something that I didn't eat.'

He hurried to put matters straight. 'Not that I'm doing any killing, brother. You know that.'

'Of course not,' said the wolf.

Bruin closed his small eyes lazily, opened them and blinked. 'Not, you understand, that I don't turn over a rock once in a while and lap up an ant or two.'

'I don't believe the Dogs would consider that killing,' Lupus told him gravely. 'Insects are a little different than animals and birds. No one has ever told us we can't kill insect life.'

'That's where you're wrong,' said Bruin. 'The Canons say so very distinctly. You must not destroy life. You must not take another's life.'

'Yes, I guess they do,' the wolf admitted sanctimoniously. 'I guess you're right, at that, brother. But even the Dogs aren't too fussy about a thing like insects. Why, you know, they're trying all the time to make a better flea powder. And what's flea powder for, I ask you? Why, to kill fleas. That's what it's for. And fleas are life. Fleas are living things.'

Bruin slapped viciously at a small green fly buzzing past his nose.

'I'm going down to the feeding station,' said the wolf. 'Maybe you would like to join me.'

'I don't feel hungry,' said the bear. 'And, besides, you're a bit too early. Ain't time for feeding yet.'

Lupus ran his tongue around his muzzle. 'Sometimes I just

drift in, casual-like you know, and the webster that's in charge gives me something extra.'

'Want to watch out,' said Bruin. 'He isn't giving you something extra for nothing. He's got something up his sleeve. I don't trust them websters.'

'This one's all right,' the wolf declared. 'He runs the feeding station and he doesn't have to. Any robot could do it. But he went and asked for the job. Got tired of lolling around in them foxed-up houses, with nothing to do but play. And he sits around and laughs and talks, just like he was one of us. That Peter is a good Joe.'

The bear rumbled in his throat. 'One of the Dogs was telling me that Jenkins claims webster ain't their name at all. Says they aren't websters. Says that they are men—'

'What's men?' asked Lupus.

'Why, I was just telling you. It's what Jenkins says—'

'Jenkins,' declared Lupus, 'is getting so old he's all twisted up. Too much to remember. Must be all of a thousand years.'

'Seven thousand,' said the bear. 'The Dogs are figuring on having a big birthday party for him. They're fixing up a new body for him for a gift. The old one he's got is wearing out – in the repair shop every month or two.'

The bear wagged his head sagely. 'All in all, Lupus, the Dogs have done a lot for us. Setting up feeding stations and sending out medical robots and everything. Why, only last year. I had a raging toothache—'

The wolf interrupted. 'But those feeding stations might be better. They claim that yeast is just the same as meat, has the same food value and everything. But it don't taste like meat—'

'How do you know?' asked Bruin.

The wolf's stutter lasted one split second. 'Why . . . why, from what my granddad told me. Regular old hellion, my granddad. He had him some venison every now and then. Told me how red meat tasted. But then they didn't have so many wardens as they have nowadays.'

Bruin closed his eyes, opened them again. 'I been wondering how fish taste,' he said. 'There's a bunch of trout down in Pine

Tree creek. Been watching them. Easy to reach down with my paw and scoop me out a couple.'

He added hastily. 'Of course, I never have.'

'Of course not,' said the wolf.

One world and then another, running like a chain. One world treading on the heels of another world that plodded just ahead. One world's to-morrow, another world's to-day. And yesterday is to-morrow and to-morrow is the past.

Except, there wasn't any past. No past, that was, except the figment of remembrance that flitted like a night-winged thing in the shadow of one's mind. No past that one could reach. No pictures painted on the wall of time. No film that one could run backward and see what-once-had-been.

Joshua got up and shook himself, sat down and scratched a flea. Ichabod sat stiffly at the table, metal fingers tapping.

'It checks,' the robot said. 'There's nothing we can do about it. The factors check. We can't travel in the past.'

'No,' said Joshua.

'But,' said Ichabod, 'we know where the cobblies are.'

'Yes,' said Joshua, 'we know where the cobblies are. And maybe we can reach them. Now we know the road to take.'

One road was open, but another road was closed. Not closed, of course, for it had never been. For there wasn't any past, there never had been any, there wasn't room for one. Where there should have been a past there was another world.

Like two dogs walking in one another's tracks. One dog steps out and another dog steps in. Like a long, endless row of ballbearings running down a groove, almost touching, but not quite. Like the links of an endless chain running on a wheel with a billion billion sprockets.

'We're late,' said Ichabod, glancing at the clock. 'We should be getting ready to go to Jenkins' party.'

Joshua shook himself again. 'Yes, I suppose we should. It's a great day for Jenkins, Ichabod. Think of it . . . seven thousand years.'

'I'm all fixed up,' Ichabod said proudly. 'I shined myself this morning, but you need a combing. You've got all tangled up.'

'Seven thousand years,' said Joshua. 'I wouldn't want to live that long.'

Seven thousand years and seven thousand worlds stepping in one another's tracks. Although it would be more than that. A world a day. Three hundred and sixty-five times seven thousand. Or maybe a world a minute. Or maybe even one world every second. A second was a thick thing – thick enough to separate two worlds, large enough to hold two worlds. Three hundred and sixty-five times seven thousand times twenty-four times sixty times sixty—

A thick thing and a final thing. For there was no past. There was no going back. No going back to find out about the things that Jenkins talked about – the things that might be truth or twisted memory warped by seven thousand years. No going back to check up on the cloudy legends that told about a house and a family of websters and a closed dome of nothingness that squatted in the mountains far across the sea.

Ichabod advanced upon him with a comb and brush and Joshua winced away.

'Ah, shucks,' said Ichabod, 'I won't hurt you any.'

'Last time,' said Joshua, 'you damn near skinned me alive. Go easy on those snags.'

The wolf had come in, hoping for a between-meals snack, but it hadn't been forthcoming and he was too polite to ask. So now he sat, bushy tail tucked neatly around his feet, watching Peter work with the knife upon the slender wand.

Fatso, the squirrel, dropped from the limb of an over-hanging tree, lit on Peter's shoulder.

'What you got?' he asked.

'A throwing stick,' said Peter.

'You can throw any stick you want to,' said the wolf. 'You don't need a fancy one to throw. You can pick up just any stick and throw it.'

'This is something new,' said Peter. 'Something I thought up. Something that I made. But I don't know what it is.'

'It hasn't got a name?' asked Fatso.

'Not yet,' said Peter. 'I'll have to think one up.'

'But,' persisted the wolf, 'you can throw a stick. You can throw any stick you want to.'

'Not as far,' said Peter. 'Not as hard.'

Peter twirled the wand between his fingers, feeling the smooth roundness of it, lifted it and sighted along it to make sure that it was straight.

'I don't throw it with my arm,' said Peter. 'I throw it with another stick and a cord.'

He reached out and picked up the thing that leaned against the tree trunk.

'What I can't figure out,' said Fatso, 'is what you want to throw a stick for.'

'I don't know,' said Peter. 'It is kind of fun.'

'You websters,' said the wolf severely, 'are funny animals. Sometimes I wonder if you have good sense.'

'You can hit any place you aim at,' said Peter, 'if your throwing stick is straight and your cord is good. You can't just pick up any piece of wood. You have to look and look—'

'Show me,' said Fatso.

'Like this,' said Peter, lifting up the shaft of hickory. 'It's tough, you see. Springy. Bend it and it snaps back into shape again. I tied the two ends together with a cord and I put the throwing stick like this, one end against the string and then pull back—'

'You said you could hit anything you wanted to,' said the wolf. 'Go ahead and show us.'

'What shall I hit?' asked Peter. 'You pick it out—'

Fatso pointed excitedly. 'That robin, sitting in the tree.'

Swiftly Peter lifted his hands, the cord came back and the shaft to which the cord was tied bent into an arc. The throwing stick whistled in the air. The robin toppled from the branch in a shower of flying feathers. He hit the ground with a soft, dull thud and lay there on his back – tiny, helpless, clenched claws

188

pointing at the treetops. Blood ran out of his beak to stain the leaf beneath his head.

Fatso stiffened on Peter's shoulders and the wolf was on his feet. And there was a quietness, the quietness of unstirring leaf, of floating clouds against the blue of noon.

Horror slurred Fatso's words. 'You killed him! He's dead! You killed him!'

Peter protested, numb with dread. 'I didn't know. I never tried to hit anything alive before. I just threw the stick at marks—'

'But you killed him. And you should never kill.'

'I know,' said Peter. 'I know you never should. But you told me to hit him. You showed him to me. You—'

'I never meant for you to kill him,' Fatso screamed. 'I just thought you'd touch him up. Scare him. He was so fat and sassy—'

'I told you the stick went hard.'

The Webster stood rooted to the ground.

Far and hard, he thought. *Far and hard – and fast.*

'Take it easy, pal,' said the wolf's soft voice. 'We know you didn't mean to. It's just among us three. We'll never say a word.'

Fatso leaped from Peter's shoulder, screamed at them from the branch above. 'I will,' he shrieked. 'I'm going to tell Jenkins.'

The wolf snarled at him with a sudden, red-eyed rage. 'You dirty little squealer. You lousy tattle-tale.'

'I will so,' yelled Fatso. 'You just wait and see. I'm going to tell Jenkins.'

He flickered up the tree and ran along a branch, leaped to another tree.

The wolf moved swiftly.

'Wait,' said Peter, sharply.

'He can't go in the trees all the way,' the wolf said swiftly. 'He'll have to come down to the ground to get across the meadow. You don't need to worry.'

189

'No,' said Peter. 'No more killings. One killing is enough.'

'He will tell, you know.'

Peter nodded. 'Yes, I'm sure he will.'

'I could stop him telling.'

'Someone would see you and tell on you,' said Peter. 'No, Lupus, I won't let you do it.'

'Then you better take it on the lam,' said Lupus. 'I know a place where you could hide. They'd never find you, not in a thousand years.'

'I couldn't get away with it,' said Peter. 'There are eyes watching in the woods. Too many eyes. They'd tell where I had gone. The day is gone when anyone can hide.'

'I guess you're right,' the wolf said slowly. 'Yes, I guess you're right.'

He wheeled around and stared at the fallen robin.

'What you say we get rid of the evidence?' he asked.

'The evidence—'

'Why, sure—' The wolf paced forward swiftly, lowered his head. There was a crunching sound. Lupus licked his chops and sat down, wrapped his tail around his feet.

'You and I could get along,' he said. 'Yes, sir, I have the feeling we could get along. We're so very much alike.'

A telltale feather fluttered on his nose.

The body was a lulu.

A sledge hammer couldn't dent it and it would never rust. And it had more gadgets than you could shake a stick at.

It was Jenkins' birthday gift. The line of engraving on the chest said so very neatly:

TO JENKINS FROM THE DOGS

But I'll never wear it, Jenkins told himself. It's too fancy for me, too fancy for a robot that's as old as I am. I'd feel out of place in a gaudy thing like that.

He rocked slowly back and forth in the rocking chair, listening to the whimper of the wind in the eaves.

They meant well. And I wouldn't hurt them for the world. I'll have to wear it once in a while just for the looks of things. Just to please the Dogs. Wouldn't be right for me not to wear it when they went to so much trouble to get it made for me. But not for every day – just for my very best.

Maybe to the Webster picnic. Would want to look my very best when I go to the picnic. It's a great affair. A time when all the Websters in the world, all the Websters left alive, get together. And they want me with them. Ah, yes, they always want me with them. For I am a Webster robot. Yes, sir, always was and always will be.

He let his head sink and mumbled words that whispered in the room. Words that he and the room remembered. Words from long ago.

A rocker squeaked and the sound was one with the time-stained room. One with the wind along the eaves and the mumble of the chimney's throat.

Fire, thought Jenkins. It's been a long time since we've had a fire. Men used to like a fire. They used to like to sit in front of it and look into it and build pictures in the flames. And dream—

But the dreams of men, said Jenkins, talking to himself – the dreams of men are gone. They've gone to Jupiter and they're buried at Geneva and they sprout again, very feebly, in the Websters of to-day.

The past, he said. The past is too much with me. And the past has made me useless. I have too much to remember – so much to remember that it becomes more important than the things there are to do. I'm living in the past and that is no way to live.

For Joshua says there is no past and Joshua should know. Of all the Dogs, he's the one to know. For he tried hard enough to find a past to travel in, to travel back in time and check up on the things I told him. He thinks my mind is failing and that I spin old robot tales, half-truth, half-fantasy, touched up for the telling.

He wouldn't admit it for the world, but that's what the rascal thinks. He doesn't think I know it, but I do.

He can't fool me, said Jenkins, chuckling to himself. None of them can fool me. I know them from the ground up – I know what makes them tick. I helped Bruce Webster with the first of them. I heard the first word that any of them said. And if they've forgotten, I haven't – not a look or word or gesture.

Maybe it's only natural that they should forget. They have done great things. I have let them do them with little interference, and that was for the best. That was the way Jon Webster told me it should be, on that night of long ago. That was why Jon Webster did whatever he had to do to close off the city of Geneva. For it was Jon Webster. It had to be. It could be no one else.

He thought he was sealing off the human race to leave the earth clear for the dogs. But he forgot one thing. Oh, yes, said Jenkins, he forgot one thing. He forgot his own son and the little band of bow and arrow faddists who had gone out that morning to play at being cavemen – and cavewomen, too.

And what they played, thought Jenkins, became a bitter fact. A fact for almost a thousand years. A fact until we found them and brought them home again. Back to the Webster House, back to where the whole thing started.

Jenkins folded his hands in his lap and bent his head and rocked slowly to and fro. The rocker creaked and the wind raced in the eaves and a window rattled. The fireplace talked with its sooty throat, talked of other days and other folks, of other winds that blew from out the west.

The past, thought Jenkins. It is a footless thing. A foolish thing when there is so much to do. So many problems that the Dogs have yet to meet.

Over-population, for example. That's the thing we've thought about and talked about too long. Too many rabbits because no wolf or fox may kill them. Too many deer because the mountain lions and the wolves must eat no venison. Too many skunks, too many mice, too many wildcats. Too many squirrels, too many porcupines, too many bear.

Forbid the one great check of killing and you have too many

lives. Control disease and succour injury with quick-moving robot medical technicians and another check is gone.

Man took care of that, said Jenkins. Yes, men took care of that. Men killed anything that stood within their path – other men as well as animals.

Man never thought of one great animal society, never dreamed of skunk and coon and bear going down the road of life together, planning with one another, helping one another – setting aside all natural differences.

But the Dogs had. And the Dogs had done it.

Like a Br'er Rabbit story, thought Jenkins. Like the child-hood fantasy of a long gone age. Like the story in the Good Book about the Lion and the Lamb lying down together. Like a Walt Disney cartoon except that the cartoon never had rung true, for it was based on the philosophy of mankind.

The door creaked open and feet were on the floor. Jenkins shifted in his chair.

'Hello, Joshua,' he said. 'Hello, Ichabod. Won't you please come in? I was just sitting here and thinking.'

'We were passing by,' said Joshua, 'and we saw a light.'

'I was thinking about the lights,' said Jenkins, nodding soberly. 'I was thinking about the night five thousand years ago. Jon Webster had come out from Geneva, the first man to come here for many hundred years. And he was upstairs in bed and all the Dogs were sleeping and I stood there by the window looking out across the river. And there were no lights. No lights at all. Just one great sweep of darkness. And I stood there, re-membering the day when there had been lights and wondering if there ever would be lights again.'

'There are lights now,' said Joshua, speaking very softly. 'There are lights all over the world to night. Even in the caves and dens.'

'Yes, I know,' said Jenkins. 'It's even better than it was before.'

Ichabod clumped across the floor to the shining robot body

standing in the corner, reached out one hand and stroked the metal hide, almost tenderly.

'It was very nice of the Dogs,' said Jenkins, 'to give me the body. But they shouldn't have. With a little patching here and there, the old one's good enough.'

'It was because we love you,' Joshua told him. 'It was the smallest thing the Dogs could do. We have tried to do other things for you, but you'd never let us do them. We wish that you would let us build you a new house, brand new, with all the latest things.'

Jenkins shook his head. 'It wouldn't be any use, because I couldn't live there. You see, this place is home. It has always been my home. Keep it patched up like my body and I'll be happy in it.'

'But you're all alone.'

'No, I'm not,' said Jenkins. 'The house is simply crowded.'

'Crowded?' asked Joshua.

'People that I used to know,' said Jenkins.

'Gosh,' said Ichabod. 'what a body! I wish I could try it on.'

'Ichabod!' yelled Joshua. 'You come back here. Keep your hands off that body—'

'Let the youngster go,' said Jenkins. 'If he comes over here some time when I'm not busy—'

'No,' said Joshua.

A branch scraped against the eave and tapped with tiny fingers along the windowpane. A shingle rattled and the wind marched across the roof with tripping, dancing feet.

'I'm glad you stopped by,' said Jenkins. 'I want to talk to you.'

He rocked back and forth and one of the rockers creaked.

'I won't last forever,' Jenkins said. 'Seven thousand years is longer than I had a right to expect to hang together.'

'With the new body,' said Joshua, 'you'll be good for three times seven thousand more.'

Jenkins shook his head. 'It's not the body I'm thinking of. It's the brain. It's mechanical, you see. It was made well, made to last a long time, but not to last forever. Sometime something will go wrong and the brain will quit.'

The rocker creaked in the silent room.

'That will be death,' said Jenkins. 'That will be the end of me.

'And that's all right. That's the way it should be. For I'm no longer any use. Once there was a time when I was needed.'

'We will always need you,' Joshua said softly. 'We couldn't get along without you.'

But Jenkins went on, as if he had not heard him.

'I want to tell you about the Websters. I want to talk about them. I want you to understand.'

'I will try to understand,' said Joshua.

You Dogs call them websters and that's all right,' said Jenkins. 'It doesn't matter what you call them, just so you know what they are.'

'Sometimes,' said Joshua, 'you call them men and sometimes you call them websters. I don't understand.'

'They were men,' said Jenkins, 'and they ruled the earth. There was one family of them that went by the name of Webster. And they were the ones who did this great thing for you.'

'What great thing?'

Jenkins hitched the chair around and held it steady.

'I am forgetful,' he mumbled. 'I forget so easily. And I get mixed up.'

'You were talking about a great thing the websters did for us.'

'Eh,' said Jenkins. 'Oh, so I was. So I was. You must watch them. You must care for them and watch them. Especially you must watch them.'

He rocked slowly to and fro and thoughts ran in his brain, thoughts spaced off by the squeaking of the rocker.

You almost did it then, he told himself. You almost spoiled the dream.

But I remembered in time. Yes. Jon Webster, I caught myself in time. I kept faith, Jon Webster.

I did not tell Joshua that the Dogs once were pets of men, that men raised them to the place they hold to-day. For they must never know. They must hold up their heads. They must carry on their work. The old fireside tales are gone and they must stay gone forever.

Although I'd like to tell them, Lord knows, I'd like to tell them. Warn them against the thing they must guard against. Tell them how we rooted out the old ideas from the cavemen we brought back from Europe. How we untaught them the many things they knew. How we left their minds blank of weapons, how we taught them love and peace.

And how we must watch against the day when they'll pick up those trends again – the old human way of thought.

'But you said . . .' persisted Joshua.

Jenkins waved his hand. 'It was nothing, Joshua. Just an old robot's mumbling. At times my brain gets fuzzy and I say things that I don't mean. I think so much about the past – and you say there isn't any past.'

Ichabod squatted on his haunches on the floor and looked up at Jenkins.

'There sure ain't none,' he said. 'We checked her, forty ways from Sunday, and all the factors check. They all add up. There isn't any past.'

'There isn't any room,' said Joshua. 'You travel back along the line of time and you don't find the past, but another world, another bracket of consciousness. The earth would be the same, you see, or almost the same. Same trees, same rivers, same hills, but it wouldn't be the world we know. Because it has lived a different life, it has developed differently. The second back of us is not the second back of us at all, but another second, a totally separate sector of time. We live in the same second all the time. We move along within the bracket of that second, that tiny bit of time that has been allotted to our particular world.'

'The way we keep time was to blame,' said Ichabod. 'It was the thing that kept us from thinking of it in the way it really was. For we thought all the time that we were passing through time when we really weren't, when we never have. We've just been moving along with time. We said, there's another second gone, there's another minute and another hour and another day, when, as a matter of fact the second or the minute or the hour was never gone. It was the same one all the time. It had just moved along and we had moved with it.'

Jenkins nodded. 'I see. Like driftwood on the river. Chips moving with the river. And the scene changes along the river bank, but the water is the same.'

'That's roughly it,' said Joshua. 'Except that time is a rigid stream and the different worlds are more firmly fixed in place than the driftwood on the river.'

'And the cobblies live in those other worlds?'

Joshua nodded. 'I'm sure they must.'

'And now,' said Jenkins, 'I suppose you are figuring out a way to travel to those other worlds.'

Joshua scratched softly at a flea.

'Sure he is,' said Ichabod. 'We need the space.'

'But the cobblies—'

'The cobblies might not be on all the worlds,' said Joshua. 'There might be some empty worlds. If we can find them, we need those empty worlds. If we don't find space, we are up against it. Population pressure will bring on a wave of killing. And a wave of killing will set us back to where we started out.'

'There's already killing,' Jenkins told him quietly.

Joshua wrinkled his brow and laid back his ears. 'Funny killing. Dead, but not eaten. No blood. As if they just fell over. It has our medical technicians half crazy. Nothing wrong. No reason that they should have died.'

'But they did,' said Ichabod.

Joshua hunched himself closer, lowered his voice. 'I'm afraid, Jenkins. I'm afraid that—'

'There's nothing to be afraid of.'

'But there is. Angus told me. Angus is afraid that one of the cobblies . . . that one of the cobblies got through.'

*

A gust of wind sucked at the fireplace throat and gamboled in the eaves. Another gust hooted in some near, dark corner. And fear came out and marched across the roof, marched with thumping, deadened footsteps up and down the shingles.

Jenkins shivered and held himself tight and rigid against another shiver. His voice grated when he spoke.

'No one has seen a cobbly.'

'You might not see a cobbly.'

'No,' said Jenkins. 'No. You might not see one.'

And that is what Man had said before. You did not see a ghost and you did not see a haunt – but you sensed that one was there. For the water tap kept dripping when you had shut it tight and there were fingers scratching at the pane and the dogs would howl at something in the night and there'd be no tracks in the snow.

And there were fingers scratching on the pane.

Joshua came to his feet and stiffened, a statue of a dog, one paw lifted, lips curled back in the beinning of a snarl. Ichabod crouched, toes dug into the floor – listening, waiting.

The scratching came again.

'Open the door,' Jenkins said to Ichabod. 'There is something out there wanting to get in.'

Ichabod moved through the hushed silence of the room. The door creaked beneath his hand. As he opened it, the squirrel came bounding in, a grey streak that leaped for Jenkins and landed in his lap.

'Why, Fatso,' Jenkins said.

Joshua sat down again and his lips uncurled, slid down to hide his fangs, Ichabod wore a silly metal grin.

'I saw him do it,' screamed Fatso. 'I saw him kill the robin. He did it with a throwing stick. And the feathers flew. And there was blood upon the leaf.'

'Quiet,' said Jenkins gently. 'Take your time and tell me. You are too excited. You saw someone kill a robin.'

Fatso sucked in a breath and his teeth were chattering.

'It was Peter,' he said.

'Peter?'

'Peter, the webster.'

'You said he threw a stick?'

'He threw it with another stick. He had the two ends tied together with a cord and he pulled on the cord and the stick bent—'

'I know,' said Jenkins. 'I know.'

'You know! You know all about it?'

'Yes,' said Jenkins, 'I know all about it. It was a bow and arrow.'

And there was something in the way he said it that held the other three to silence, making the room seem big and empty and the tapping of the branch against the pane a sound from far away, a hollow, ticking voice that kept on complaining without the hope of aid.

'A bow and arrow?' Joshua finally asked. 'What is a bow and arrow?'

And what was it, thought Jenkins.

What is a bow and arrow?

It is the beginning of the end. It is the winding path that grows to the roaring road of war.

It is a plaything and a weapon and a triumph in human engineering.

It is the first faint stirring of an atom bomb.

It is a symbol of a way of life.

And it's a line in a nursery rhyme.

Who killed Cock Robin
I, said the sparrow.
With my bow and arrow,
I killed Cock Robin.

And it was a thing forgotten. And a thing relearned.

It is the thing that I've been afraid of.

He straightened in his chair, came slowly to his feet.

'Ichabod,' he said, 'I will need your help.'

'Sure,' said Ichabod. 'Anything you like.'

'The body,' said Jenkins. 'I want to wear my new body. You'll have to unseat my brain case—'

Ichabod nodded. 'I know how to do it, Jenkins.'

Joshua's voice had a sudden edge of fear. 'What is it, Jenkins? What are you going to do?'

'I'm going to the Mutants,' Jenkins said, speaking very slowly. 'After all these years, I'm going to ask their help.'

The shadow slithered down the hill, skirting the places where the moonlight flooded through forest openings. He glimmered in the moonlight – and he must not be seen. He must not spoil the hunting of the others that came after.

There would be others. Not in a flood, of course, but carefully controlled. A few at a time and well spread out so that the life of this wondrous world would not take alarm.

Once it did take alarm, the end would be in sight.

The shadow crouched in the darkness, low against the ground, and tested the night with twitching, high-strung nerves. He separated out the impulses that he knew, cataloguing them in his knife-sharp brain, filing them neatly away as a check against his knowledge.

And some he knew and some were mystery and others he would guess at. But there was one that held a hint of horror.

He pressed himself close against the ground and held his ugly head out straight and flat and closed his perceptions against the throbbing of the night, concentrating on the thing that was coming up the hill.

There were two of them and the two were different. A snarl rose in his mind and bubbled in his throat and his tenuous body tensed into something that was half slavering expectancy and half cringing outland terror.

He rose from the ground, still crouched, and flowed down the hill, angling to cut the path of the two who were coming up.

Jenkins was young again, young and strong and swift – swift of brain and body. Swift to stride along the wind-swept, moon-drenched hills. Swift to hear the talking of the leaves and the sleepy chirp of birds – and more than that.

Yes, much more than that, he admitted to himself.

The body was a lulu. A sledge hammer couldn't dent it and it would never rust. But that wasn't all.

Never figured a body'd make this much difference to me. Never knew how ramshackle and worn out the old one really was. A poor job from the first, although it was the best that could be done in the days when it was made. Machinery sure is wonderful, the tricks they can make it do.

It was the robots, of course. The wild robots. The Dogs had fixed it up with them to make the body. Not very often the Dogs had much truck with the robots. Got along all right and all of that – but they got along because they let one another be, because they didn't interfere, because neither one was nosey.

There was a rabbit stirring in his den – and Jenkins knew it. A raccoon was out on a midnight prowl and Jenkins knew that, too – knew the cunning, sleek curiosity that went on within the brain behind the little eyes that stared at him from the clump of hazel brush. And off to the left, curled up beneath a tree, a bear was sleeping and dreaming as he slept – a glutton's dream of wild honey and fish scooped out of a creek, with ants licked from the underside of an upturned rock as relish for the feast.

And it was startling – but natural. As natural as lifting one's feet to walk, as natural as normal hearing was. But it wasn't hearing and it wasn't seeing. Nor yet imagining. For Jenkins knew with a cool, sure certainty about the rabbit in the den and the coon in the hazel brush and the bear who dreamed in his sleep beneath the tree.

And this, he thought, is the kind of bodies the wild robots have – for certainly if they could make one for me, they'd make them for themselves.

They have come a long ways, too, in seven thousand years, even as the Dogs have travelled far since the exodus of humans. But we paid no attention to them, for that was the way it had to be. The robots went their way and the Dogs went theirs and they did not question what one another did, had no curiosity about what one another did. While the robots were building spaceships and shooting for the stars, while they built bodies, while they worked with mathematics and mechanics, the Dogs had worked with animals, had forged a brotherhood of the things that had been wild and hunted in the days of Man – had listened to the cobblies and tried to probe the depths of time to find there was no time.

And certainly if the Dogs and robots have gone as far as this, the Mutants had gone farther still. And they will listen to me, Jenkins said, they will have to listen, for I'm bringing them a problem that falls right into their laps. Because the Mutants are men – despite their ways, they are the sons of Man. They can bear no rancour now, for the name of Man is a dust that is blowing with the wind, the sound of leaves on a summer day – and nothing more.

Besides, I haven't bothered them for seven thousand years – not that I ever bothered them. Joe was a friend of mine, or as close to a friend as a Mutant ever had. He'd talk with me when he wouldn't talk with men. They will listen to me – they will tell me what to do. And they will not laugh.

Because it's not a laughing matter. It's just a bow and arrow, but it's not a laughing matter. It might have been at one time, but history takes the laugh out of many things. If the arrow is a joke, so is the atom bomb, so is the sweep of disease-laden dust that wiped out whole cities, so is the screaming rocket that arcs and falls ten thousand miles away and kills a million people.

Although now there are no million people. A few hundred, more or less, living in the houses that the Dogs built for them because then the Dogs still knew what human beings were, still knew the connection that existed between them and looked on men as gods. Looked on men as gods and told the old tales before the fire of a winter evening and built against the day when Man might return and pat their heads and say, 'Well done, thou good and faithful servant.'

And that wasn't right, said Jenkins striding down the hill, that wasn't right at all. For men did not deserve that worship, did not deserve the godhood. Lord knows I loved them well enough, myself. Still love them, for that matter – but not because they are men, but because of the memory of a few of the many men.

It wasn't right that the Dogs should build for Man. For they were doing better than Man had ever done. So I wiped the memory out and a long, slow work it was. Over the long years I took away the legends and misted the memory and now they call men websters and think that's what they are.

I wondered if I had done right I felt like a traitor and I spent bitter nights when the world was asleep and dark and I sat in the rocking chair and listened to the wind moaning in the eaves. For it was a thing I might not have the right to do. It was a thing the Websters might not have liked. For that was the hold they had on me, that they still have on me, that over the stretch of many thousand years I might do a thing and worry that they might not like it.

But now I know I'm right. The bow and arrow is the proof of that. Once I thought that Man might have got started on the wrong road, that somewhere in the dim, dark savagery that was his cradle and his toddling place, he might have got off on the wrong foot, might have taken the wrong turning. But I see that I was wrong. There's one road and one road alone that Man may travel – the bow and arrow road.

I tried hard enough, Lord knows I really tried.

When we rounded up the stragglers and brought them home to Webster House, I took away their weapons, not only from their hands but from their minds. I re-edited the literature that could be re-edited and I burned the rest I taught them to read again and sing again and think again. And the books had no trace of war or weapons, no trace of hate or history, for history is hate – no battles or heroics, no trumpets.

But it was wasted time, Jenkins said to himself. I know now that it was wasted time. For a man will invent a bow and arrow, no matter what you do.

He had come down the long hill and crossed the creek that tumbled towards the river and now he was climbing again, climbing against the dark, hard uplift of the cliff-crowned hill.

There were tiny rustlings and his new body told his mind that it was mice, mice scurrying in the tunnels they had fashioned in the grass. And for a moment he caught the little happiness that went with the running, playful mice, the little, unformed, uncoagulated thoughts of happy mice.

A weasel crouched for a moment on the bole of a fallen tree and his mind was evil, evil with the thought of mice, evil with remembrance of the old days when weasels made a meal of mice. Blood hunger and fear, fear of what the Dogs might do if he killed a mouse, fear of the hundred eyes that watched against the killing that once had stalked the world.

But a man had killed. A weasel dare not kill, and a man had killed. Without intent, perhaps, without maliciousness. But he had killed. And the Canons said one must not take a life.

In the years gone by others had killed and they had been punished. And the man must be punished, too. But punishment was not enough. Punishment, alone, would not find the answer. The answer must deal not with one man alone, but with all men, with the entire race. For what one of them had done, the rest were apt to do. Not only apt to do, but bound to do – for they were men, and men had killed before and would kill again.

The Mutant castle reared black against the sky, so black that it shimmered in the moonlight. No light came from it and that was not strange at all, for no light had come from it ever. Nor, so far as anyone could know, had the door ever opened into the outside world. The Mutants had built the castles, all over the world, and had gone into them and that had been the end. The Mutants had meddled in the affairs of men, had fought a sort of chuckling war with men and when the men were gone, the Mutants had gone, too.

Jenkins came to the foot of the broad stone steps that led up to the door and halted. Head thrown back, he stared at the building that reared its height above him.

I suppose Joe is dead, he told himself. Joe was long-lived, but he was not immortal. He would not live forever. And it will seem strange to meet another Mutant and know it isn't Joe.

He started the climb, going very slowly, every nerve alert,

waiting for the first sign of chuckling humour that would descend upon him.

But nothing happened.

He climbed the steps and stood before the door and looked for something to let the Mutants know that he had arrived.

But there was no bell. No buzzer. No knocker. The door was plain, with a simple latch. And that was all.

Hesitantly, he lifted his fist and knocked and knocked again, then waited. There was no answer. The door was mute and motionless.

He knocked again, louder this time. Still there was no answer.

Slowly, cautiously, he put out a hand and seized the latch, pressed down with his thumb. The latch gave and the door swung open and Jenkins stepped inside.

'You're cracked in the brain,' said Lupus. 'I'd make them come and find me. I'd give them a run they would remember. I'd make it tough for them.'

Peter shook his head. 'Maybe that's the way you'd do it, Lupus, and maybe it would be right for you. But it would be wrong for me. Websters never run away.'

'How do you know?' the wolf asked pitilessly. 'You're just talking through your hair. No webster had to run away before and if no webster had to run away before, how do you know they never—'

'Oh, shut up,' said Peter.

They travelled in silence up the rocky path, breasting the hill.

'There's something trailing us,' said Lupus.

'You're just imagining,' said Peter. 'What would be trailing us?'

'I don't know, but—'

'Do you smell anything?'

'Well, no.'

'Did you hear anything or see anything?'

'No, I didn't, but—'

'Then nothing's following us,' Peter declared, positively. 'Nothing ever trails anything any more.'

The moonlight filtered through the treetops, making the forest a mottled black and silver. From the river valley came the muffled sound of ducks in midnight argument. A soft breeze came blowing up the hillside, carrying with it a touch of river fog.

Peter's bowstring caught in a piece of brush and he stopped to untangle it. He dropped some of the arrows he was carrying and stooped to pick them up.

'You better figure out some other way to carry them things,' Lupus growled at him. 'You're all the time getting tangled up and dropping them and—'

'I've been thinking about it,' Peter told him, quietly. 'Maybe a bag of some sort to hang around my shoulder.'

They went on up the hill.

'What are you going to do when you get to Webster House?' asked Lupus.

'I'm going to see Jenkins,' Peter said. 'I'm going to tell him what I've done.'

'Fatso's already told him.'

'But maybe he told him wrong. Maybe he didn't tell it right. Fatso was excited.'

'Lame-brained, too,' said Lupus.

They crossed a patch of moonlight and plunged on up the darkling path.

'I'm getting nervous,' Lupus said. 'I'm going to go back. This is a crazy thing you're doing. I've come part way with you, but—'

'Go back, then,' said Peter bitterly. 'I'm not nervous. I'm—'

He whirled around, hair rising on his scalp.

For there was something wrong – something in the air he breathed, something in his mind – an eerie, disturbing sense of danger and, much more than danger, a loathsome feeling that clawed at his shoulder blades and crawled along his back with a million prickly feet.

'Lupus!' he cried. 'Lupus!'

A bush stirred violently down the trail and Peter was running, pounding down the trail. He ducked around a bush and skidded to a halt. His bow came up and with one motion he picked an arrow from his left hand, nocked it to the cord.

Lupus was stretched upon the ground, half in shade and half in moonlight. His lip was drawn back to show his fangs. One paw still faintly clawed.

Above him crouched a shape. A shape – and nothing else. A shape that spat and snarled, a stream of angry sound that screamed in Peter's brain. A tree branch moved in the wind and the moon showed through and Peter saw the outline of the face – a faint outline, like the half erased chalk lines upon a dusty board. A skull-like face with mewling mouth and slitted eyes and ears that were tufted with tentacles.

The bow cord hummed and the arrow splashed into the face – splashed into it and passed through and fell upon the ground. And the face was there, still snarling.

Another arrow nocked against the cord and back, far back, almost to the ear. An arrow driven by the snapping strength of well-seasoned straight-grained hickory – by the hate and fear and loathing of the man who pulled the cord.

The arrow spat against the chalky outlines of the face, slowed and shivered, then fell free.

Another arrow and back with the cord. Farther yet this time. Farther for more power to kill the thing that would not die when an arrow struck it. A thing that only slowed an arrow and made it shiver and then let it pass on through.

Back and back – and back. And then it happened.

The bow string broke.

For an instant, Peter stood there with the useless weapon dangling in one hand, the useless arrow hanging from the other. Stood and stared across the little space that separated him from the shadow horror that crouched across the wolf's grey body.

And he knew no fear. No fear, even though the weapon was

no more. But only flaming anger that shook him and a voice that hammered in his brain with one screaming word:

KILL-KILL-KILL.

He threw away the bow and stepped forward, hands hooked at his side, hooked into puny claws.

The shadow backed away – backed away in a sudden pool of fear that lapped against its brain – fear and horror at the flaming hatred that beat at it from the thing that walked towards it. Hatred that seized and twisted it. Fear and horror it had known before – fear and horror and disquieting resignation – but this was something new. This was a whiplash of torture that seared across its nerves, that burned across its brain.

This was hatred.

The shadow whimpered to itself – whimpered and mewed and backed away and sought with frantic fingers of thought within its muddled brain for the symbols of escape.

The room was empty – empty and old and hollow. A room that caught up the sound of the creaking door and flung it into muffled distances, then hurled it back again. A room heavy with the dust of forgetfulness, filled with the brooding silence of aimless centuries.

Jenkins stood with the door pull in his hand, stood and flung all the sharp alertness of the new machinery that was his body into the corners and the darkened alcoves. There was nothing. Nothing but the silence and the dust and darkness. Nor anything to indicate that for many years there had been anything but silence, dust and darkness. No faintest tremor of a residuary thought, no footprints on the floor, no fingermarks scrawled across the table.

An old song, an incredibly old song – a song that had been old when he had first been forged, crept out of some forgotten corner of his brain. And he was surprised that it still was there, surprised that he had ever known it – and knowing it, dismayed at the swirl of centuries that it conjured up, dismayed at the remembrance of the neat white houses that had stood upon a million hills, dismayed at the thought of men who had loved their acres and walked them with the calm and quiet assurance of their ownership.

Annie doesn't live here any more.

Silly, said Jenkins to himself. Silly that some absurdity of an all-but-vanished race should rise to haunt me now. Silly.

Annie doesn't live here any more.

Who killed Cock Robin? I, said the sparrow—

He closed the door behind him and walked across the room.

Dust-covered furniture stood waiting for the man who had not returned. Dust-covered tools and gadgets lay on the table tops. Dust covered the titles of the rows of books that filled the massive bookcase.

They are gone, said Jenkins, talking to himself. And no one knew the hour or the reason of their going. Nor even where they went. They slipped off in the night and told no one they were leaving. And sometimes, no doubt, they think back and chuckle – chuckle at the thought of our thinking that they still are here, chuckle at the watch we keep against their coming out.

There were other doors and Jenkins strode to one. With his hand upon the latch he told himself the futility of opening it, the futility of searching any further. If this one room was old and empty, so would be all the other rooms.

His thumb came down and the door came open and there was a blast of heat, but there was no room. There was desert – a gold and yellow desert stretching to a horizon that was dim and burnished in the heat of a great blue sun.

A green and purple thing that might have been a lizard, but wasn't, skittered like a flash across the sand, its tiny feet making the sound of eerie whistling.

Jenkins slammed the door shut, stood numbed in mind and body.

A desert. A desert and a thing that skittered. Not another room, not a hall, nor yet a porch – but a desert.

And the sun was blue – blue and blazing hot.

Slowly, cautiously, he opened the door again, at first a crack and then a little wider.

The desert still was there.

Jenkins slammed the door and leaned with his back against it, as if he needed the strength of his metal body to hold out the desert, to hold out the implication of the door and desert.

They were smart, he told himself. Smart and fast on their mental feet. Too fast and too smart for ordinary men. We never knew just how smart they were. But now I know they were smarter than we thought.

This room is just an anteroom to many other worlds, a key that reaches across unguessable space to other planets that swing around unknown suns. A way to leave this earth without ever leaving it – a way to cross the void by stepping through a door.

There were other doors and Jenkins stared at them, stared and shook his head.

Slowly he walked across the room to the entrance door. Quietly, unwilling to break the hush of the dust-filled room, he lifted the latch and let himself out and the familiar world was there. The world of moon and stars, of river fog drifting up between the hills, of treetops talking to one another across the notches of the hills.

The mice still ran along their grassy burrows with happy mouse thoughts that were scarcely thoughts. An owl sat brooding in the tree and his thoughts were murder.

So close, thought Jenkins. So close to the surface still, the old blood-hunger, the old bone-hate. But we're giving them a better start than Man had – although probably it would have made no difference what kind of a start mankind might have had.

And here it is again, the old blood-lust of Man, the craving to be different and to be stronger, to impose his will by things of his devising – things that make his arm stronger than any other arm or paw, to make his teeth sink deeper than any natural fang, to reach and hurt across distances that are beyond his own arm's reach.

I thought I could get help. That is why I came here. And there is no help.

No help at all. For the Mutants were the only ones who might have helped and they have gone away.

It's up to you, Jenkins told himself, walking down the stairs. Mankind's up to you. You've got to stop them, somehow. You've got to change them somehow. You can't let them mess up the thing the Dogs are doing. You can't let them turn the world again into a bow and arrow world.

He walked through the leafy darkness of the hollow and knew the scent of mouldy leaves from the autumn's harvest beneath the new green of growing things and that was something, he told himself, he'd never known before.

His old body had no sense of smell.

Smell and better vision and a sense of knowing, of knowing what a thing was thinking, to read the thoughts of raccoons, to guess the thoughts of mice, to know the murder in the brains of owls and weasels.

And something more – a faint and wind-blown hatred, an alien scream of terror.

It flicked across his brain and stopped him in his tracks, then sent him running, plunging up the hillside, not as a man might run in darkness, but as a robot runs, seeing in the dark and with the strength of metal that has no gasping lungs or panting breath.

Hatred – and there could be one hatred only that could be like that.

The sense grew deeper and sharper as he went up the path in leaping strides and his mind moaned with the fear that sat upon it – the fear of what he'd find.

He plunged around a clump of bushes and skidded to a halt.

The man was walking forward, with his hands clenched at his side and on the grass lay the broken bow. The wolf's grey body lay half in the moonlight, half in shadow and backing away from it was a shadowy thing that was half-light, half-shadow, almost seen but never surely, like a phantom creature that moves within one's dream.

'Peter!' cried Jenkins, but the words were soundless in his mouth.

For he sensed the frenzy in the brain of the half-seen creature, a frenzy of cowering terror that cut through the hatred of the man who walked forward towards the drooling, spitting blob of shadow. Cowering terror and frantic necessity – a necessity of finding, of remembering.

The man was almost on it, walking straight and upright – a man with puny body and ridiculous fists – and courage. Courage, thought Jenkins, courage to take on hell itself. Courage to go down into the pit and rip up the quaking flagstones and shout a lurid, obscene jest at the keeper of the damned.

Then the creature had it – had the thing it had been groping for, knew the thing to do. Jenkins sensed the flood of relief, that flashed across its being, heard the thing, part word, part symbol, part thought, that it performed. Like a piece of mumbo-jumbo, like a spoken charm, like an incantation, but not entirely that. A mental exercise, a thought that took command of the body – that must be nearer to the truth.

For it worked.

The creature vanished. Vanished and was gone – gone out of the world.

There was no sign of it, no single vibration of its being. As if it had never been.

And the thing it had said, the thing that it had thought? It went like this. Like this—

Jenkins jerked himself up short. It was printed on his brain and he knew it, knew the word and thought and the right inflection – but he must not use it, he must forget about it, he must keep it hidden.

For it had worked on the cobbly. And it would work on him. He knew that it would work.

The man had swung around and now he stood limp, hands dangling at his side, staring at Jenkins.

His lips moved in the white blur of his face. 'You . . . you—'

'I am Jenkins,' Jenkins told him. 'This is my new body.'

'There was something here,' said Peter.

'It was a cobbly,' said Jenkins. 'Joshua told me one had gotten through.'

'It killed Lupus,' said Peter.

Jenkins nodded. 'Yes, it killed Lupus. And it killed many others. It was the thing that has been killing.'

'And I killed it,' said Peter. 'I killed it . . . or drove it away . . . or something.'

'You frightened it away,' said Jenkins. 'You were stronger than it was. It was afraid of you. You frightened it back to the world it came from.'

'I could have killed it,' Peter boasted, 'but the cord broke—'

'Next time,' said Jenkins quietly, 'you must make stronger cords. I will show you how it's done. And a steel tip for your arrow—'

'For my what?'

'For your arrow. The throwing stick is an arrow. The stick and cord you throw it with is called a bow. All together, it's called a bow and arrow.'

Peter's shoulders sagged. 'It was done before, then. I was not the first?'

Jenkins shook his head. 'No, you were not the first.'

Jenkins walked across the grass and lay his hand upon Peter's shoulder.

'Come home with me, Peter.'

Peter shook his head. 'No. I'll sit here with Lupus until the morning comes. And then I'll call in his friends and we will bury him.'

He lifted his head to look into Jenkins' face. 'Lupus was a friend of mine. A great friend, Jenkins.'

'I know he must have been,' said Jenkins. 'But I'll be seeing you?'

'Oh, yes,' said Peter. 'I'm coming to the picnic. The Webster picnic. It's in a week or so.'

'So it is,' said Jenkins, speaking very slowly, thinking as he spoke. 'So it is. And I will see you then.'

He turned around and walked slowly up the hill.

Peter sat down beside the dead wolf, waiting for the dawn. Once or twice, he lifted his hand to brush at his cheeks.

They sat in a semi-circle facing Jenkins and listened to him closely.

'Now, you must pay attention,' Jenkins said, 'That is most important. You must pay attention and you must think real hard and you must hang very tightly to the things you have – to the lunch baskets and the bows and arrows and the other things.'

One of the girls giggled. 'Is this a new game, Jenkins?'

'Yes,' said Jenkins, 'sort of. I guess that is what it is – a new game. And an exciting one. A most exciting one.'

Someone said: 'Jenkins always thinks up a new game for the Webster picnic.'

'And now,' said Jenkins, 'you must pay attention. You must look at me and try to figure out the thing I'm thinking—'

'It's a guessing game,' shriekd the giggling girl. 'I love guessing games.'

Jenkins made his mouth into a smile. 'You're right,' he said. 'That's exactly what it is – a guessing game. And now if you will pay attention and look at me—'

'I want to try out these bows and arrows,' said one of the men. 'After this is over, we can try them out, can't we, Jenkins?'

'Yes,' said Jenkins patiently, 'after this is over you can try them out.'

He closed his eyes and made his brain reach out for each of them, ticking them off individually, sensing the thrilled expectancy of the minds that yearned towards his, felt the little probing fingers of thought that were dabbing at his brain.

'Harder,' Jenkins thought. 'Harder! Harder!'

A quiver went across his mind and he brushed it away. Not

hypnotism – nor yet telepathy, but the best that he could do. A drawing together, a huddling together of minds – and it was all a game.

Slowly, carefully, he brought out the hidden symbol – the words, the thought and the inflection. Easily he slid them into his brain, one by one, like one would speak to a child, trying to teach it the exact tone, the way to hold its lips, the way to move its tongue.

He let them lay there for a moment, felt the other minds touching them, felt the fingers dabbing at them. And then he thought them aloud – thought them as the cobbly had thought them.

And nothing happened. Absolutely nothing. No click within his brain. No feeling of falling. No vertigo. No sensation at all.

So he had failed. So it was over. So the game was done.

He opened his eyes and the hillside was the same. The sun still shone and the sky was robin's egg.

He sat stiffly, silently and felt them looking at him.

Everything was the same as it had been before.

Except—

There was a daisy where the clump of Oswego tea had bloomed redly before. There was a pasture rose beside him and there had been none when he had closed his eyes.

'Is that all there's to it?' asked the giggly girl, plainly disappointed.

'That is all,' said Jenkins.

'Now we can try out the bows and arrows?' asked one of the youths.

'Yes,' said Jenkins, 'but be careful. Don't point them at one another. They are dangerous. Peter will show you how.'

'We'll unpack the lunch,' said one of the women. 'Did you bring a basket, Jenkins?'

'Yes,' said Jenkins. 'Esther has it. She held it when we played the game.'

'That's nice,' said the woman. 'You surprise us every year with the things you bring.'

215

And you'll be surprised this year, Jenkins told himself. You'll be surprised at packages of seeds, all very neatly labelled.

For we'll need seeds, he thought to himself. Seeds to plant new gardens and to start new fields – to raise food once again. And we'll need bows and arrows to bring in some meat. And spears and hooks for fish.

Now other little things that were different began to show themselves. The way a tree leaned at the edge of the meadow. And a new kink in the river far below.

Jenkins sat quietly in the sun, listening to the shouts of the men and boys, trying out the bows and arrows, hearing the chatter of the women as they spread the cloth and unpacked the lunches.

I'll have to tell them soon, he told himself. I'll have to warn them to go easy on the food – not to gobble it up all at one sitting. For we will need that food to tide us over the first day or two, until we can find roots to dig and fish to catch and fruit to pick.

Yes, pretty soon I'll have to call them in and break the news to them. Tell them they're on their own. Tell them why. Tell them to go ahead and do anything they want to. For this is a brand-new world.

Warn them about the cobblies.

Although that's the least important. Man has a way with him – a very vicious way. A way of dealing with anything that stands in his path.

Jenkins sighed.

Lord help the cobblies, he said.

NOTES ON THE EIGHTH TALE

There is some suspicion that the eighth and final tale may be a fraud, that it has no place in the ancient legend, that it is a more recent story made up by some storyteller hungering for public acclamation.

Structurally, it is an acceptable story, but the phraseology of it does not measure up to the narrative skill that goes into the others. Another thing is that it is too patently a story. It is too clever in its assembly of material, works the several angles from the other tales too patly together.

And yet, while no trace of historic basis can be found in any of the other tales, which are indisputably legendary, there is historic basis for this tale.

It is a matter of record that one of the closed worlds is closed because it is a world of ants. It is now an ant world – has been an ant world for uncounted generations.

There is no evidence that the ant world is the original world on which the Dogs arose, but neither is there evidence that it is not. The fact that research has not uncovered any world which can lay claim to being the original world would seem to indicate that the ant world might in fact be the world that was called the Earth.

If that is so, all hope of finding further evidence of the legend's origin may be gone forever, for only on the first world could there be artifacts which might prove beyond contention the origin of the legend. Only there could one hope to find the answer to the basic question of Man's existence or his non-existence. If the ant world is the Earth, then the closed city of Geneva and the house on Webster Hill are lost to us forever.

VIII
The Simple Way

Archie, the little renegade raccoon, crouched on the hillside, trying to catch one of the tiny, scurrying things running in the grass. Rufus, Archie's robot, tried to talk to Archie, but the raccoon was too busy and he did not answer.

Homer did a thing no Dog had ever done before. He crossed the river and trotted into the wild robots' camp and he was scared, for there was no telling what the wild robots might do to him when they turned around and saw him. But he was worried worse than he was scared, so he trotted on.

Deep in a secret nest, ants dreamed and planned for a world they could not understand. And pushed into that world, hoping for the best, aiming at a thing no Dog, or robot, or man could understand.

In Geneva, Jon Webster rounded out his ten-thousandth year of suspended animation and slept on, not stirring. In the street outside, a wandering breeze rustled the leaves along the boulevard, but no one heard and no one saw.

Jenkins strode across the hill and did not look to either left or right, for there were things he did not wish to see. There was a tree that stood where another tree had stood in another world. There was the lay of ground that had been imprinted on his brain with a billion footsteps across ten thousand years.

And, if one listened closely, one might have heard laughter echoing down the ages . . . the sardonic laughter of a man named Joe.

*

Archie caught one of the scurrying things and held it clutched within his tight-shut paw. Carefully he lifted the paw and opened it and the thing was there, running madly, trying to escape.

'Archie,' said Rufus, 'you aren't listening to me.'

The scurrying thing dived into Archie's fur, streaked swiftly up his forearm.

'Might have been a flea,' said Archie. He sat up and scratched his belly.

'New kind of flea,' he said. 'Although I hope it wasn't. Just the ordinary kind are bad enough.'

'You aren't listening,' said Rufus.

'I'm busy,' said Archie. 'The grass is full of them things. Got to find out what they are.'

'I'm leaving you, Archie.'

'You're what!'

'Leaving you,' said Rufus. 'I'm going to the Building.'

'You're crazy,' fumed Archie. 'You can't do a thing like that to me. You've been tetched ever since you fell into that ant hill . . .'

'I've had the Call,' said Rufus. 'I just got to go.'

'I've been good to you,' the raccoon pleaded. 'I've never overworked you. You've been like a pal of mine instead of like a robot. I've always treated you just like an animal.'

Rufus shook his head stubbornly. 'You can't make me stay,' he said. 'I couldn't stay, no matter what you did. I got the Call and I got to go.'

'It isn't like I could get another robot,' Archie argued. 'They drew my number and I ran away. I'm a deserter and you know I am. You know I can't get another robot with the wardens watching for me.'

Rufus just stood there.

'I need you,' Archie told him. 'You got to stay and help me rustle grub. I can't go near none of the feeding places or the wardens will nab me and drag me up to Webster Hill. You got to help me dig a den. Winter's coming on and I will need a den.

It won't have heat or light, but I got to have one. And you've got to . . .'

Rufus had turned around and was walking down the hill, heading for the river trail. Down the river trail . . . travelling towards the dark smudge above the far horizon.

Archie sat hunched against the wind that ruffled through his fur, tucked his tail around his feet. The wind had a chill about it, a chill it had not held an hour or so before. And it was not the chill of weather, but the chill of other things.

His bright, beady eyes searched the hillside and there was no sign of Rufus.

No food, no den, no robot. Hunted by the wardens. Eaten up by fleas.

And the Building, a smudge against the farther hills across the river valley.

A hundred years ago, so the records said, the Building had been no bigger than the Webster House.

But it had grown since . . . a place that never was completed. First it had covered an acre. And then a square mile. Now finally a township. And still it grew, sprawling out and towering up.

A smudge above the hills and a cloudy terror for the little, superstitious forest folks who watched it. A word to frighten kit and whelp and cub into sudden quiet.

For there was evil in it . . . the evil of the unknown, an evil sensed and attributed rather than seen or heard or smelled. A sensed evil, especially in the dark of night, when the lights were out and the wind keened in the den's mouth and the other animals were sleeping, while one lay awake and listened to the pulsing *otherness* that sang between the worlds.

Archie blinked in the autumn sunlight scratched furtively at his side.

Maybe some-day, he told himself, someone will find a way to handle fleas. Something to rub on one's fur so they will stay away. Or a way to reason with them, to reach them and talk things over with them. Maybe set up a reservation for them, a place where they could stay and be fed and not bother animals. Or something of the sort.

As it was, there wasn't much that could be done. You scratched yourself. You had your robot pick them off, although the robot usually got more fur than fleas. You rolled in the sand or dust. You went for a swim and drowned some of them . . . well, you really didn't drown them; you just washed them off and if some of them drowned that was their own tough luck.

You had your robot pick them off . . . but now there was no robot.

No robot to pick off fleas.

No robot to help him hunt for food.

But, Archie remembered, there was a black haw tree down in the river bottom and last night's frost would have touched the fruit. He smacked his lips, thinking of the haws. And there was a cornfield just over the ridge. If one was fast enough and bided his time and was sneaky about it, it was no trouble at all to get an ear of corn. And if worse came to worse there always would be roots and wild acorns and that patch of wild grapes over on the sand bar.

Let Rufus go, said Archie, mumbling to himself. Let the Dogs keep their feeding stations. Let the wardens go on watching.

He would live his own life. He would eat fruit and grub for roots and raid the cornfields, even as his remote ancestors had eaten fruits and grubbed for roots and raided fields.

He would live as the other raccoons had lived before the Dogs had come along with their ideas about the Brotherhood of Beasts. Like animals had lived before they could talk with words, before they could read the printed books that the Dogs provided, before they had robots that served in lieu of hands, before there was warmth and light for dens.

Yes, and before there was a lottery that told you if you stayed on Earth or went to another world.

The Dogs, Archie remembered, had been quite persuasive about it, very reasonable and suave. Some animals, they said, had to go to the other worlds or there would be too many

222

animals on Earth. Earth wasn't big enough, they said, to hold everyone. And a lottery, they pointed out was the fair way to decide which of them would go to the other worlds.

And, after all, they said, the other worlds would be almost like the Earth. For they were just extensions of the Earth. Just other worlds following in the track of Earth. Not quite like it, perhaps, but very close. Just a minor difference here and there. Maybe no tree where there was a tree on Earth. Maybe an oak tree where Earth had a walnut tree. Maybe a spring of fresh, cold water where there was no such spring on Earth.

Maybe, Homer had told him, growing very enthusiastic . . . maybe the world he would be assigned to would be a better world than Earth.

Archie hunched against the hillside, felt the warmish sun of autumn cutting through the cold chill of autumn's wind. He thought about the black haws. They would be soft and mushy and there would be some of them lying on the ground. He would eat those that were on the ground, then he'd climb the tree and pick some more and then he'd climb down again and finish off the ones he had shaken loose with his climbing of the tree.

He'd eat them and take them in his paws and smear them on his face. He might even roll in them.

Out of the corner of one eye, he saw the scurrying things running in the grass. Like ants, he thought, only they weren't ants. At least, not like any ants he'd ever seen before.

Fleas, maybe. A new kind of flea.

His paw darted out and snatched one up. He felt it running in his palm. He opened the paw and saw it running there and closed the paw again.

He raised his paw to his ear and listened.

The thing he'd caught was ticking!

The wild robot camp was not at all the way Homer had imagined it would be. There were no buildings, just launching ramps and three spaceships and half a dozen robots working on one of the ships.

Although, come to think of it. Homer told himself, one should have known there would be no buildings in a robot camp. For the robots would have no use of shelter and that was all a building was.

Homer was scared, but he tried hard not to show it. He curled his tail over his back and carried his head high and his ears well forward and trotted towards the little group of robots, never hesitating. When he reached them, he sat down and lolled out his tongue and waited for one of them to speak.

But when none of them did, he screwed up his courage and spoke to them, himself.

'My name is Homer,' he said, 'and I represent the Dogs. If you have a head robot, I would like to talk to him.'

The robots kept on working for a minute, but finally one of them turned around and came over and squatted down beside Homer so that his head was level with the dog's head. All the other robots kept on working as if nothing had happened.

'I am a robot called Andrew,' said the robot squatting next to Homer, 'and I am not what you would call the head robot, for we have no such thing among us. But I can speak with you.'

'I came to you about the Building,' Homer told him.

'I take it,' said the robot called Andrew, 'that you are speaking of the structure to the north-east of us. The one you can see from here if you just turn around.'

'That's the one,' said Homer. 'I came to ask why you are building it.'

'But we aren't building it,' said Andrew.

'We have seen robots working on it.'

'Yes, there are robots working there. But we are not building it.'

'You are helping someone else?'

Andrew shook his head. 'Some of us get a call . . . a call to go and work there. The rest of us do not try to stop them, for we are all free agents.'

'But who is building it?' asked Homer.

'The ants,' said Andrew.

Homer's jaw dropped slack.

224

'Ants? You mean the insects. The little things that live in ant hills?'

'Precisely,' said Andrew. He made the fingers of one hand ran across the sand like a harried ant.

'But they couldn't build a place like that,' protested Homer. 'They are stupid.'

'Not any more,' said Andrew.

Homer sat stock still, frozen to the sand, felt chilly feet of terror run along his nerves.

'Not any more,' said Andrew, talking to himself. 'Not stupid any more. You see once upon a time, there was a man named Joe . . .'

'A man? What's that?' asked Homer.

The robot made a clucking noise, as if gently chiding Homer.

'Men were animals,' he said. 'Animals that went on two legs. They looked very much like us except they were flesh and we are metal.'

'You must mean the websters,' said Homer. 'We know about things like that, but we call them websters.'

The robot nodded slowly. 'Yes, the websters could be men. There was a family of them by that name. Lived just across the river.'

'There's a place called Webster House,' said Homer. 'It stands on Webster's Hill.'

'That's the place,' said Andrew.

'We keep it up,' said Homer. 'It's a shrine to us, but we don't understand just why. It is the word that has been passed down to us . . . we must keep Webster House.'

'The websters,' Andrew told him, 'were the ones that taught you Dogs to speak.'

Homer stiffened. 'No one taught us to speak. We taught ourselves. We developed in the course of many years. And we taught the other animals.'

Andrew, the robot, sat hunched in the sun, nodding his head as if he might be thinking to himself.

'Ten thousand years,' he said. 'No, I guess it's nearer twelve. Around eleven, maybe.'

Homer waited and as he waited he sensed the weight of years that pressed against the hills . . . the years of river and of sun, of sand and wind and sky.

And the years of Andrew.

'You are old,' he said. 'You can remember that far back?'

'Yes,' said Andrew. 'Although I am one of the last of the man-made robots, I was made just a few years before they went to Jupiter.'

Homer sat silently, tumult stirring in his brain.

Man . . . a new word.

An animal that went on two legs.

An animal that made the robots, that taught the Dogs to talk.

And, as if he might be reading Homer's mind. Andrew spoke to him.

'You should not have stayed away from us,' he said. 'We should have worked together. We worked together once. We both would have gained if we had worked together.'

'We were afraid of you,' said Homer. 'I am still afraid of you.'

'Yes,' said Andrew. 'Yes, I suppose you would be. I suppose Jenkins kept you afraid of us. For Jenkins was a smart one. He knew that you must start fresh. He knew that you must not carry the memory of Man as a dead weight on your necks.'

Homer sat silently.

'And we,' the robot said, 'are nothing more than the memory of Man. We do the things he did, although more scientifically, for, since we are machines, we must be scientific. More patiently than Man, because we have forever, and he had a few short years.'

Andrew drew two lines in the sand, crossed them with two other lines. He made an X in the open square in the upper left hand corner.

'You think I'm crazy,' he said. 'You think I'm talking through my hat.'

226

Homer wriggled his haunches deeper into the sand.

'I don't know what to think,' he said. 'All these years . . .'

Andrew drew an O with his finger in the centre square of the cross-hatch he had drawn in the sand.

'I know,' he said. 'All these years you have lived with a dream. The idea that the Dogs were the prime movers. And the facts are hard to understand, hard to reconcile. Maybe it would be just as well if you forgot what I said. Facts are painful things at times. A robot has to work with them, for they are the only things he has to work with. We can't dream, you know. Facts are all we have.'

'We passed fact long ago,' Homer told him. 'Not that we don't use it, for there are times we do. But we work in other ways. Intuition and cobblying and listening.'

'You aren't mechanical,' said Andrew. 'For you, two and two are not always four, but for us it must be four. And sometimes I wonder if tradition doesn't blind us. I wonder sometimes if two and two may not be something more or less than four.'

They squatted in silence, watching the river, a flood of molten silver tumbling down a coloured land.

Andrew made an X in the upper right hand corner of the cross-hatch, an O in the centre upper space, and X in the centre lower space. With the flat of his hand, he rubbed the sand smooth.

'I never win,' he said. 'I'm too smart for myself.'

'You were telling me about the ants,' said Homer. 'About them not being stupid any more.'

'Oh, yes,' said Andrew. 'I was telling you about a man named Joe . . .'

Jenkins strode across the hill and did not look to either left or right, for there were things he did not wish to see, things that struck too deeply into memory. There was a tree that stood where another tree had stood in another world. There was the lay of ground that had been imprinted on his brain with a billion footsteps across ten thousand years.

The weak winter sun of afternoon flickered in the sky, flickered like a candle guttering in the wind, and when it steadied and there was no flicker it was moonlight and not sunlight at all.

Jenkins checked his stride and swung around and the house was there . . . low-set against the ground, sprawled across the hill, like a sleepy young thing that clung close to mother earth.

Jenkins took a hesitant step and as he moved his metal body glowed and sparkled in the moonlight that had been sunlight a short heartbeat ago.

From the river valley came the sound of a night bird crying and a raccoon was whimpering in a cornfield just below the ridge.

Jenkins took another step and prayed the house would stay . . . although he knew it couldn't because it wasn't there. For this was an empty hilltop that had never known a house. This was another world in which no house existed.

The house remained, dark and silent, no smoke from the chimneys, no light from the windows, but with remembered lines that one could not mistake.

Jenkins moved slowly, carefully, afraid the house would leave, afraid that he would startle it and it would disappear.

But the house stayed put. And there were other things. The tree at the corner had been an elm and now it was an oak, as it had been before. And it was autumn moon instead of winter sun. The breeze was blowing from the west and not out of the north.

Something happened, thought Jenkins. The thing that has been growing on me. The thing I felt and could not understand. An ability developing? Or a new sense finally reaching light? Or a power I never dreamed I had.

A power to walk between the worlds at will. A power to go anywhere I choose by the shortest route that the twisting lines of force and happenstance can conjure up for me.

He walked less carefully and the house still stayed, unfrightened, solid and substantial.

He crossed the grass-grown patio and stood before the door.

Hesitantly, he put out a hand and laid it on the latch. And the latch was there. No phantom thing, but substantial metal.

Slowly he lifted it and the door swung in and he stepped across the threshold.

After five thousand years, Jenkins had come home . . . back to Webster House.

So there was a man named Joe. Not a Webster, but a man. For a webster was a man. And the Dogs had not been first.

Homer lay before the fire, a limp pile of fur and bone and muscle, with his paws stretched out in front of him and his head resting on his paws. Through half-closed eyes he saw the fire and shadow, felt the heat of the blazing logs reach out and fluff his fur.

But inside his brain he saw the sand and the squatting robot and the hills with the years upon them.

Andrew had squatted in the sand and talked, with the autumn sun shining on his shoulders . . . had talked of men and dogs and ants. Of a thing that had happened when Nathaniel was alive, and that was a time long gone, for Nathaniel was the first Dog.

There had been a man named Joe . . . a mutant-man, a more-than-man . . . who had wondered about ants twelve thousand years ago. Wondered why they had progressed so far and then no farther, why they had reached the dead end of destiny.

Hunger, perhaps, Joe had reasoned . . . the ever-pressing need to garner food so that they might live. Hibernation, perhaps, the stagnation of the winter sleep, the broken memory chain, the starting over once again, each year a genesis for ants.

So, Andrew said, his bald pate gleaming in the sun. Joe had picked one hill, had set himself up as a god to change the destiny of ants. He had fed them, so that they need not strive with hunger. He had enclosed their hill in a dome of glassite and had heated it so they need not hibernate.

And the thing had worked. The ants advanced. They fashioned carts and they smelted ore. This much one could know, for the carts were on the surface and acrid smelting smoke came from the chimneys that thrust up from the hill. What other things they did, what other things they learned, deep down in their tunnels, there was no way of knowing.

Joe was crazy, Andrew said. Crazy . . . and yet, maybe not so crazy either.

For one day he broke the dome of glassite and tore the hill asunder with his foot, then turned and walked away, not caring any more what happened to the ants.

But the ants had cared.

The hand that broke the dome, the foot that ripped the hill had put the ants on the road to greatness. It had made them fight . . . fight to keep the things they had, fight to keep the bottleneck of destiny from closing once again.

A kick in the pants, said Andrew. A kick in the pants for ants. A kick in the right direction.

Twelve thousand years ago a broken, trampled hill. To-day a mighty building that grew with each passing year. A building that had covered a township in one short century, that would cover a hundred townships in the next. A building that would push out and take the land. Land that belonged, not to ants, but animals.

A building . . . and that was not quite right, although it had been called the Building from the very start. For a building was a shelter, a place to hide from storm and cold. The ants would have no need of that, for they had their tunnels and their hills.

Why would an ant build a place that sprawled across a township in a hundred years and yet that kept on growing? What possible use could an ant have for a place like that?

Homer nuzzled his chin deep into his paws, growled inside his throat.

There was no way of knowing. For first you had to know how an ant would think. You would have to know her ambition and her goal. You would have to probe her knowledge.

Twelve thousand years of knowledge. Twelve thousand years from a starting point that itself was unknowable.

But one had to know. There must be a way to know.

For, year after year, the Building would push out. A mile across, and then six miles and after that a hundred. A hundred miles and then another hundred and after that the world.

Retreat, thought Homer. Yes, we could retreat. We could migrate to those other worlds, the worlds that follow us in the stream of time, the worlds that tread on one another's heels. We could give the Earth to ants and there still would be space for us.

But this is home. This is where the Dogs arose. This is where we taught the animals to talk and think and act together. This is the place where we created the Brotherhood of Beasts.

For it does not matter who came first . . . the webster or the dog. This place is home. Our home as well as Webster's home. Our home as well as ants'.

And we must stop the ants.

There must be a way to stop them. A way to talk to them, find out what they want. A way to reason with them. Some basis for negotiation. Some agreement to be reached.

Homer lay motionless on the hearth and listened to the whisperings that ran through the house, the soft, far-off padding of robots on their rounds of duties, the muted talk of Dogs in a room upstairs, the crackling of the flames as they ate along the log.

A good life, said Homer, muttering to himself. A good life and we thought we were the ones who made it. Although Andrew says it wasn't us. Andrew says we have not added one iota to the mechanical skill and mechanical logic that was our heritage . . . and that we have lost a lot. He spoke of chemistry and he tried to explain, but I couldn't understand. The study of elements, he said, and things like molecules and atoms. And electronics . . . although he said we did certain things without the benefit of electronics more wonderfully than man could have done with all his knowledge. You might study electronics for a million years, he said, and not reach those other worlds, not even know they're there . . . and we did it, we did a thing a webster could not do.

Because we think differently than a webster does. No, it's man, not webster.

And our robots. Our robots are no better than the ones that were left to us by man. A minor modification here and there . . . an obvious modification, but no real improvement.

Who ever would have dreamed there could be a better robot?

A better ear of corn, yes. Or a better walnut tree. Or a wild rice that would grow a fuller head. A better way to make the yeast that substitutes for meat.

But a better robot . . . why, a robot does everything we might wish that it could do. Why should it be better?

And yet . . . the robots receive a call and go off to work on the Building, to build a thing that will push us off the Earth.

We do not understand. Of course, we cannot understand. If we knew our robots better, we might understand. Understanding, we might fix it so that the robots would not receive the call, or, receiving it, would pay it no attention.

And that, of course, would be the answer. If the robots did not work, there would be no building. For the ants, without the aid of robots, could not go on with their building.

A flea ran along Homer's scalp and he twitched his ear.

Although Andrew might be wrong, he told himself. We have our legend of the rise of the Brotherhood of Beasts and the wild robots have their legend of the fall of man. At this date, who is there to tell which of the two is right?

But Andrew's story does tie in. There were Dogs and there were robots and when man fell they went their separate ways . . . although we kept some of the robots to serve as hands for us. Some robots stayed with us, but no dogs stayed with the robots.

A late autumn fly buzzed out of a corner, bewildered in the firelight. It buzzed around Homer's head and settled on his nose. Homer glared at it and it lifted its legs and insolently brushed its wings. Homer dabbed at it with a paw and it flew away.

A knock came at the door.

Homer lifted his head and blinked at the knocking sound. 'Come in,' he finally said.

It was the robot, Hezekiah.

'They caught Archie,' Hezekiah said.

'Archie?'

'Archie, the raccoon.'

'Oh, yes,' said Homer. 'He was the one that ran away.'

'They have him out here now,' said Hezekiah. 'Do you want to see him?'

'Send them in,' said Homer.

Hezekiah beckoned with his finger and Archie ambled through the door. His fur was matted with burs and his tail was dragging. Behind him stalked two robot wardens.

'He tried to steal some corn,' one of the wardens said, 'and we spotted him, but he led us quite a chase.'

Homer sat up ponderously and stared at Archie. Archie stared straight back.

'They never would have caught me,' Archie said, 'if I'd still had Rufus. Rufus was my robot and he would have warned me.'

'And where is Rufus now?'

'He got the call to-day,' said Archie, 'and left me for the Building.'

'Tell me,' said Homer. 'Did anything happen to Rufus before he left? Anything unusual? Out of the ordinary?'

'Nothing,' Archie told him. 'Except that he fell into an ant hill. He was a clumsy robot. A regular stumble bum . . . always tripping himself, getting tangled up. He wasn't co-ordinated just the way he should be. He had a screw loose some place.'

Something black and tiny jumped off of Archie's nose, raced along the floor. Archie's paw went out in a lightning stroke and scooped it up.

'You better move back a ways,' Hezekiah warned Homer. 'He's simply dripping fleas.'

'It's not a flea,' said Archie, puffing up in anger. 'It is some thing else. I caught it this afternoon. It ticks and it looks like an ant, but it isn't one.'

233

The thing that ticked oozed between Archie's claws and tumbled to the floor. It landed right side up and was off again. Archie made a stab at it, but it zigzagged out of reach. Like a flash it reached Hezekian and streaked up his leg.

Homer came to his feet in a sudden flash of knowledge.

'Quick!' he shouted. 'Get it! Catch it! Don't let it . . .'

But the thing was gone.

Slowly Homer sat down again. His voice was quiet now, quiet and almost deadly.

'Wardens,' he said, 'take Hezekiah into custody. Don't leave his side, don't let him get away. Report to me everything he does.'

Hezekiah backed away.

'But I haven't done a thing.'

'No,' said Homer softly. 'No, you haven't yet. But you will. You'll get the Call and you'll try to desert us for the Building. And before we let you go, we'll find out what it is that made you do it. What it is and how it works.'

Homer turned around, a doggish grin wrinkling up his face.

'And, now, Archie . . .'

But there was no Archie.

There was an open window. And there was no Archie.

Homer stirred on his bed of hay, unwilling to awake, a growl gurgling in his throat.

Getting old, he thought. Too many years upon me, like the years upon the hills. There was a time when I'd be out of bed at the first sound of something at the door, on my feet, with hay sticking in my fur, barking my head off to let the robots know.

The knock came again and Homer staggered to his feet.

'Come in,' he yelled. 'Cut out the racket and come in.'

The door opened and it was a robot, but a bigger robot than Homer had ever seen before. A gleaming robot, huge and massive, with a polished body that shone like slow fire even in the dark. And riding on the robot's shoulder was Archie, the raccoon.

'I am Jenkins,' said the robot. 'I came back to-night.'

234

Homer gulped and sat down very slowly.

'Jenkins,' he said. 'There are stories . . . legends . . . from the long ago.'

'No more than a legend?' Jenkins asked.

'That's all,' said Homer. 'A legend of a robot that looked after us. Although Andrew spoke of Jenkins this afternoon as if he might have known him. And there is a story of how the Dogs gave you a body on your seven thousandth birthday and it was a marvellous body that . . .'

His voice ran down . . . for the body of the robot that stood before him with the raccoon perched on his shoulder . . . that body could be none other than the birthday gift.

'And Webster House?' asked Jenkins. 'You still keep Webster House?'

'We still keep Webster House,' said Homer. 'We keep it as it is. It's a thing we have to do.'

'The websters?'

'There aren't any websters.'

Jenkins nodded at that. His body's hair-trigger sense had told him there were no websters. There were no webster vibrations. There was no thought of websters in the minds of things he'd touched.

And that was as it should be.

He came slowly across the room, soft-footed as a cat despite his mighty weight, and Homer felt him moving, felt the friendliness and kindness of the metal creature, the protectiveness of the ponderous strength within him.

Jenkins squatted down beside him.

'You are in trouble,' Jenkins said.

Homer stared at him.

'The ants,' said Jenkins. 'Archie told me. Said you were troubled by the ants.'

'I went to Webster House to hide,' said Archie. 'I was scared you would hunt me down again and I thought that Webster House . . .'

'Hush, Archie,' Jenkins told him. 'You don't know a thing

about it. You told me that you didn't. You just said the Dogs were having trouble with the ants.'

He looked at Homer.

'I suppose they are Joe's ants,' he said.

'So you know about Joe,' said Homer. 'So there was a man called Joe.'

Jenkins chuckled. 'Yes, a troublemaker. But likeable at times. He had the devil in him.'

Homer said: 'They're building. They get the robots to work for them and they are putting up a building.'

'Surely,' said Jenkins, 'even ants have the right to build.'

'But they're building too fast. They'll push us off the Earth. Another thousand years or so and they'll cover the whole Earth if they keep on building at the rate they've been.'

'And you have no place to go? That's what worries you.'

'Yes, we have a place to go. Many places. All the other worlds. The cobbly worlds.'

Jenkins nodded gravely. 'I was in a cobbly world. The first world after this. I took some websters there five thousand years ago. I just came back to-night. And I know the way you feel. No other world is home. I've hungered for the Earth for almost every one of those five thousand years. I came back to Webster House and I found Archie there. He told me about the ants and so I came up here. I hope you do not mind.'

'We are glad you came,' said Homer softly.

'These ants,' said Jenkins. 'I suppose you want to stop them.'

Homer nodded his head.

'There is a way,' said Jenkins. 'I know there is a way. The websters had a way if I could just remember. But it's so long ago. And it's a simple way, I know. A very simple way.'

His hand came up and scraped back and forth across his chin.

'What are you doing that for?' Archie asked.

'Eh?'

'Rubbing your face that way. What do you do it for?'

Jenkins dropped his hand. 'Just a habit. Archie. A webster gesture. A way they had of thinking. I picked it up from them.'

236

'Does it help you think?'

'Well, maybe. Maybe not. It seemed to help the websters. Now what would a webster do in a case like this? The websters could help us. I know they could . . .'

'The websters in the cobbly world,' said Homer.

Jenkins shook his head. 'There aren't any websters there.'

'But you said you took some back.'

'I know. But they aren't there now. I've been alone in the cobbly world for almost four thousand years.'

'Then there, aren't websters anywhere. The rest went to Jupiter. Andrew told me that. Jenkins, where is Jupiter?'

'Yes, there are,' said Jenkins. 'There are some websters left, I mean. Or there used to be. A few left at Geneva.'

'It won't be easy,' Homer said. 'Not even for a webster. Those ants are smart. Archie told you about the flea he found.'

'It wasn't any flea,' said Archie.

'Yes, he told me,' Jenkins said. 'Said it got on to Hezekiah.'

'Not on to,' Homer told them. 'Into is the word. It wasn't a flea . . . it was a robot, a tiny robot. It drilled a hole in Hezekiah's skull and got into his brain. It sealed the hole behind it.'

'And what is Hezekiah doing now?'

'Nothing,' said Homer. 'But we are pretty sure what he will do as soon as the ant robot gets the set-up fixed. He'll get the Call. He'll get the call to go and work on the Building.'

Jenkins nodded. 'Taking over,' he said. 'They can't do a job like that themselves, so they take control of things that can.'

He lifted his hand again and scraped it across his chin.

'I wonder if Joe knew,' he mumbled. 'When he played god to the ants I wonder if he knew.'

But that was ridiculous. Joe never could have known. Even a mutation like Joe could not have looked twelve thousand years ahead.

'So long ago, thought Jenkins. So many things have happened. Bruce Webster was just starting to experiment with dogs, had no more than dreamed his dream of talking, thinking dogs that would go down the path of destiny paw in hand with

237

Man . . . not knowing then that Man within a few short centuries would scatter to the four winds of eternity and leave the Earth to robot and to dog. Not knowing then that even the name of Man would be forgotten in the dust of years, that the race would come to be known by the name of a single family.

And yet, thought Jenkins, if it was to be any family, the Websters were the ones. I can remember them as if it were yesterday. Those were the days when I thought of myself as a Webster, too.

Lord knows, I tried to be. I did the best I could. I stood by the Webster dogs when the race of men had gone and finally I took the last bothersome survivors of that madcap race into another world to clear the way for Dogs . . . so that the Dogs could fashion the Earth in the way they planned.

And now even those last bothersome survivors have gone . . . Some place, somewhere . . . I wish that I could know. Escaped into some fantasy of the human mind. And the men on Jupiter are not even men, but something else. And Geneva is shut off . . . blocked off from the world.

Although it can't be farther away or blocked more tightly than the world from which I came. If only I could learn how it was I travelled from the exile cobbly world back to Webster House . . . then, maybe, perhaps, somehow or other, I could reach Geneva.

A new power, he told himself. A new ability. A thing that grew upon me without my knowing that it grew. A thing that every man and every robot . . . and perhaps every dog . . . could have if he but knew the way.

Although it may be my body that made it possible . . . this body that the Dogs gave me on my seven thousandth birthday. A body that has more than any body of flesh and blood has ever quite attained. A body that can know what a bear is thinking or a fox is dreaming, that can feel the happy little mouse thoughts running in the grass.

Wish fulfilment. That might be it. The answer to the strange, illogical yearnings for things that seldom are and often cannot be. But all of which are possible if one knows the way, if one can grow or develop or graft on to oneself the new ability that directs the mind and body to the fulfilment of the wish.

I walked the hill each day, he remembered. Walked there because I could not stay away, because the longing was so strong, steeling myself against looking too closely, for there were differences I did not wish to see.

I walked there a million times and it took that many times before the power within me was strong enough to take me back.

For I was trapped. The word, the thought, the concept that took me into the cobbly world was a one way ticket and while it took me there it could not take me back. But there was another way, a way I did not know. That even now I do not know.

'You said there was a way,' urged Homer.

'A way?'

'Yes, a way to stop the ants.'

Jenkins nodded. 'I am going to find out I'm going to Geneva.'

Jon Webster awoke.

And this is strange, he thought, for I said eternity.

I was to sleep forever and forever has no end.

All else was mist and the greyness of sleep forgetfulness, but this much stood out with mind-sharp clarity. Eternity, and this was not eternity.

A word ticked at his mind, like feeble tapping on a door that was far away.

He lay and listened to the tapping and the word became two words . . . words that spoke his name:

'Jon Webster. Jon Webster.' On and on, on and on. Two words tapping at his brain.

'Jon Webster.'

'Jon Webster.'

'Yes,' said Webster's brain and the words stopped and did not come again.

Silence and the thinning of the mists of forgetfulness. And the trickling back of memory. One thing at a time.

There was a city and the name of the city was Geneva.

Men lived in the city, but men without a purpose.

The Dogs lived outside the city . . . in the whole world outside the city. The Dogs had purpose and a dream.

Sara climbed the hill to take a century of dreams.

And I . . . I, thought Jon Webster, climbed the hill and asked for eternity. This is not eternity.

'This is Jenkins, Jon Webster.'

'Yes, Jenkins,' said Jon Webster, and yet he did not say it, not with lip and tongue and throat, for he felt the fluid that pressed around his body inside its cylinder, fluid that fed him and kept him from dehydrating. Fluid that sealed his lips and eyes and ears.

'Yes, Jenkins,' said Webster, speaking with his mind. 'I remember you. I remember you now. You were with the family from the very first. You helped us teach the Dogs. You stayed with them when the family was no more.'

'I am still with them,' said Jenkins.

'I sought eternity,' said Webster. 'I closed the city and sought eternity.'

'We often wondered,' Jenkins told him. 'Why did you close the city?'

'The Dogs,' said Webster's mind. 'The Dogs had to have their chance. Man would have spoiled their chance.'

'The dogs are doing well,' said Jenkins.

'But the city is open now?'

'No, the city still is closed.'

'But you are here.'

'Yes, but I'm the only one who knows the way. And there will be no others. Not for a long time, anyway.'

'Time,' said Webster. 'I had forgotten time. How long is it, Jenkins?'

'Since you closed the city? Ten thousand years or so.'

'And there are others?'

'Yes, but they are sleeping.'

'And the robots? The robots still keep watch?'

'The robots still keep watch.'

Webster lay quietly and a peace came upon his mind. The city still was closed and the last of men were sleeping. The Dogs were doing well and the robots stayed on watch.

'You should not have wakened me,' he said. 'You should have let me sleep.'

'There was a thing I had to know. I knew it once, but I have forgotten and it is very simple. Simple and yet terribly important.'

Webster chuckled in his brain. 'What is it, Jenkins?'

'It's about ants,' said Jenkins. 'Ants used to trouble men. What did you do about it?'

'Why, we poisoned them,' said Webster.

Jenkins gasped. 'Poisoned them!'

'Yes,' said Webster. 'A very simple thing. We used a base of syrup, sweet, to attract the ants. And we put poison in it, a poison that was deadly to ants. But we did not put in enough of it to kill them right away. A slow poison, you see, so they would have time to carry it to the nest. That way we killed many instead of just two or three.'

Silence hummed in Webster's head . . . the silence of no thought, no words.

'Jenkins,' he said. 'Jenkins, are you . . .'

'Yes, Jon Webster, I am here.'

'That is all you want?'

'That is all I want.'

'I can go to sleep again.'

'Yes, Jon Webster. Go to sleep again.'

Jenkins stood upon the hilltop and felt the first rough fore-running wind of winter whine across the land. Below him the slope that ran down to the river was etched in black and grey with the leafless skeletons of trees.

To the north-east rose the shadow-shape, the cloud of evil omen that was called the Building. A growing thing spawned in the mind of ants, built for what purpose and to what end no thing but an ant could even closely guess.

But there was a way to deal with ants.

The human way.

The way Jon Webster had told him after ten thousand years of sleep. A simple way and a fundamental way, a brutal, but efficient way. You took some syrup, sweet, so the ants would like it, and you put some poison in it . . . slow poison so it wouldn't work too fast.

The simple way of poison. Jenkins said. The very simple way.

Except it called for chemistry and the Dogs knew no chemistry.

Except it called for killing and there was no killing.

Not even fleas, and the Dogs were pestered plenty by the fleas. Not even ants . . . and the ants threatened to dispossess the animals of the world they called their birthplace.

There had been no killing for five thousand years or more. The idea of killing had been swept from the minds of things.

And it is better that way, Jenkins told himself. Better that one should lose a world than go back to killing.

He turned slowly and went down the hill.

Homer would be disappointed, he told himself.

Terribly disappointed when he found the websters had no way of dealing with the ants . . .

Clifford D. Simak was born in Wisconsin in 1904. After leaving university he began work with a number of Midwest newspapers. His first published story appeared in *Wonder Stories* in 1931, though he only became a full-time writer of SF after his retirement. Simak's novels included *Cosmic Engineers, City, Time is the Simplest Thing, They Walked Like Men* and *The Visitors*. During his career he won three Hugo Awards, as well as the Grand Master Nebula Award in 1977. He died in 1988.

SF MASTERWORKS

A Case of Conscience James Blish

A Fall of Moondust Arthur C. Clarke

A Maze of Death Philip K. Dick

Arslan M. J. Engh

A Scanner Darkly Philip K. Dick

Babel-17 Samuel R. Delaney

Behold the Man Michael Moorcock

Blood Music Greg Bear

Bring the Jubilee Ward Moore

Cat's Cradle Kurt Vonnegut

Childhood's End Arthur C. Clarke

Cities in Flight James Blish

City Clifford Simak

Dancers at the End of Time
Michael Moorcock

Dark Benediction Walter M. Miller

Dhalgren Samuel R. Delany

Do Androids Dream of Electric
Sheep? Philip K. Dick

Downward to Earth Robert Silverberg

Dr Bloodmoney Philip K. Dick

Dune Frank Herbert

Dying Inside Robert Silverberg

Earth Abides George R. Stewart

Emphyrio Jack Vance

Eon Greg Bear

Flow My Tears, the Policeman Said
Philip K. Dick

Flowers for Algernon Daniel Keyes

Gateway Frederik Pohl

Grass Sheri S. Tepper

Greybeard Brian Aldiss

Helliconia Brian Aldiss

I am Legend Richard Matheson

Inverted World Christopher Priest

Jem Frederik Pohl

Last and First Men Olaf Stapledon

Life During Wartime Lucius Shepard

Lord of Light Roger Zelazny

Man Plus Frederik Pohl

Mission of Gravity Hal Clement

Mockingbird Walter Tevis

More Than Human Theodore Sturgeon

Non-Stop Brian Aldiss

Nova Samuel R. Delany

Now Wait for Last Year* Philip K. Dick

Pavane Keith Roberts

Rendezvous with Rama
Arthur C. Clarke

Ringworld Larry Niven

Roadside Picnic Boris Strugatsky,
Arkady Strugatsky

Sirius Olaf Stapledon

Stand on Zanzibar John Brunner

Star Maker Olaf Stapledon

Tau Zero Poul Anderson

The Body Snatchers Jack Finney

The Book of Skulls Robert Silverberg

The Centauri Device M. John Harrison

The Child Garden Geoff Ryman

* no longer available

The City and the Stars
Arthur C. Clarke

The Complete Roderick John Sladek

The Demolished Man Alfred Bester

The Difference Engine William Gibson
and Bruce Stirling

The Dispossessed Ursula Le Guin

The Drowned World* J. G. Ballard

The Female Man Joanna Russ

The Fifth Head of Cerberus
Gene Wolfe

The First Men in the Moon
H. G. Wells

The Food of the Gods
H. G. Wells

The Forever War Joe Haldeman

The Fountains of Paradise
Arthur C. Clarke

The Invisible Man H. G. Wells

The Island of Doctor Moreau
H. G. Wells

The Lathe of Heaven Ursula le
Guin

The Man in the High Castle
Philip K. Dick

The Martian Time-Slip
Philip K. Dick

The Moon is a Harsh Mistress
Robert A. Heinlein

The Penultimate Truth Philip K. Dick

The Prestige Christopher Priest

The Rediscovery of Man
Cordwainer Smith

The Shrinking Man Richard Matheson

The Simulacra Philip K. Dick

The Sirens of Titan Kurt Vonnegut

The Space Merchants Frederik Pohl
and C. M. Kornbluth

The Stars My Destination
Alfred Bester

**The Three Stigmata of Palmer
Eldritch** Philip K. Dick

The Time Machine H. G. Wells

**The Time Machine/The War of the
Worlds** H. G. Wells

Time Out of Joint Philip K. Dick

Timescape Greg Benford

Ubik Philip K. Dick

Valis Philip K. Dick

Where Late the Sweet Birds Sang
Kate Wilhelm

BEYOND
SPACE AND TIME

ESSENTIAL
CONTEMPORARY
CLASSICS